An Impossible Confession

FAIR WARNING

Miss Helen Fairmead could not argue when Mary, her maid, reproached her. 'Miss Fairmead, you were very unwise to permit Lord Drummond such liberties.'

'I know,' Helen said.

'And as for returning his kiss like that, oh, miss, if it ever got out you'd have no reputation left.'

'I know that, too,' replied Helen softly.

'He's a man of the world, miss, and it's my belief he's made love to a hundred ladies.'

Helen nodded. 'I know all you say about him could be true. He could be a libertine, a wicked lord with a dark past, intent only on adding me to his list of easy conquests. But when he kissed me. . . . Oh, Mary, I've never felt like that before, it was the most wonderful feeling in the world.'

An Impossible Confession

SANDRA HEATH

ROBERT HALE · LONDON

© Sandra Heath 1988, 2007
First published in Great Britain 2007

ISBN-978-0-7090-8087-9

Robert Hale Limited
Clerkenwell House
Clerkenwell Green
London EC1R 0HT

The right of Sandra Heath to be identified as
author of this work has been asserted by her
in accordance with the Copyright, Designs and
Patents Act 1988

2 4 6 8 10 9 7 5 3 1

Typeset in 11/13½pt Classical Garamond Roman
by Derek Doyle & Associates, Shaw Heath
Printed and bound in Great Britain by
Biddles Limited, King's Lynn

CHAPTER 1

The blue post chaise left the exclusive Cheltenham school, driving smartly out through the tall wrought iron gates. The fashionable spa was quiet in the early morning sun, and the villa gardens were bright with mid-May flowers, but the chaise's two passengers, a young lady and her maid, were too excited to take note of anything but the dazzling new life they were embarking upon.

Soon the town was behind them, and the London road began the long climb into the Cotswold hills. The yellow-jacketed post-boy urged his team to greater effort, kicking his heels to keep them at it all the way to the top. Far from being a boy, he was nearly fifty years old, and he'd driven this road countless times. He knew every bend and incline, and he drove like the wind, living up to the nickname by which his kind were known, the 'yellow bounders.'

There wasn't much traffic at such an early hour, but a detachment of horse artillery was moving slowly in the same direction as the chaise, impeding its progress for a while. The soldiers were en route from their Herefordshire barracks to the distant port of Dover, where they would embark for the Low Countries. On such a beautiful spring morning, it was hard to remember that 1815 was a year of war, and that near Brussels a final confrontation was soon expected with Bonaparte's France.

Passing the column of horse artillery at last, the chaise continued on its way. A day's journey lay ahead before it reached its destination, the magnificent estate of Bourne End, near Ascot in Berkshire, but after setting off so promptly, there was little doubt that it would cover the distance before nightfall.

The young lady gazed impatiently out of the chaise window. Her name was Miss Helen Fairmead, and at the age of nineteen she had at last completed her education, being now deemed ready for her first London Season. From now on, her home would be with her sister and brother-in-law, Colonel and Mrs Gregory Bourne, one of society's most popular and sought-after young couples. Gregory was a devotee of the turf, one of its leading lights, and owned a stud of thoroughbreds that was reckoned to be the finest in the land. Bourne End, newly rebuilt in the latest picturesque style, was a very desirable address indeed, and Helen was assured of every advantage. Exclusive doors would be opened for her, her name would grace all the best invitation lists, and vouchers for Almack's, that temple of the highest fashion, would not be difficult for her to obtain.

She was striking rather than beautiful, for her green eyes were a little too large, and her mouth too wide, but she had a glory of long honey-colored hair, and a complexion of the softest pink and white. Her figure was curving and slender-waisted, and looked good in all the latest modes. Today she'd chosen to wear a lavender silk spencer over her long-sleeved white lawn gown. The spencer was unbuttoned to reveal the pretty white embroidery on the gown's high-waisted bodice, and her white shoes and gloves were slashed with lavender. The hem of the gown was fashionably stiffened with rouleaux and more embroidery, to give the triangular shape that was all the rage, and she carried a lavender velvet reticule. Her hair was dressed up into a knot beneath a stylish straw bonnet, and her only jewelry, apart from a signet ring, was a dainty gold fob watch given to her by her sister, Margaret. All in all, she was a young woman of elegance and fashion, and very much a credit to her couturière, Madame Rosalie of The Promenade, Cheltenham, whose talents would soon take her to the more superior circles of London.

Helen's entire wardrobe was by Madame Rosalie, and the chaise boot was packed to capacity with trunks containing an almost bewildering variety of gowns, pelisses, spencers, hats, bonnets, shoes, shawls, and petticoats. The requirements of a young lady setting out on her first Season were many and expensive, but Colonel Gregory Bourne's generosity and fondness were such that he hadn't stinted by so much as a pin; indeed, he'd even supplied his sister-in-law with a collection of beautiful jewelry.

As the chaise reached the top of the climb into the hills, Helen attempted to apply herself to the pages of Miss Austen's *Mansfield Park*, but she was too excited to concentrate. How different her life was going to be from now on; indeed, how different she was from the rather timid young girl who'd arrived at Miss Figgis's Seminary for the Daughters of Gentlefolk five years before. Then she'd merely been the younger daughter of a modest Worcestershire landowner, overcome with envy that her elder sister had just gone to London to enjoy an unexpected Season because of the beneficence of a distant relative. Margaret Fairmead had been very fortunate indeed. Helen could not have hoped then for a similar stroke of luck; the highlight of her social calender was likely to be the annual subscription ball at the assembly rooms in Worcester. But Margaret's Season had changed everything, for although she hadn't been a beauty, or 'a fortune,' she'd still managed to snap up one of England's most eligible young gentlemen. Colonel Gregory Bourne was not only handsome and privileged, he was also something of a hero, having distinguished himself in Spain at the battle of Vimiero in 1808, when his personal heroism had saved his men from certain extinction. He'd received wounds that had led to him being invalided out of the army, and he'd returned to London to find himself the object of much romantic attention from hopeful ladies. He could have taken his pick, but once his glance fell upon Margaret, he'd lost his heart completely. Theirs had been a match to set society by the ears, for no one had expected him to take such an insignificant bride, and their marriage at St George's, Hanover Square, had been one of the most extravagant occasions that year.

Margaret had been pampered with love and luxury from the outset of the marriage, and she and Gregory had adored each other in a way that made theirs a love match of the highest order. They'd lived at first in a fine town house in Park Lane, waiting until Bourne End was rebuilt in the very latest style. The work had finished two summers before, but Helen had yet to see the new house, although she knew of it from Margaret's letters. Margaret and Gregory were all the family she had now, for her parents had both been killed in a carriage overturn during her second year at

Cheltenham, and the elderly great-aunt she'd stayed with during subsequent school vacations had died the previous autumn, but she'd always been close to her sister, and on the occasions she'd met Gregory, she'd liked him very much indeed. The new life now stretching before her was everything she could have ever wished for, and she couldn't wait for it to begin. Royal Ascot was in two weeks' time, and it was at this prestigious event that she'd make her first appearance in society.

The postboy hurled the chaise toward the end of the first stage, which was at the Frogmill Inn. He took on and passed every vehicle on the road, from a Cheltenham 'Flyer' stagecoach to a rather startled military gentleman driving a gig, and as the chaise lurched and swayed alarmingly, Helen's thoughts were dragged momentarily away from the delicious contemplation of her fortunate circumstances. Posting was always a somewhat hazardous method of traveling, because it was so fast, and she was to have made the journey in Gregory's carriage, but when Miss Figgis had been persuaded to let her leave two days earlier than previously agreed, it was an escape that could not be refused. Five years was a horrid long time to be incarcerated in school, even one as superior as the seminary, and Helen hadn't been able to wait to get away. She'd hired the first available chaise, and now would be at Bourne End before Gregory dispatched his private carriage.

The rigors of the chaise's pace didn't alarm the maid, who was so tired after staying up half the night packing for the unexpected departure that her head was lolling against the back of the seat. Mary Caldwell was the same age as her mistress, and had been in her service for just over a year. She was Cheltenham born and bred, and sharp enough to have used her time at the school to lose as much of her country ways and accent as possible. She was small and dark-haired, with brown eyes and a liberal sprinkling of freckles on her snub nose. Her clothes were plain, a light-blue linen dress beneath a gray cape, and her mobcap was very stiffly starched. To Helen, she was more than just a maid, she was a friend too, and so was accorded the privilege of speaking her mind from time to time, a liberty she used whenever she felt it was in the interests of her rather impetuous mistress. Discreet, wise beyond her years, and intensely loyal, she thought the world of Helen, whose welfare she guarded like a tiger. Like Helen, she was excited about the new life at Bourne End, and she'd been determined to stay awake and see every inch of the journey, but her eyes had closed, and now she was fast asleep.

The Frogmill Inn loomed ahead, and at last the postboy maneuvered his tired team into the yard, where stagecoaches and mails always made their last stop in, and first stop out of Cheltenham. Helen glanced at the clock on the wall of the ticket office next to the taproom door. It was a quarter to eight. Frowning, she looked at her fob watch, which indicated that it was only twenty-five past seven. She'd forgotten to wind it the night before, and it was running slow again. She really would have to get into a proper routine, otherwise she'd never know the right time. Adjusting it, she settled back in the seat, and almost immediately the chaise started forward again, the swift change of team accomplished very deftly.

As the postboy brought the fresh horses up to a spanking pace, she noticed that there was more traffic on the road now. There were a number of stagecoaches and slow-moving wagons and carts, to say nothing of a variety of private carriages, from landaus and barouches to cabriolets and curricles. The *beau monde* was always to be found on the road from London to fashionable Cheltenham spa, just as it was to be found on the road to Bath.

There were no more columns of horse artillery to hinder progress; indeed, there was very little sign of anything military. The hills were beautiful at this time of year, the fields fresh and bright and the woods dazzling with bluebells. There were mellow stone hamlets, flocks of sheep with lambs, hedges bowing beneath the weight of hawthorn blossoms, and valleys where cool streams wound between mossy banks; the war in Europe was a world away. In London the newspapers were increasingly uneasy, and the citizens were said to be quite agitated about the situation across the Channel, fearing invasion at any moment, but here, in the serenity of the countryside, Napoleon Bonaparte was but a name to frighten the children into good behavior.

It wasn't long after the end of the second stage of the journey that Helen's day began to go wrong. They'd just passed the wool town of Northleach, and she and Mary were sharing the light meal of cold chicken and salad packed for them at the seminary, when quite suddenly the chaise drew to a standstill on the open road and the rather disgruntled postboy came to the door to inform them that one of the horses had gone lame. He rode on to the next inn for a replacement, and more than an hour was lost. Then no less than five hours were lost on the next stage, because repairs had to be carried out on a faulty wheel. Realizing that her intention of reaching Bourne End before nightfall was in jeopardy, Helen endeavored to hire another chaise, but there wasn't one to be had, and so she and Mary resigned themselves to a long wait in the house of an obliging clergyman while the chaise was made good again.

It was well on in the afternoon when they were at last able to set off again, and by then Helen knew they'd have to travel by night in order to complete the journey, it being unthinkable that an unescorted young lady should stay at an inn, even a superior posting house. But she reckoned without the intervention of the weather, or the existence of a highwayman by the name of Lord Swag, whose after-dark activities on the road beyond the village of Upper Ballington had recently been causing much alarm. Highwaymen were scarce these days, but this impudent fellow had been doing very well for himself out of travelers grown complacent about such things.

The weather changed quite abruptly at six o'clock in the evening. Clouds stole swiftly over the clear May skies, and the sunshine was shut out as a torrential downpour set in. In a very short time the road was dirty and difficult to traverse as puddles and rivulets formed, and the chaise could only move slowly. The horse's heads were low and dejected as they plodded through the rain toward the end of the stage, which lay beyond Upper Ballington at the Rose Tree Inn, on a stretch of road where Lord Swag was particularly active. There should have been several hours of daylight left, but the weather was so bad that darkness came very early. The road was almost deserted, all other travelers wisely having broken their journey, and just as the outlying houses of Upper Ballington appeared ahead, the postboy reined in and dismounted, coming to the door.

'Beggin' your pardon, miss,' he said, the rain dripping from the brim of his beaver hat, 'but there's no 'ope of reachin' anywhere tonight, 'ceptin' the village just up the road.'

Helen was dismayed. 'But I have to reach Ascot.'

'That's not possible, miss,' he replied firmly.

'But. . . .'

'Not only is the weather against us, there's also Lord Swag to consider now it's as good as dark.'

'Lord Swag?' She hadn't heard of the highwayman.

'The, er, gentleman of the road, miss.'

'But there aren't any highwaymen anymore,' she protested.

'Beggin' your pardon, miss, but there's Lord Swag, and a little rough weather won't keep 'im inside. Them as is foolish enough to stay on the road in conditions like this, will be sittin' targets for 'im. I don't know what you've got in all that there luggage we loaded up, but I reckon 'e'd find it mortal interestin'.'

He would, for her jewelry was in one of the valises. She drew a long, resigned breath. 'What do you intend to do, then?'

'I'm stoppin' at the Cat and Fiddle in Upper Ballington. It's about a quarter of a mile ahead. You might be able to 'ire another chaise there, if you're that set on riskin' it, but my advice is to call a 'alt tonight and carry on in the mornin'. Lord Swag don't come out in daylight.'

He didn't wait for her to reply, but slammed the door and went to remount. A moment later the chaise continued at its crawling pace.

Helen looked unhappily at Mary. 'What am I to do? I'm not supposed to even set foot in an inn, let alone get myself benighted at one.'

'I know, miss.'

'Oh, I can hear Miss Figgis now. Unmarried ladies never enter wayside inns unescorted, so do not, whatever the temptation, be so foolish as to stay at one. Your reputation must be considered before all else, Miss Fairmead, so do not forget it.' She mimicked the headmistress's thin voice very accurately indeed, making Mary giggle in spite of the quandary they were in.

The maid glanced out at the fading light, and the downpour. 'You don't really have any choice, miss. The postboy has no intention of continuing, and I don't think it's very likely you'll get another carriage, not in weather like this, with a highwayman to avoid.'

'But an inn is quite out of the question, Mary. To stay at one amounts to a heinous sin, or so I've been lectured for the past five years.'

'The circumstances are rather exceptional, miss. Why, I haven't seen anyone else on the road for at least half an hour now.'

Even as she spoke the sound of hooves carried clearly into the chaise, coming up smartly from behind. Helen's breath caught in alarm, for she thought instantly of the highwayman. Lowering the glass to look out, she saw to her relief that the hooves belonged to a high-stepping team of perfectly matched bays pulling a dashing bright red curricie. The little vehicle was moving at a spanking pace in spite of the weather, and a gentleman of fashion was at the ribbons, his top hat pulled low over his forehead. His modish traveling cloak was soaked through as he eased the blood team effortlessly past the slow-moving chaise, and he didn't even glance at the other vehicle as he drove on by.

Helen drew back inside, raising the glass again. 'It wasn't Lord Swag, it was a gentleman who looked as if he had but five minutes in which to reach Hyde Park.'

At last the chaise approached the Cat and Fiddle, a large old stone building with mullioned windows and a rambling, gabled roof. Behind it were stables and coach-houses, and beyond them some tall elms where rooks could be heard settling down for the night. The scraping sound of a fiddle emanated from the tap room, and the smell of cooking drifted from the kitchens as the chaise approached the archway leading into the courtyard.

Helen glanced out in time to see a notice fixed to the wall. *No horses, links, lanterns, or vehicles for hire.* Her last hope faded away; now she *had* to stay at the inn. She looked at Mary. 'One day out of Cheltenham, and already my reputation is to suffer. Unless. . . .' A thought struck her.

'Miss Fairmead?' Mary looked at her in concern, for she knew that note in her mistress's voice.

'I've just remembered something else Miss Figgis was fond of drumming into me. She said that single and married ladies only stayed at inns if escorted, but widows were allowed more latitude.'

She removed her gloves, transferring her signet ring to her left hand, and turning it so that only the band of gold could be seen.

Mary watched in dismay. 'Oh, Miss Fairmead, I don't think you should. . . .'

'It's inspired, Mary Caldwell. Widows are permitted to stay at inns, so I must become a widow for the night. I shall be Mrs er, Brown. Yes, that will do nicely.'

'But. . . .'

'Don't find fault, Mary, for I think it's an excellent notion. No one need know my real name, and therefore my reputation will not suffer at all. No one will ever know that Miss Helen Fairmead stayed the night at the Cat and Fiddle Inn, Upper Ballington.'

But it wasn't going to be as simple as that, as she was going to find out to her cost.

CHAPTER TWO

Two other vehicles were in the courtyard, a London-bound stagecoach that had been about to depart, but had at the last moment cried off because of Lord Swag, and the bright red curricle that had overtaken the chaise a short while before. The enclosed space seemed to amplify the noise of the rain, and it was a dark, shadowy place, in spite of the lanterns suspended beneath the gallery giving access to the rooms on the first floor.

The stagecoachman was disgruntled at not being able to complete his journey to the capital, but the passengers, having heard in the inn about the advent of the nocturnal highwayman, had decided *en bloc* not to travel any further until the next day. Seated wetly on his box, the stagecoachman was engaged in an ill-tempered altercation with an ostler, and the very name Lord Swag was cursed roundly more than once. In the ticket office the clerk was dealing with an anxious man who wanted to reach Northleach that night to see a sick relative, and from the adjacent kitchen door a maid emerged to empty a bucket of water into the overflowing gutter. A thin black lurcher was tethered to an iron hoop in the wall next to some large water butts, and its attention was riveted on the maid, whom it evidently hoped was going to bring food.

The gentleman with the curricle was standing in the shelter afforded by the gallery, instructing a groom concerning the precise care of his valuable vehicle and team. He was near one of the lanterns, and Helen could see him quite clearly. He'd removed his top hat and cloak, and was revealed as very much a man of fashion, tall, supremely elegant, and exceedingly handsome. There was something unmistakably aristocratic about his finely made profile, and something very arresting about the piercing blue of his eyes as he glanced briefly toward the chaise without noticing her face at the window. His tousled black hair was worn just a little longer than was the vogue, and it became him very well. He was dressed in the excellence only Bond Street could provide, his mulberry coat boasting a high stand-fall collar and a superbly tailored line that showed off his manly figure to perfection. His long legs were encased in extremely tight light-gray corduroy trousers, and his gray-and-white-striped Valencia waistcoat was partly unbuttoned to reveal the frills of his shirt. A jeweled pin glittered in the folds of his neckcloth, a bunch of seals hung from his fob, and he held the curricle whip in one gloved hand, tapping it against his rain-spattered Hessian boots. He certainly didn't look as if a minute or so before he'd been driving like the devil through the torrential downpour; indeed, he could have just stepped from a drawing room.

In those brief moments, as the chaise joined the other vehicles and the postboy dismounted, Helen found herself secretly apprais-ing the gentleman, whom she thought devastatingly attractive.

'Miss Fairmead?' Mary hadn't noticed the gentleman, and was looking curiously at her.

'Mm?'

'Shall we alight?'

'Yes, of course. Please bring the little valise from the boot, the one with my jewelry. I'd rather have it with me.'

'Yes, miss. I packed your night things in the brown trunk, shall I bring them as well?'

'Yes. And remember, I'm Mrs Brown from now on.'

Mary was unhappy about the pretense, but nodded.

Helen opened the chaise door, and immediately the damp evening air swept over her. The noise of the rain was all around, and she could hear the stagecoachman and groom arguing loudly. The postboy had been inspecting the bridle of one of the horses, but as he heard the chaise door open, he came around to assist her. But the moment he stepped into view, his yellow jacket seemed to antagonize the hitherto quiet lurcher. With a savage volley of barks and snarls, it flung itself at him, coming up sharply because of the leash, but then hurling forward again, determined to somehow get to the object of its hatred. The postboy halted in alarm, backing instinctively away, and the sight of its prey moving further out of reach infuriated the lurcher still more. It was like something possessed, goaded beyond belief by the mere sight of a yellow jacket.

The uproar frightened the various teams in the courtyard, that of the stagecoach particularly so, for they were facing the almost demented dog. They tossed their heads nervously, dragging the stagecoach forward a little and causing the stagecoachman to reach instinctively for the reins. For the postboy, discretion proved the better part of valor, and he decided to leave Helen to her own devices. Turning on his heel, he hurried away, and his departure drove the lurcher to further distraction. It flung itself after him with such force that it seemed it must tear the iron hoop from the wall. The horses were increasingly restive, and the stagecoachman was having a great deal of trouble calming his frightened team.

Helen had no option but to alight unaided, and as she did so the stagecoachman lost his battle to hold his team back. They started forward, anxious to get away from the dog, and Helen stepped down right into their path. They surged toward her, and she turned with a frightened gasp, screaming as they towered over her, their eyes rolling as they fought against the bit.

Mary screamed as well, certain she was about to see her beloved mistress trampled to death, but then, at the eleventh hour, Helen was snatched to safety, and pressed back against the wall by someone as the coach horses clattered past, so close that they splashed water over her hem. She closed her eyes, her heart pounding with dread as she clung fearfully to her rescuer. She heard the stage-coachman's shouts, and the clatter of hooves as the team were at last brought under control, but she was still too afraid to open her eyes.

All was confusion in the yard, with ostlers calling out in alarm, Mary bursting into tears, and the lurcher keeping up its wretched noise as if compelled to do so by some unseen force. Helen continued to cling to her rescuer, her face pressed against his shoulder. She was trembling from head to toe, only too aware of how close a scrape it had been.

'Are you all right?' Her deliverer gently relaxed his hold, looking anxiously at her.

She opened her eyes then raising her head to look into the vivid blue gaze of the Bond Street gentleman.

'Are you all right?' he asked again, more than a little concerned.

She managed to nod. 'Yes, I – I think so.'

But she swayed a little, and he tightened his hold immediately, glancing across the courtyard at the main doorway into the inn. The door was ajar and he could see a bright passageway where tables stood against the wall with the bowls of water and fresh handtowels always put out for newly arriving guests; he also saw a settle, which was the very thing for a lady in distress. He steered her quickly across to the doorway, ushered her inside and seated her carefully on the settle. 'Shall I have someone bring you a glass of water?' he asked, glancing around for a sign of a waiter or a maid.

'No, thank you. I just need a moment.'

'Of course. That was a little too close for comfort, I think.'

'It was indeed.' She looked up at him. 'I believe I owe you my life, Mr. . . ?'

'Lord Drummond of Wintervale.' He inclined his head and made a gesture of bowing.

'Oh. Forgive me, I didn't realize.'

'Why should you? I don't wear a sign around my neck.' He replied, a little amused. 'Actually, I happen to be Adam Drummond – Lord Drummond of Wintervale, my family name and title being one and the same, a distinction I share with a number of my peers, including Earl Spencer of Althorp.' He smiled.

It was a smile that devastated her defenses, arousing all manner of thoughts that no young lady fresh from Miss Figgis's Seminary should ever think. Helen was caught off guard by her own reaction, and had to look away in some confusion.

He watched her. 'You now have the advantage of me, I think, for although you know who I am, your identity remains a mystery.'

For a moment she was in danger of blurting out the truth, but she remembered just in time. 'My – my name is Mrs Brown, my lord.'

'Mr Brown is indeed a fortunate man to have such a lovely wife.'

She colored at the compliment, but was regaining her composure with each passing moment. 'My husband is dead, my lord,' she replied, feeling horridly guilty as she uttered the words, but all she could think of was the harm that would be done to her reputation should her real identity be known.

He looked a little uncomfortable. 'I beg your pardon, I trust my remark didn't cause distress.'

'Of course not, my lord.'

'It didn't occur to me that you might be a widow, for you wear no hint of mourning.'

'I've been a widow for some years, sir.' Oh, dear, the fibs were coming one after the other.

She was spared from having to tell further untruths by the sudden appearance of the landlord, who'd been drawn at last from his comfortable chair in the kitchens by the noise and disturbance in the courtyard. He'd ordered, the lurcher to be taken away to the stables, and had learned of the miraculous prevention of a terrible accident. He came reluctantly into the passage, for he knew full well he was going to receive a sharp rebuke from the owner of the curricle. A large man with a pot belly and jowls that bulged above his tight collar, he came unwillingly toward them. He was wiping his hands on his starched apron, his eyes meeting theirs for as brief a moment as possible.

'I trust the lady is unharmed, sir.'

'She is, but that's not thanks to your thoughtlessness. What on earth possessed you to leave that black brute in the courtyard, it's quite obviously untrained.' Lord Drummond's blue eyes were cold, and his tone was sharply clipped.

'The dog was once badly beaten by a postboy, sir, that's why he behaved as he did.'

'Indeed, and is it also why you tied him up in a place where he's almost certain to see postboys?' inquired his lordship dryly.

The man shifted guiltily. 'We don't get many postboys here, sir.'

'You're on the London road,' came the somewhat acid response.

'Yes, sir.'

'So I think it reasonable to expect the occasional postboy to appear in your yard. In future, I trust you'll show more basic sense, and keep that damned cur well away from innocent travelers.'

'Yes, sir. I will, sir.'

Lord Drummond looked at Helen. 'Are you intending to lodge here for the night?'

'The weather and Lord Swag leave me no choice in the matter, sir.'

'We're both in the same predicament, I fancy, for it's too important that I reach London for a meeting in the very early morning for me to risk an encounter with a gentleman of the road. I'll have to leave at dawn,' He smiled, turning back sternly to the landlord. 'I expect you to make some restitution to this lady for the terrible distress your carelessness has caused.'

'Restitution, sir?' The man's face fell.

'Yes. I expect you to provide her with your best room for the night.'

'Certainly, sir.'

'And then I expect you to provide me with your next best room.'

'Yes, sir.'

'And I certainly expect your kitchens to provide something more palatable than the usual fodder you undoubtedly place before your unfortunate guests.'

'The Cat and Fiddle has always provided a good table, sir,' replied the man, drawing himself up proudly.

'I trust that doesn't prove an idle boast. Now, see to it that Mrs Brown's chaise is properly attended to, and then have her postboy present himself to me, for I intend to have words with him concerning the way he deserted his duty.'

'Yes, sir.' The man hurried thankfully out again, just as Mary came timidly in, still sniffing a little tearfully and clutching the valise containing Helen's jewelry, as well as a discreet bundle of night attire wrapped in a shawl.

Helen smiled at her. 'I'm all right, Mary.'

'Are you sure, miss?'

'Quite sure, but please try and remember that I'm Mrs Brown, not your previous mistress.' Helen eyed her warningly.

'Yes, madam. Forgive me.' Mary met her gaze a little guiltily.

Lord Drummond saw nothing untoward in the exchange, and looked at Helen again. 'I take it you're traveling with just your maid?'

'Yes.'

'Then would you do me the inestimable honor of dining with me? Fate has conspired to halt our journeys in this odious establishment, and so it seems to me that we could make the stay much more agreeable by enjoying each other's company. At least, I shall enjoy yours, and I trust you will feel the same about mine.' He smiled again.

Her defenses were reduced to tatters. His smiles rendered her totally vulnerable, and made her want to throw caution to the winds. She'd already broken a cardinal rule by staying in this place; she'd be breaking another if she went so far as to dine with a gentleman she hardly knew, even if he had just saved her life. She hesitated, feeling Mary's horrified gaze upon her.

He misinterpreted the hesitation, thinking he'd appeared more than a little forward. 'Forgive me, I meant nothing improper by the invitation, Mrs Brown. I merely think that dinner is much more enjoyable when taken in company. I loathe dining alone.'

She looked quickly at him. 'So do I, my lord. I gladly accept your invitation.' She felt rather than heard Mary's dismayed gasp.

He was smiling again. 'Excellent. Shall we say in one hour's time wherever mine host directs? I understand from the groom that there's to be a rather rowdy reunion dinner in the main dining room, which will make it crowded and exceeding disagreeable for those not involved.'

She nodded. 'In one hour's time.'

He took her hand to kiss it, and she had to suppress a frisson of wayward pleasure, for it was as if she wore no gloves and his lips touched her bare skin.

As he walked back out to the rainswept courtyard, Mary came closer, still clutching the valise and night things. She looked unhappily at her mistress. 'Oh, Miss Fairmead, you really shouldn't have accepted, you don't know anything about him.'

'I know.'

'Miss Figgis said. . . .'

'I'm well aware of what Miss Figgis said.' Helen gave a rather reckless smile. 'I know I shouldn't feel like this, but I'm really beginning to enjoy myself.'

'But he might be really wicked!'

'He might be, but I'm sure he isn't. Besides, I'm not Miss

Fairmead, I'm the widowed Mrs Brown. She's the one who's staying here, and she's the one who's going to dine with Lord Drummond.'

'But he's a stranger, miss.'

'Mary Caldwell, if you say one more word I shall make you sleep in the chaise. I know I'm behaving improperly, I know I shouldn't have even *thought* of accepting his invitation, but I have, and now I intend to enjoy myself to the full.'

'But, what if. . . ?'

'There's no such thing as "what if," not tonight,' declared Helen firmly.

Mary sighed and fell silent. This was all the height of madness, and nothing good was going to come of it, nothing good at all.

CHAPTER 3

One hour later, Helen was almost ready to keep her dinner appointment. She sat before the candlelit dressing table while Mary put the finishing touches to her hair.

Outside, it was still raining heavily, but in the Cat and the Fiddle's best room it was dry, warm, and very comfortable. The room occupied a prime position at the front of the inn, with windows facing the London road, but was so large that it also had a window and door opening onto the gallery above the courtyard. It was a handsome chamber, beamed and paneled, and in view of the terrible weather, which made the night unseasonably cool, a fire had been lit in the immense hearth.

Apart from the dressing table, the room boasted a particularly fine old four-poster bed hung with pale blue damask, and there was a vast wardrobe with enough space for the clothes of half a dozen ladies of fashion. A table stood in one corner, with a porcelain jug and bowl, and a chest of drawers occupied another corner, so far beyond the arc of candlelight that it was barely visible in the shadows. At the foot of the bed there was a pallet, brought in especially for Mary, and it looked rather small beside the great four-poster, which was so high there were steps to climb into it.

Helen's reflection looked back at her from the mirror on the dressing table. She wore the same white gown she'd traveled in, it hardly being practical to unpack and press another one just for this evening, but she wasn't displeased, for the gown was one of what Madame Rosalie called her 'amiable creations,' because it could be dressed up or down to suit the occasion. Tonight she'd chosen to wear her mother's diamonds with it, and they glittered and flashed as the candlelight moved. Her hair was twisted up into an elaborate knot from which tumbled several heavy ringlets, and there was a froth of little curls framing her face.

Mary put the last pin in place and looked at her in the mirror. 'There, miss, I've finished.'

'You've done it beautifully, Mary. Thank you.'

'Thank you, miss.'

Their eyes met again, and Helen sighed. 'Oh, all right, say it again if you must.'

'I can't help it, miss, I'm worried about tonight. There's still time for you to change your mind, you could plead a headache.'

'I could, but I'm not going to. Mary, I'm having dinner with him, not slipping into his bed.'

Mary was shocked. 'Oh, Miss Fairmead, you shouldn't say such things. Besides. . . .'

'Yes?'

'That isn't why I'm worried, for I'm sure Lord Drummond is a fine and honorable gentleman.'

'I'm sure he is, too. Why are you worried then?'

'I think you know.'

'Because I could meet him again some time and he'd know I'd been masquerading as a widow?'

'Yes, miss.'

'That's a remote chance I intend to take.'

'Remote, miss? It seems to me that the whole of society goes to Bourne End.'

The maid was right, but Helen didn't want to think about it, not tonight. She got up, causing a draft that set the candle flames dancing. 'Mary, I've spent the last five years paying attention to rules, learning them all by heart so that when I reach Bourne End I can spend the rest of my life abiding by them. But tonight, just for tonight, there aren't any rules, there isn't even a Helen Fairmead.'

'I don't know what's come over you, Miss Fairmead, for this isn't like you at all.'

'What's come over me?' Helen smiled suddenly, snatching up her shawl. 'A Cat and Fiddle tarradiddle, that's what's come over me. I've told a fib, and I'm free for an evening.'

Determined not to hear any more common sense from the maid, she hurried from the room, closing the door firmly behind her.

Tonight was going to be an adventure, a stolen excitement that was most strictly forbidden; the prospect of spending time in Lord Drummond's company was too tempting to allow the sobering thought of possible consequences to stand in the way.

The Cat and Fiddle's passages rambled, and its floorboards were squeaky and uneven. She descended the staircase to the wide passage where earlier she'd sat on the settle recovering from the incident in the courtyard. The row of bowls on the tables had all been used, the water in them was dirty and the towels equally so. The settle was laden with wet cloaks and hats, and the noise of male laughter and conversation emanated from behind a door. The reunion dinner was evidently well in progress, and the guests well in drink.

As she reached the bottom, the landlord appeared from the cellars, wiping a dusty bottle on his apron. He paused immediately when he saw her. 'Good evening, ma'am.'

'Good evening.'

'I trust the room is to your satisfaction?'

'Yes. Thank you.'

There was a sudden gust of laughter from the dining room, and the landlord hastily put the bottle down. 'If you'll come this way, ma'am, I'll take you to Lord Drummond.'

She followed him along the hallway toward the rear of the inn. Sporting prints lined the paneled walls, and doorways were graced by antler trophies, giving the establishment a distinctly masculine atmosphere that made her feel out of place in her diamonds and white lawn.

The landlord opened a door at the very end of the passage, standing aside for her to enter as he announced her name. The room was small and private, lit by a four-branched candleholder on the paneled wall and by a single candlestick on the white-clothed table set for two. There were comfortable chairs on either side of the fireplace, and a large sofa against another wall. Crimson velvet curtains hung at the single tall window that looked out at the courtyard, directly opposite the archway from the London road.

Lord Drummond stood by the window, holding the curtain aside to look at the endless rain. He wore the same mulberry coat and light-gray trousers as before, and he turned quickly to smile at her. 'Good evening, Mrs Brown.'

'Good evening, my lord.'

He nodded at the landlord, who was waiting in the doorway. 'You may serve dinner now.'

'My lord.'

The door closed and he returned his attention to Helen, taking her hand and raising it to his lips. 'I trust the notion of dining *à deux* with me isn't too disagreeable, but the stagecoach passengers have elected to eat in their rooms, and as you will no doubt have gathered, the reunion dinner is in full rumbustious possession of the main dining room.'

'And threatening to become more rumbustious still before much longer,' she replied, conscious that this time his lips had indeed touched her bare skin, and that the sensation was far too pleasing for comfort.

He conducted her to the table and drew out one of the chairs, waiting until she had settled before sitting down himself directly opposite. 'I'm afraid dinner is a choice of good Cotswold mutton or good Cotswold mutton.'

'It can indeed be very good, sir.'

'So I understand,' he replied, smiling.

'From which reply I guess you do not hail from these parts.'

'You guess correctly. I'm here at the moment because I've been visiting my sister, Lady Bowes-Fenton, in Burford, and I'm now on my way to an important war office meeting in London in the morning. My personal neck of the woods is in Sussex.'

'Wintervale?' she asked, remembering how he'd introduced himself earlier.

'Yes, do you know it?'

'I'm afraid not, I don't know Sussex at all.'

'Wintervale is on the edge of the South Downs. It's an extremely large, extremely ancient estate attached to a small village, and has been owned by the Drummond family since the time of Henry III. To be honest, there are unkind souls who've been heard to mutter that Wintervale's plumbing and general discomfort must have been known personally to that same monarch.' He smiled.

'You don't believe in improving, my lord?'

'I happen to like Wintervale as it is. If I require a taste of modern luxury, I take myself to my house in Berkeley Square.'

'The best of both worlds?'

'Indeed so. But enough of me, let's turn to you. Since you appear to be acquainted with the delights of Cotswold mutton, I imagine you reside somewhere in these hills?'

'Not exactly, I come from Worcestershire,' she replied honestly.

'Indeed?' He sat forward with interest. 'It's a county I know well, for I have relatives there. I'm sure you must know the Tancreds of Malvern?'

Abruptly the conversation became awkward for her, because she did indeed know the Tancreds, they were very prominent in Worcestershire affairs, but she could hardly say that to him without inviting further questions about her background. For a moment she could only stare at him, her mind racing, then she smiled and shook her head. 'No, I'm afraid not.' It was her first fib of the evening.

'I confess I'm surprised, for I've been led to believe they have a finger firmly set in every available pie in the county.'

To her relief the landlord chose that moment to appear with a waiter carrying the dinner. A maid followed with a bottle of wine. When the food had been set on the table and the door closed once more, Lord Drummond poured the wine and glanced appreciatively at their plates. 'I must say it looks exceeding appetizing, so perhaps mine host's boasts regarding his table are justified after all.'

'The strip you tore off him earlier was probably warning enough that he'd better not displease you again, my lord.'

'It was no more than he deserved, and probably a good deal less. The same is probably true of your postboy, who promises me that from now on he'll convey you as carefully and attentively as if you were royalty.'

She smiled. 'You evidently have a way with words, sir.'

'Oh, I do, believe me. Your health, Mrs Brown.' He raised his glass.

'And yours, Lord Drummond.' She raised hers as well.

The mutton was very succulent indeed, the vegetables cooked to perfection, and the gravy light and tasty; the conversation, however, was soon uncomfortable for her again.

Lord Drummond smiled at her. 'Are you *en route* for town, Mrs Brown?'

'For Ascot.'

'To be in good time for the races?'

'To live there.'

'By coincidence I shall shortly be temporarily residing six miles away at Windsor, I've taken 5 King Henry Crescent while my Berkeley Square property has gas lighting installed. Perhaps our paths will cross, for I understand Ascot shops in Windsor.'

'I think it highly unlikely we'll meet, my lord, for I do not intend to go to Windsor.' It was the second fib, for she knew that Margaret shopped a great deal in that town, and that therefore she would too.

His glance moved briefly over her. 'Where will you be residing in Ascot?'

This was dreadful. 'I – I believe it's somewhere near the racecourse,' she replied vaguely.

'Don't you know?' he asked in surprise.

'No, as it happens, I don't. A property has been obtained for me by my solicitor.' The Cat and Fiddle tarradiddles were coming thick and fast now.

'I see. Well, since you're going to be close to the racecourse, I can only imagine you have an interest in the turf. Am I right?'

'I don't know the first thing about horseracing,' she replied, at last managing to be honest.

'You'll be the only such soul in Ascot.'

'Are you a racing man, Lord Drummond?' she asked, her fingers crossed beneath the table that he wasn't, for if he was, he'd probably know Gregory.

'I used to be,' he replied shortly.

This was no mistaking the abrupt edge that had entered his voice. She began to uncross her fingers. 'You aren't now?'

'I attend the races, but I no longer own racehorses.'

'May I be so bold as to ask why?'

'My name was involved in an unpleasant *cause célèbre* last summer, and the experience was enough to persuade me to withdraw. My presence at Royal Ascot this year will undoubtedly raise a great many eyebrows, and if it hadn't been for my sister, Lady Bowes-Fenton, I'd have stayed away, but she persuaded me that nonattendance would be construed in some quarters as proof of a guilty conscience.'

She stared. 'It sounds very serious, Lord Drummond.'

'It's ancient history to me now, and to those who matter to me. The rest can think what they choose.'

She wondered what it was all about, but only briefly, for she was too concerned about one discomforting fact; he was going to be attending Royal Ascot. She would be as well, and not only that, she'd be rather conspicuous in the Bourne private box, which was second only to the royal stand itself in importance. Mary's warnings were suddenly beginning to sound ominously appropriate, and she, Helen, was beginning to wish she hadn't invented Mrs Brown, but had elected to tell the truth from the outset. She managed a smile, however, in an effort not only to hide her own unease, but to smooth over the awkwardness that had arisen in the conversation. 'I – I may not know anything about horseracing, Lord Drummond, but since I understand the queen herself likes to place a bet or three, perhaps I will be allowed a similar indulgence. Do you have a tip for me?'

'Do I look like a knowing one, Mrs Brown?' he asked, smiling a little.

'I really have no idea, sir.'

'Well, it so happens that there is one piece of advice I can give you, and that is to follow horses owned by Colonel Gregory Bourne.'

Helen couldn't hide the start this caused her; indeed, she was caught so off guard that she dropped her knife and fork with a clatter.

He looked at her in concern. 'Are you all right, Mrs Brown?'

'Er, yes. Quite all right, I – I just thought I heard someone at the door.'

'I didn't hear anything.' He got up and went to see, looking out into the empty hallway. The sound of the reunion dinner carried clearly, but there was no sign of anyone. He closed the door again and returned to his seat, smiling. 'Now then, where were we? Ah, yes, I was recommending Bourne's nags. He always has the finest blood in his stables, and since Royal Ascot is the be all and end all of his existence, well, he usually turns out a liberal sprinkling of winners.'

He sounded as if he knew Gregory well. Alarm spread unnervingly through her. Oh, surely fate couldn't have been mean enough to thrust her into the society of a man who could tell her family all about her escapade! 'Is – is Colonel Bourne a friend of yours?' she asked, dreading what his reply might be.

'He was, but now most definitely is not; indeed, there's only one man on earth I like less.'

Beyond the flood of relief that swept over her, she couldn't help wondering why he apparently loathed Gregory, who was always so agreeable, charming, and generally likeable.

He refilled their wine glasses. 'Enough of Bourne, the thought of him gives me indigestion. Would you mind if I asked you a rather personal question, Mrs Brown?'

'That depends on the question, sir.'

'When we first met you said you no longer wore mourning because you'd been a widow for a number of years.'

'Yes.' Oh, please don't ask me something that requires another fib.

'It's just that you're still so young, you hardly seem more than nineteen, which makes me wonder how old you actually were when you married.'

She made herself look directly into his eyes. 'Looks are deceiving, Lord Drummond. I married at eighteen, was widowed at twenty, and am now twenty-three.' Three more tarradiddles. She was thoroughly ashamed of herself.

'I wonder if I was ever acquainted with your husband? What was his first name?'

'I – I'd rather not talk about my marriage, Lord Drummond.' She felt trapped and couldn't think of any other way out.

'Forgive me, I didn't mean to tread upon painful memories.'

Again she was saved from embarrassment by the arrival of the landlord, waiter, and maid, this time to clear away the first course and serve the dessert, apple pie and thick cream.

Helen found herself relaxing again, thinking she'd parried all awkward questions quite well, but as he poured the last of the wine she soon realized she'd aroused too much of his curiosity after all.

'You never did tell me where exactly you come from in Worcestershire, Mrs Brown.'

'Didn't I?' She quickly sampled the apple pie. 'I do believe this is as excellent as the first course, Lord Drummond.'

He eyed her, swirling his glass of wine for a long moment. 'I think it's time to stop this verbal fencing, Mrs Brown.'

'Verbal fencing?' Her heart sank once more

'Yes. So far tonight you've avoided giving me any information about yourself, apart from the facts that you're twenty-three, a widow from Worcestershire, and you're going to reside in Ascot. I have the uncomfortable feeling that you think I'm trying to subtly interrogate you, which, believe me, I'm not. My questions have all been asked in complete innocence, but your reaction to them suggests the existence of secrets you're anxious to preserve at all costs.'

She looked guiltily at him, not knowing quite what to say.

'You're perfectly entitled to your privacy, Mrs Brown,' he went on, 'and what you do, where you go, and who you go to are your business and no one else's. Least of all mine.'

She suddenly realized what he was thinking. He believed she was going to a secret rendezvous with a lover! 'Lord Drummond, I rather fear you've jumped to the wrong conclusion.'

'I haven't jumped to any conclusion at all,' he replied diplomatically.

'Oh, yes, you have, you think I have a lover,' she retorted with a boldness born of three glasses of red wine.

There was amusement in his glance. 'Very well, I admit that that *is* what I was thinking.'

'You're entirely wrong.'

'Then I humbly crave your pardon. He smiled then. 'But for all that, it was a natural enough assumption, for you are indeed a very beautiful young woman, and I'll warrant you have admirers in plenty.'

'You flatter me, I think,' she answered, coloring.

'No, Mrs Brown, I pay you a deserved compliment.' He hesitated, swirling his wine again. 'Perhaps I should explain why I so readily jumped to the wrong conclusion. You see, your manner tonight has put me very much in mind of another lady, one I know very well indeed. You are a widow, and therefore a free agent, but she is very much married, to a harsh, vindictive, and jealous man who wouldn't hesitate to cast her off and deny her access to her children if he knew she'd briefly indulged in a passionate love affair. Please don't think I'm in any way likening you to an adulterous wife, it's just that while she was involved in that affair, she behaved with the same air of mystery that I now perceive in you.' He gave a disarming smile. 'I accept that I'm totally in error where you're concerned, and you have my abject apologies for embarrassing you.'

She had the grace to look exceeding guilty. 'Lord Drummond, I cannot allow you to apologize so profusely without offering some apology myself. You are right to think my conduct a little secretive, but wrong as to my reasons.' She swallowed, feeling very self-conscious indeed. 'Does – does the lady now live happily with her husband?'

'She exists with him, but that's all I can really say. The only time I saw her really happy was when she was embroiled in the affair.' He gave a rather ironic laugh. 'She may have been happy then, but it was an affair that cost *me* very dear indeed.'

'I don't understand. Unless, of course . . . I mean. . . .' She broke off in confusion.

He smiled. 'No, Mrs Brown, I was not the lover. So, now who's leaping to the wrong conclusions, mm?'

'It just suddenly seemed obvious,' she replied lamely, horridly aware of the flaming color on her cheeks.

'I know the feeling,' he murmured, still smiling.

'Forgive me for being so blatantly curious, but why did her affair cost you dear?' she asked, too intrigued to be discreet.

'It's a little involved. You see, someone else, another man, found out about the affair, and also that I was at pains to protect the lady concerned. This man for some reason wished to do me harm; and he proceeded to vilely blacken my character, threatening to expose the lady's secret if I attempted to clear my name.'

'But that's dreadful,' she gasped. 'It's – it's blackmail!'

'Yes, it is, but it's blackmail to which I submit, since the alternative is the ruining of the lady's life. She made a mistake when she broke her marriage vows, but it was only one mistake, and she doesn't deserve to suffer the awful fate that would certainly result if her affair was revealed. She loves her children very much, but would lose them, and that is something I could not have on my conscience.'

'So you submit to this man's will?'

'That's one way of putting it.' He smiled a little wryly.

'I didn't mean it in a derogatory way, Lord Drummond. Indeed, I think your actions very honorable.'

He seemed to see some irony in this. 'You're exceeding good for my morale, Mrs Brown. To be perfectly honest with you, I don't know why I've told you any of this, for I've never told anyone before.'

'Perhaps it's because I was rude enough to ask.'

'Perhaps.'

'May I be even more rude?'

He laughed. 'Oh, please, feel absolutely free.'

'You've asked me questions about my husband, but I've been wondering about you. Are you married, my lord?' She could hardly believe she was being forward enough to ask such a question, but it was something she really wanted to know.

He sat back, surveying her for a moment. 'Why, Mrs Brown, I'm of a mind to be flattered by your interest.'

She blushed.

'There is no Lady Drummond; indeed, there's no lady in my life at all at the moment.'

'I find that difficult to believe, sir.'

'As difficult as I find it to believe there's no man in yours?' he murmured, a certain devilment in his eyes.

'That's hardly the same. You're so. . . .' She broke off, flustered.

Her embarrassment amused him. 'Now I'm definitely of a mind to be flattered, for I do believe you're about to pay me a handsome compliment. So let me compliment you as well, my mysterious Mrs Brown, for I think you should know I find you very intriguing.' He spoke softly, and there was a disturbing warmth in his eyes.

Suddenly the atmosphere had changed, and she felt unprotected.

'I – I think it's time I retired to my room, Lord Drummond,' she said a little lamely.

He smiled, putting his napkin on the table and getting up. 'Oh Mrs Brown, if only you knew how alluring you are when you're all embarrassment, I vow you'd be very shocked indeed.'

She was sharply conscious of how attracted to him she was, and knowing that he wasn't indifferent to her came as a heady realization. Her pulse began to quicken, and to hide her confusion she made much of folding her own napkin.

He came around the table. 'Don't be alarmed,' he said, 'for although the base thought of seducing you has persisted all evening, I promise I don't intend to take advantage of you, tempting though the thought may be.'

She was very conscious of his closeness as he drew the chair away for her, and she knew how totally defenseless she was. Had he indeed chosen to take advantage, her treacherous senses would have betrayed her into offering little or no resistance. She was shocked by her thoughts. Had the wine affected her? Could she blame red Burgundy for her weakness? No, she couldn't, for even if she'd sipped water during dinner, she knew she'd still be feeling the same about Adam Drummond, Lord Drummond of Wintervale.

She was deeply dismayed with herself, and bewildered by the complete demolishment of the values impressed upon her during her five years at Cheltenham. All those lessons, warnings, and lectures about how to go on had been in vain, failing to turn her into anything remotely approaching a proper young lady of impeccable virtue; there was nothing proper about the emotion this man had aroused in her, and certainly nothing virtuous. What on earth had come over her?

He took a candle to escort her to her room. The inn was now resounding to the noise of the reunion dinner, which promised to go on for some hours yet. They'd reached the stage of singing bawdy songs, but she hardly heard anything, she was too preoccupied with her thoughts, and with her breathless awareness of how warm his hand was on her elbow as they ascended the staircase.

At her door she turned to face him, her diamonds glittering in the light of the candle. Her acquaintance with Lord Drummond was over, for he'd have left for his meeting at the War Office before she'd even risen from her bed the next morning. The charged atmosphere between them still lingered, and she managed a slightly self-conscious smile. 'Thank you for this evening, my lord. I – I hope you arrive in London in good time for your meeting.'

'I'm sure I will, but if I don't, it will be my own fault for chancing it until the last moment in order to enjoy another day with my sister and her children. Failure to arrive in time will result in endless lectures from my redoubtable uncle, Lord Llancwm, who is very definitely a soldier of the old school, expecting everything to be done yesterday. There are times when I wonder if I was wise to agree to dabble in government business for my good friend, Lord Liverpool, who thinks I have an aptitude for diplomacy. I was persuaded to believe him, which means I'm only too often seated across a Whitehall table from my uncle, who insists I should be away fighting with Wellington.'

'But Lord Liverpool prefers you to be in London?'

'Yes. He dispatches me on every errand he shrinks from himself.' He smiled. 'I've been described as the First Lord of the Treasury's running footman.'

She smiled too. 'I'm sure you belittle your role, sir.'

'Possibly.' The candlelight reflected in his eyes. 'You thanked me for tonight, but I should equally thank you. I've enjoyed this evening very much indeed, and I trust this isn't going to be a final good-bye, for it would please me immensely if we encountered each other again.'

She lowered her eyes, thinking that even if she hadn't fibbed from the moment she'd entered the inn, the antagonism that apparently existed between him and Gregory would have made any future contact very inadvisable indeed; but, oh how she'd have liked to see him again.

He took her hand, raising it to his lips. 'Good night, Mrs Brown.'

'Good night, Lord Drummond.'

He opened her door for her, and then turned to walk away, his shadow leaping against the passage walls as the candle guttered and smoked. He didn't look back as he turned the corner and vanished from her sight.

She stood in the faint pool of light from her room. He'd stepped out of her life as abruptly as he'd stepped into it, and now her stolen evening was over. But would anything ever be the same for her again? Tonight she'd been exposed to the tempting charm of a man who'd treated her in a rather more worldly way than he would had he realized she was so young and unmarried; it was an experience she'd liked very much, in spite of her own faux pas causing the occasional awkwardness, and she knew that any more time spent with him would have been very hazardous indeed for her heart and her virtue. It was as well that this brief encounter was at an end, for where he was concerned it would have been dangerously easy to allow her heart to rule her head.

She went into her room, closing the door softly behind her. But she wasn't closing it on a fleeting chapter of her life, for she was destined to see him again before he left, and in circumstances that were alarming, to say the least.

CHAPTER 4

Just as dawn was breaking, Helen was awakened by a stifled scream from the courtyard. Her eyes flew open and she sat up sharply in the bed, her hair tumbling loose about her shoulders. Sleep clung confusingly, and she didn't know what had disturbed her.

Everything was quiet now, there wasn't a sound except for Mary's rhythmic breathing as she slept on the pallet. The night candle burned steadily, and outside it had stopped raining. She leaned over to pick up her watch. It was nearly half past four. She replaced the watch on the little table and drew a long breath, gazing at the window on to the gallery. It was still dark outside, but a faint glimmer of silver told of dawn's approach. Would she hear Lord Drummond drive away?

Slowly, she wriggled back down under the warm bedclothes. She didn't want to hear him leave, she didn't want to know the very moment he quitted her life. She closed her eyes to try to sleep again, but as she did so another muffled cry came from the courtyard. With a startled gasp she sat up once more, pushing her hair back from her face as she looked toward the gallery door and window.

Slowly, she pushed the bedclothes aside and slipped from the bed, picking up her light-blue frilled muslin wrap and moving hesitantly toward the door. Behind her, Mary continued to sleep, sighing as she turned over on the pallet. Helen put the wrap on, and then quietly opened the gallery door to peep out into the gloom of first light.

The air was damp and cool as she stepped outside. The light blue of her wrap was turned to a ghostly white, and a gentle dawn breeze stirred her tangled hair as she placed her shaking hands on the rail to look cautiously down into the shadowy courtyard below.

Everything was utterly silent again, and the only sign of anyone's being about was a shaft of light from an open kitchen door. The moments passed, and still the courtyard remained silent, although she became aware, of sounds from the stables. She didn't need to be told that those sounds were of Lord Drummond's curricle being made ready. Suddenly there was a stealthy scuffling in the courtyard and her eyes flew fearfully back to search the inky shadows below. Someone was down there!

Her pulse quickened and her hands trembled on the rail. She couldn't see anyone. The faint light from the kitchen door shone on cobbles that were still damp from the rain, and she could make out the steps leading down from the gallery. The water butts loomed dark against the inn wall, and the archway out to the London road was as black as pitch, but the iron hoop where the lurcher had been tied was a vague metallic glimmer in the darkness.

A lamp was lit suddenly in one of the ground floor rooms, and in the seconds before the curtains were closed the light flooded out over the yard. A faint movement caught Helen's eye. It was by another water butt she hadn't noticed before, standing in a far corner beyond the ticket office, and as the curtains closed and the darkness engulfed everything again, Helen realized she'd seen the frantic beating of a woman's hand upon the burly shoulder of an assailant.

Helen's heart almost stopped as she concentrated on that dark corner. She leaned forward, staring intently, determined to be quite sure what she'd seen. Her eyes seemed to become accustomed to things, and she could see the struggling woman doing all she could to break free from her rough attacker. It was the maid who'd served dinner, and the man was the stagecoachman whose team had so nearly caused a fatal accident when Helen had arrived. The maid's bodice was ripped and her hair was loose, jolted from its pins by the savagery of the attack. She was at the man's mercy, unable to scream for help because his huge hand was clamped over her mouth.

Helen's reaction was immediate and instinctive. She began to raise the alarm at the top of her lungs. 'Help! Come quickly! Please!' Her cries for assistance pierced the silence, startling the rooks from the elms behind the inn so that they rose in a noisy cloud.

Mary ran out to her straightaway, her eyes wide with fright. 'Miss Fairmead? Whatever is it?'

'Down there. That coachman is attacking a maid!' Helen pointed, but the moment she'd screamed the man had dragged his victim right behind the water butt and all was suddenly completely still.

Mary peered down. 'I can't see anything, miss.'

'He's got her there, I know he has.' Helen drew another breath and started to call out for help again. 'Come quickly, someone! Help! Please!'

Further along the gallery several doors opened and some rather bleary faces peered out, only to withdraw sharply as Helen directed her pleas to them.

The courtyard became brighter once more as the curtains below were flung open again. There were more lights in the kitchens; too, and a scullery maid and a fat cook emerged brandishing brooms. They stared up at Helen and Mary on the gallery, but took fright almost immediately, hurrying back inside and bolting the door.

Helen stared down helplessly. Would no one go to the maid's rescue? Even as she thought this, Lord Drummond hurried from the direction of the stables, his traveling cloak billowing as he paused, looking straight up at her. She pointed toward the corner. 'Over there, a coachman has one of the maids! You must help her.'

He whirled around in the direction she pointed, but everything was utterly still. Helen could have wept with frustration, and gathering her skirts she hurried along the gallery toward the steps, Mary loyally following. They descended to the courtyard, and Helen ran to him. 'There is a man there, my lord, and he's forcing himself upon the maid. I saw it all, truly I did!'

He put out a hand to stop her. 'Go back to the steps, Mrs Brown, this is no place for—' He said no more, for at that moment the terrified maid managed to cry out.

'Help me! *Please!*'

The coachman relaxed his grip and she tore herself free. Bruised and battered, her bodice torn, she ran weeping toward Helen, who drew her to the foot of the steps, well away from the coachman, who'd emerged at last, revealing by his staggering gait that he was dangerously in drink.

He had no intention of surrendering without a fight, and with sudden agility darted to one side to snatch up a pitch-fork that rested against the wall. Helen stifled a cry as the sharp prongs were stabbed viciously toward Lord Drummond, coming within inches of their target.

Lord Drummond's agility was more than a match. He moved nimbly back, circling as his huge opponent kept jabbing the pitch-fork at him without success.

Helen held the sobbing maid, who was so distraught that she knew nothing of the drama behind her. Mary stood nearby, her eyes huge with fear as she watched the two men.

Lord Drummond moved tantalizingly close, inviting another lunge, and the coachman obliged, stabbing the pitchfork wildly at him and missing. Again and again this happened, with Lord Drummond moving easily back out of reach. The coachman became enraged, thrusting forward far too violently at last and losing his balance. It was the moment Lord Drummond had been waiting for, and as the drunken man stumbled forward he moved in, felling him completely with a single blow to the jaw. The pitchfork clattered to the cobbles and the coachman lay senseless where he fell.

For a moment Helen closed her eyes with unutterable relief, but then she turned as the kitchen door opened again and the fat cook came out to belatedly usher the weeping maid to safety. Helen caught the woman's eye accusingly.

Faces were now gazing down from the gallery, faces that were much the worse for wear and belonged to the dinner revelers. A trio of stagecoach passengers were together near the top of the steps, gazing down in consternation as they saw Lord Drummond crouch by their coachman for a moment before ordering some ostlers, who'd appeared from the stables, to drag the unconscious man away and lock him up somewhere in readiness for a visitation from the constables.

The faces withdrew from the gallery as Lord Drummond approached Helen, his glance taking in her disheveled hair and the way her muslin wrap outlined her figure. 'So, we meet again after all, Mrs Brown,' he said softly.

'Do – do you always make such dramatic appearances on the scene, sir?' she inquired, managing to somehow inject a note of lightness into her voice.

'I'm afraid I'm a very vain St George, always ready to demonstrate my peerless qualities as a rescuer of damsels in distress,' he replied, smiling, but then became more serious. 'It seems I must ask you yet again if you're all right?'

'Yes, thank you. Are you?'

'I had little enough to do – it's simple enough to keep out of the way of a man who's completely in drink.'

'You were the only one brave enough to go to the rescue.'

'Not quite, for you showed remarkable courage yourself.'

'Me? But I did nothing.'

'Which is why you're down here, and not safely up on the gallery or even still in your room?' He smiled. 'We can both take a bow, I think.'

She suddenly remembered she was in her undress, and lowered her eyes in some embarrassment. 'You probably think me very indiscreet.'

'Indiscreet?' There was a touch of humor in his voice. 'Why on earth should I think that?'

'Because I'm staying in this place, because I so readily accepted your invitation to dinner, and because I've now appeared in public in my undress.' She couldn't meet his eyes, and suddenly felt dreadful. She'd behaved apallingly, and now, in the cold light of dawn, she was only too conscious of the fact.

'Mrs Brown, I promise you I don't think anything ill of your conduct; indeed, it has been quite obvious to me that having to lodge here has been very difficult for you. As I said earlier, I can't begin to guess what your secrets are, and it isn't my place to guess anyway, but that doesn't stop me wishing I did know everything about you. If it hadn't been for the importance of my appointment in town, I'd have stayed here a little longer in the hope of furthering our acquaintance.'

She stared at him. 'You – you would?'

'How can you really doubt it? Haven't I made it plain enough that I find you devilishly attractive? Perhaps I should make it plainer.' He put his hand to her waist, drawing her close to kiss her on the lips. It was no brief caress, but a leisurely arousal of her already susceptible body. She was enveloped by a sweet, beguiling ecstasy, his to do with as he pleased, and her lips parted willingly as her body melted against him. She surrendered to the wild feelings tumbling through her, returning the kiss with an unqualified honesty that hid nothing.

Mary watched in the utmost dismay, unable to believe that her chaste, if a little impetuous, mistress was really behaving in this wanton way.

His lips moved richly over Helen's as for a long, long moment he dwelt on the kiss, but at last he drew slowly away. 'I sincerely hope that this is to be *au revoir* and not good-bye,' he said softly, his eyes very dark.

She couldn't say anything. Her heart was pounding so much it was unbearable, and the tumult of emotion throbbing through her was so wild and exciting that she was in danger of forgetting she was in this place under false pretenses, in danger of forgetting that he and Gregory viewed each other with a deep dislike.

He saw the warm flush on her face. 'You're a sweet mystery to me, and it may be that you have no choice but to remain a mystery, so please believe me when I say that if this is the case, then you will never know a moment's embarrassment because of me. If we should come face to face under circumstances that are an anxiety to you, and you need to forget we are acquainted, then I will bow to your wishes.'

She wanted to say so much to him, but as she struggled to find the right words, Mary knew it was time to intervene. 'Madam, you really should go back inside, it's not right to stay out here in only your wrap.'

The note of warning was timely, and in a cold wash of sanity Helen strove to collect herself. What would he think of her if he knew she'd told him nothing but lies since they met? And what would he say if he knew she was the sister-in-law of Colonel Gregory Bourne? She wanted to see him again, but everything conspired to make that a very unwise decision indeed.

He put his hand to her cheek. 'If by any lucky chance you do wish to further our acquaintance, well, there are three addresses which will find me; Drummond House in Berkeley Square, Wintervale itself, and 5 King Henry Crescent, Windsor. I will not embarrass you by attempting to seek you out in Ascot, for I respect your right to every privacy. The ball is very firmly in your court, Mrs Brown.' His thumb moved gently against her skin for a moment more, and then he turned and walked away toward the stables.

A minute later, she heard the curricle. He drove across the courtyard, and she felt his warm glance upon her before he tooled the fresh bays beneath the archway and out onto the London road. The cool dawn air didn't seem to touch her, she was still wrapped in his embrace. She gazed at the archway, listening until the sound of the curricle died away completely into the distance.

Mary looked anxiously at her. 'Miss Fairmead, you were very unwise to permit such intimate liberties.'

'I know.'

'And as for returning the kiss like that, oh, miss, if it ever got out you'd have no reputation left.'

'I know that, too,' replied Helen softly.

'Please come back inside.'

Helen hesitated. 'It would be so easy to fall in love with him, Mary.'

'He's a man of the world, miss, and it's my belief he's made love to a hundred ladies.'

Helen looked at her. 'And I'm just another to add to the list?'

'I don't know, miss, but it has to be wondered. Besides, you told me last night that he and Colonel Bourne are at odds, so perhaps you'd best remember what he said.'

'Said?'

'That if you wished not to acknowledge him when next you meet, *if* you meet, then he'd respect that wish. You just might come face to face with him, Miss Fairmead, especially if he's attending Royal Ascot, and if you do, well, you'll be living under the colonel's roof, won't you?'

Helen drew a long breath. 'Yes, I will.'

'He and the colonel have fallen out, and it could be that the colonel is in the wrong, but it could also be that Lord Drummond is in the wrong. You don't know anything about him. He mentioned that cozy thing, but. . . .'

'Cozy thing? Oh, you mean the *cause célèbre*.'

'Yes, miss. Well, he told you about it, but he didn't really give any details, did he? Maybe that's because he knows he's in the wrong.'

Helen looked at her. 'You're right, of course, except that I find it hard to believe he'd do anything wrong.'

'Do you find it easier to think the colonel could do something wrong?' persisted the maid, determined at all costs to steer her mistress away from the rash course she'd seemed set on ever since arriving at the inn, even if by presuming to steer, she was stepping a little above herself.

'No, of course not.' Helen managed a smile. 'It's all right, Mary, I know you have my best interests at heart.'

'I do, miss. Now, please come back inside, it's cold out here.'

Helen nodded and moved toward the steps, pausing at the bottom to look at the maid again: 'I know all you say about him could be true, he could be a libertine, a wicked lord with a dark past, intent only upon my seduction, even though he protests he isn't, but when he kissed me. . . . Oh, Mary, I've never felt like that before, it was the most wonderful feeling in the world.'

CHAPTER 5

As the journey to Ascot continued later that morning, Helen tried her hardest to put Lord Drummond from her mind, but it proved an impossible task. Could Mary possibly be right, was he far from the flawless hero he seemed? Or was her own instinct more accurate, and he was all she could ever wish? Whatever the truth about him, however, one thing was certain as far as she was concerned: his smiles and kisses had consigned caution to oblivion. She wondered greatly about the unexplained *cause célèbre* he'd mentioned, and about the lady whose reputation and happiness he was so anxious to protect. He'd said he hadn't been her lover, but that didn't mean he wasn't in love with her. Helen gazed out of the chaise window. Yes, from the way he'd spoken of the lady, it seemed very probable indeed that he loved her, and that if there wasn't anyone in his life at the moment, it was because this particular lady wasn't available.

It wasn't until the middle of the afternoon, as the chaise was driving over Ascot Heath, that she managed to temporarily forget Lord Drummond, or Adam, as she now found herself thinking of him, and turn her attention to the scenery outside. The race meeting wasn't for another two weeks, but already the heath bore signs of it. Makeshift stables were dotted everywhere to accommodate the many horses that were arriving from all over the country, some under their own power, others in large, slow-moving wagons. Owners liked to have their horses well settled in before a meeting, and so there weren't only stables, there were grooms, stable boys, temporary forges, sheds of hay, and everything else associated with the world of the turf. A steady flow of horses and wagons trickled along the road, all converging on the course built one hundred years before on a whim of Queen Anne's. By the opening day of the royal meeting, a veritable town of tents and booths would have sprung up behind the stands lining the course, and in this town would take place the cockfighting, prizefighting, wrestling, gambling, and drinking that were as great an attraction to the lower orders as the horse racing was to the *beau monde*. When the meeting commenced, crowds of thousands would descend upon the heath, including practically every resident of Mayfair, but for the moment, in spite of all the increased activity, it was all still quite quiet.

Leaving the racecourse behind, the chaise drove on to Bourne End, and as the lodge gates appeared ahead, she found herself wondering what her first impression of the house itself would be. She'd been told about it countless times in Margaret's letters, but she'd never seen it, having only stayed previously at the town house in Park Lane.

The chaise swept through the gates, which were set by a beautiful gothic lodge, and then entered the incomparable park, which was ablaze with the late spring glory of purple, white, and crimson rhododendrons. There may have been a great deal that was new and innovative about the house itself, but the park had been laid out by Capability Brown at the height of his brilliance, and Gregory had very wisely elected to leave it untouched.

At last the house itself came into view. The famous architect Mr Searles had been engaged to design and build the new Bourne End, and the rambling two story building, with its shallow roof and tall chimneys, spread with magnificent irregularity over a low hill in the center of the park. There was nothing symmetrical or conventional about it, every elevation was novel and different, with semicircular roofed balconies of great size supported on columns above leafy verandas. She knew from her sister's letters that there wasn't a square or rectangular room in the building, they were all oval, circular, or octagonal, and those on the ground floor could all be entered from the outside through large French windows, either directly from the grounds or through tall conservatories where tropical plants pressed luxuriantly against the glass. Informality and nature were the key, and as a consequence there were leaves and flowers everywhere, trained on trellises, up the balcony columns, and around the French windows. Spring leaves, lilac, honeysuckle, and very early roses nodded against warm brickwork, as if the house was inviting a complete invasion, and the whole was a symphony of the picturesque.

Helen drank in the scene as the chaise traveled the final few hundred yards of the journey. Behind the house there were gardens, and the immense white stableblock that was famous the length and breadth of England. The servants' wing was adjacent to the stables, joined to the house but really quite separate, which was in itself a startling departure from the usual unified design which had marked all great houses until now.

The chaise drew up at last before the main entrance, which lay beneath one of the immense roofed balconies, and Helen prepared to alight, having already decided that Bourne End was quite the most beautiful home she'd ever seen. As the crunch of hooves and wheels on gravel died away, two footmen in Gregory's gray-and-gold livery hurried to open the chaise door. One of them assisted Helen down, and as she stood by the vehicle she became aware of the rhythmic drumming of swift hooves on grass. She turned quickly to see several racehorses being exercised at full stretch across the park and away into the distance. She reflected that they were a sight and sound to which she was going to become greatly accustomed from now on.

A delighted voice drew her attention sharply back to the house, as her sister hurried out to greet her. 'Helen! Oh, Helen, we weren't expecting you just yet!'

Margaret Bourne was very like her younger sister, with the same green eyes and honey-colored hair, but she was shorter and more rounded, with a dimpled smile and plump arms. She wore a pale green silk gown that became her particularly well, and her costly cashmere shawl dragged carelessly on the ground as she ran to hug Helen.

The sisters embraced joyfully, and then Margaret stood back, her head on one side as she inspected Helen's appearance. 'My, my, how very London you are, to be sure.'

'I have Gregory to thank for my Madame Rosalie wardrobe.'

'He was only too pleased to provide for you. But why on earth are you here today?'

'I couldn't stand the thought of Miss Figgis for another minute, so I persuaded her to let me go. Five years is a horrid long time to be incarcerated at school.'

'But worth it to produce young ladies of spotless character, faultless poise, and perfect manners, which is how I trust *you* have turned out.'

How Helen managed to give an innocent smile, she didn't know; all she did know was that as her sister spoke, visions of the goings-on at the Cat and Fiddle hovered accusingly all around. Spotless character, faultless poise, and perfect manners? Nothing could have been further from the truth after her disgraceful behavior at the inn, and she only hoped Margaret would never find out how far her little sister had fallen from grace in one single day.

The footmen were unloading the trunks from the chaise boot, watched very closely by Mary, who was determined that her mistress's belongings should be handled with the utmost care. The postboy hovered anxiously nearby, having indeed adopted a different attitude for the second part of the journey, just as Adam had so dryly predicted, and the moment the last trunk was removed from the boot and the lid closed, he remounted and drove away as swiftly as the tired horses would permit.

'You should have waited for the traveling carriage,' said Margaret a little disapprovingly.

'That wouldn't have been nearly so interesting,' Helen replied, with much more meaning than her sister could possibly know.

'Interesting?'

'Well, the postboy was full of dire warnings about highwaymen.'

'Highwaymen, in *this* day and age?

'Oh, I'm reliably informed that there is one, a certain Lord Swag.'

'Good heavens, I thought they were extinct.'

Some more racehorses galloped across the park, and Margaret turned quickly to observe them. 'The light-gray is Musket, Gregory's hope for the Maisemore Stakes, and the chestnut is Lexicon, which is reckoned to have an excellent chance in the Gold Cup itself. I do so hope they both do well, for after last year's disagreeable events it would be good to carry everything off without upset.'

Helen looked at her. 'Last year's disagreeable events? But I thought all the Bourne End horses won.'

'They did, it was the behind-the-scenes trouble I was referring to.'

'What behind-the-scenes trouble? You didn't tell me anything in your letters. You gave me the impression that last year's was one of the best Royal Ascots you'd attended, with the Czar's presence, and. . . .'

'I didn't mention it because it really was too upsetting at the time. Gregory was very anxious indeed to have it all forgotten as quickly as possible, especially since the Jockey Club inquiry cleared him of all involvement. Luckily, it was all kept from the newspapers, even though there was a great deal of whispering.' Margaret smiled apologetically. 'Helen, I really wish I hadn't said anything to you, because if he knew Gregory would be very cross with me. It's all ancient history now, anyway, so please forget I ever said a word.'

Ancient history. That was how Adam had spoken of the *cause célèbre* he'd referred to but never explained. Could whatever had happened to him be the selfsame thing Margaret was at pains to avoid speaking of now? Surely it had to be. Adam and Gregory had once been friends, but now loathed each other, and now it seemed that something of considerable importance, something disagreeable, had happened in the lives of both men the previous summer. That event had led to Adam's withdrawing from further participation in horse racing except as a spectator, and whatever it was that had happened to Gregory had also been very much connected with horse racing.

Margaret linked her arm. 'Shall we go inside and see Gregory? He doesn't even know you're here; he's far too absorbed in watching his horses through his telescope. It will do him good to take his eyes away from the wretched thing for a while, for I truly believe he'll wake up one morning with one huge eye in the middle of his forehead.'

Laughing, the sisters went into the house, and Helen immediately halted in surprise, gazing around the circular entrance hall. The cream walls were hung with the many racing certificates presented to Gregory's winners, and with paintings of those winners. Three chandeliers were suspended from the ceiling, and a curving staircase followed the line of the wall, rising between fine Doric columns to a balustraded landing on the floor above. Daylight shafted in from high windows, falling on a floor of mosaic swirls of arcadian greenery. A number of fine double doors opened off the hall, and on either side of each were tables where vases of flowers and ferns had been exquisitely arranged. A basket stood next to one of these tables, and with it some more flowers, a pair of scissors, and a pair of dainty little gloves, from which Helen knew immediately that Margaret had been arranging the flowers when she'd heard the chaise arrive.

Margaret smiled at her. 'What do you think?'

'I think you've arranged them beautifully.'

'Not the flowers, silly, I mean the house.'

'Oh, it's perfect, Margaret, truly perfect.'

'I'm afraid it's already been trumped.'

'It has? Surely not.'

'I fear so, the Prince Regent has out-picturesqed us with the Royal Lodge, his new *cottage orné* in Windsor Great Park. Well, it's hardly a cottage, it's a veritable thatched palace, and when it was completed last month it was universally declared to be the most modern and superior dwelling in the land. I was quite of a mind to be miffed, but it's impossible to remain miffed with him for long, he's too charming.'

Helen gave a slight laugh. 'You know, I can still hardly believe my sister is friendly with the Prince Regent. It's a world away from our life in Worcestershire, isn't it?'

'It certainly is, and you are shortly going to meet the prince yourself. We're holding a dinner party here in a few days' time, and he's going to be the guest of honor. I trust your fortitude is up to not only the prince but also twenty-five other guests, including a number of dukes, duchesses, earls, countesses, and sundry other persons of consequence, including the Russian ambassador and at least three lady patronesses from Almack's.'

Helen felt quite pale at the prospect. 'The Prince Regent *and* three of Almack's dragons?' She murmured faintly.

'Yes, but don't fret, for I'm sure you'll carry it off with impeccable Fairmead flair. It's all a considerable coup for you, you know, for there aren't many young ladies who embark on their first Season with the Prince Regent under their belt – in a manner of speaking, of course.' Margaret grinned.

The footmen carried the first trunk in, still watched over by Mary, and as they vanished up the staircase, a butler appeared from one of the doors at the far end of the hall.

'Ah, Morris,' said Margaret, 'as you can see, Miss Fairmead has arrived a little earlier than expected. Will you send some house-maids up to see that her room is in perfect order?'

'Yes, madam.' His voice was deep and rather lugubrious, and Helen was irresistibly reminded of an undertaker she'd once encountered in Cheltenham.

'And then will you have some Pekoe and sweet almond biscuits served in the drawing room?'

'Yes, madam. Is there anything else, madam?'

'No, Morris, that is all.'

'Madam.' He bowed and withdrew again.

Margaret rolled her eyes behind his back, and it was all Helen could do not to burst into giggles. Linking arms again, the sisters proceeded toward the nearest double doors, which led to a large, extremely beautiful octagonal room with a line of four French windows opening on to a veranda beneath another of the balconies. The walls were adorned with gilt-framed mirrors, shelves of books, paintings, and display cabinets, and there were comfortable floral armchairs and plum velvet sofas. The windows were swathed with plum velvet curtains and hung with delicate nets that moved gently in the light breeze coming in through the one open French window. There were more flower arrangements, and pots containing fine plants, and the room looked very inviting indeed.

Colonel Gregory Bourne, late of the Berkshire Regiment and now commander of the local militia, was bending by his telescope, watching the progress of some of his racehorses. He was tall and fair-haired, wearing a pine-green riding coat and buckskin breeches. His top hat, gloves, and riding crop lay on a nearby table, and he remained totally unaware of his wife's entrance with her sister.

Margaret surveyed him fondly, winking at Helen before speaking to him. 'Sirrah, where are your manners?'

'Mm?'

'Lexicon's coming on reasonably, I suppose, but Musket appears to possess only three legs and doesn't stand an earthly in the Maisemore.'

'Eh?' He straightened immediately, turning crossly to face her. 'What was that you said?'

'I said it's a lovely day, made lovelier by the unexpected arrival of my only dear sister.' Margaret smiled at him.

He blinked and then noticed Helen for the first time. 'Helen! Where have you sprung from?'

'Cheltenham,' she replied dryly.

He grinned, crossing to embrace her. The only outward signs now of the dreadful injuries he'd sustained at Vimiero were his limp, the awkward set of his right arm, and the rather romantic white saber scar on his cheek. He hugged her warmly, kissing her cheek. 'Welcome to Bourne End, Helen.'

'Thank you, Gregory, it's lovely to be here at last.'

He ushered her to one of the sofas, and then escorted Margaret to one of the chairs, standing behind her with one hand protectively on her shoulder. 'Margaret, I trust you haven't been doing anything too strenuous,' he said, looking down anxiously into his wife's green eyes.

'I don't think anyone could possibly describe flower arranging as strenuous, Gregory,' she replied.

'I know, but you're quite capable of doing things the doctor has strictly forbidden.'

Helen was instantly alarmed. 'The doctor? Surely you're not ill, Margaret.'

'No, I'm just in an, er, interesting condition.'

Helen stared at her, her face breaking into a delighted smile. 'A baby? At last? Oh, I'm so pleased for you both.'

'We're quite pleased with ourselves,' Gregory observed, 'for we were beginning to think we'd remain childless.'

'When is my niece or nephew due?' asked Helen.

'Oh, another seven months yet,' replied Margaret, 'it's very early days, and I'm afraid I feel positively green in the mornings, but I'm assured that soon I'll be glowing and disgustingly healthy.'

Gregory looked a little anxious. 'I still say we should cancel the dinner party.'

'I won't hear of it!'

'Then at least promise to forgo the Farrish House ball this year.'

'I won't hear of that, either, Gregory Bourne, I only feel ill in the mornings; apart from that I'm quite all right, and you wouldn't really deny Helen her first two important social events, would you?'

'Well. . . .'

'Shame on you, sir. I notice you don't think I should avoid the four days of the race meeting.'

'That's different.'

'You, sirrah, have a selective conscience.'

'And you are too given to wrapping your waspish tongue around me,' he grumbled, grinning.

'You deserve it.'

Helen was impatient to know about the ball. 'There's to be a ball?'

'Yes,' said Margaret immediately, 'at Farrish House in Windsor on the eve of the race meeting, in about two weeks' time. It's a masked ball, and everyone who's anyone attends.'

'And I will, too?'

'Of course. I'm taking you to Windsor very shortly to choose a costume from a couturière there who specializes in such things. She's promised to keep several costumes aside just for you.'

Gregory smiled. 'All you have to remember, little sister, is that you wear the fancy dress to Farrish House, not to the Prince Regent's dinner party.'

'I think Miss Figgis taught me just about enough to get that right, thank you,' responded Helen.

The Pekoe and sweet almond biscuits were brought, and as Helen accepted her cup, the conversation suddenly took a very different turn.

Gregory leaned forward to select a biscuit. 'Tell me, Helen, at what on earth time did you leave Cheltenham this morning to reach here in the middle of the afternoon?'

'An age ago, it seems,' she replied vaguely.

'It must have been.' He didn't pursue the point.

'Helen tells me there are still highwaymen to be found terrorizing the king's highway,' said Margaret.

Gregory was immediately interested. 'Not Lord Swag, by any chance?'

'Why, yes,' replied Helen. 'You've obviously heard of him.'

'He's struck in the neighborhood of Windsor on two occasions recently. I hope you didn't encounter him.'

'No. I – I did have an alarming encounter of another sort, though. There was nearly a very nasty accident, and I might have been killed if someone's quick thinking hadn't saved me in the very nick of time.'

Margaret was alarmed. 'Oh, Helen, what on earth happened?'

Helen hesitated, but she had to mention Adam at some point in the proceedings, and now was as good a time as any. 'We'd stopped at an inn to, er, change the horses. A dog frightened the team of a stagecoach, and I was almost trampled, because I chose that of *all* moments to alight. Lord Drummond pulled me to safety in time.'

The room was suddenly so quiet, the proverbial pin could have been heard to drop. Helen looked quickly from Margaret to Gregory. Their faces were very still. 'Have I said something wrong?' she asked at last, knowing full well that she had.

Gregory put down his cup. 'Are you referring to *Adam* Drummond?' he asked stiffly.

'Yes.'

Margaret drew a long breath. 'Oh, no. Of all the men in England, it had to be him!'

Gregory looked at Helen. 'I realize you have every reason to be grateful to him, and if he saved your life, then we're grateful to him as well, but apart from that, I won't have his name mentioned in this house.'

Helen was taken aback. 'But. . . .'

'Have I made myself clear, Helen?'

She had to nod. 'Yes. Perfectly clear.'

'Good. And now, if you will both excuse me, I have much to do.' Snatching up his hat, gloves, and riding crop, he walked out past his telescope to the veranda, his limp emphasized by his anger.

Stunned, Helen stared after him. Whatever she'd been expecting from a mention of Adam, it hadn't been this. She'd never seen

Gregory so angry, He was usually so placid and amiable, but it seemed that she'd certainly found a way of touching him on a raw nerve. She looked askance at Margaret. 'Will you explain all this to me?'

'As I said earlier, it's all best left, and now that you've seen how it affects Gregory, perhaps you'll accept that I'm right. It nearly resulted in Gregory's being unfairly banned from racing, and it *did* result in Adam's withdrawing from the turf because he was shunned.'

As she'd said earlier? So, Adam's *cause célèbre* and the 'behind-the-scenes trouble' were one and the same. Helen sat back. 'Margaret you also said earlier that it was all ancient history, which it quite patently isn't.'

'Perhaps I was guilty of wishful thinking. Helen, Adam Drummond may be a paragon to you, but to us he's a low, dishonorable blackguard who betrayed our friendship and brought Bourne End's good name into disrepute. He's anathema to us now, and no matter how high he may stand in your personal esteem, I expect you, while under our roof, to observe our wishes in this. Don't mention him again.' Margaret picked up the teapot, the expression on her face indicating that the subject was most definitely closed. 'Some more tea?' she asked.

Helen longed to press her for the full story; indeed, she desperately wanted to find out what had happened, but she knew that this wasn't the time. With a sigh she nodded and held out her cup. 'Yes. Thank you.'

CHAPTER 6

Helen rose early on her first morning at Bourne End, stepping out onto the balcony of her bedroom and gazing down at the park, which was bathed in spring sunshine. The rhododendrons seemed even more magnificent and colorful than the day before, and already the drumming of hooves signified activity in the stables. A string of racehorses, their jockeys riding short in the new American style, moved swiftly over the dewy grass, vanishing from sight among the trees.

As she stood there in her light blue robe, she wondered if this new day would bring any more information about what had shattered the friendship with Adam.

At dinner the night before, both Gregory and Margaret had been at pains to behave as if the awkwardness of earlier hadn't happened. Indeed, they couldn't have been warmer or more full of the exciting things they had planned for her first Season, but not by so much as a word did they mention Adam, or what he was supposed to have done. They had mentioned another gentleman, though, and very frequently. A certain Mr Ralph St John occupied a very special place in their esteem, and they seemed to be firmly of the opinion that he would soon occupy a similar place in Helen's. He was spoken of with much approval, even his monumental gambling debts were blithely discounted, and Helen was informed that she'd soon make his highly desirable acquaintance, for he had been engaged to escort her to the dinner in a day or so's time. But she wasn't in the least bit interested in the wonderful Mr Ralph St John, her thoughts were all of Adam, Lord Drummond.

Today must surely prove more productive of information, for not only had Gregory already gone to the stables, which meant that Margaret would be alone at breakfast, but Mary had been primed to find out all she could in the servants' quarters.

She went back into her room, a handsome oval chamber with rich shell-pink Chinese silk on the walls. The bed was an elegant four-poster hung with ruched white muslin, and the chairs on either side of the marble fireplace were upholstered in rose velvet. The Axminster carpet had been specially woven in a floral design in pink, gold, and white, and the same design was picked out on the ceiling from which a crystal chandelier was suspended. Wardrobes were cunningly concealed in the walls, and their doors alternated with tall mirrors that made the room seem very light and airy.

She sat at the muslin-draped dressing table, and drew her hairbrush slowly through her hair as she waited for Mary to arrive.

At last there was a discreet knock at the door, and as the glass domed clock on the mantlepiece chimed nine, the maid came in. She looked very fresh and tidy in a gray gingham dress, white apron, and starched mob cap, and her dark hair was pinned up into a very precise knot. 'Good morning, Miss Fairmead,' she said, hurrying to take the brush and commence her morning duties.

'Good morning, Mary. Are you comfortable in your new room?'

'Oh, yes, miss. I've never had a room all to myself before, it's very grand.'

'Do you think you'll like it here?'

'Yes, miss.'

Looking at the maid's reflection in the dressing table mirror, Helen detected a certain telling flush. 'What's his name, Mary Caldwell?' she inquired in a teasing tone.

'Miss?'

'Don't look all innocence, I can read you like a book. Who is he?'

Mary colored. 'His name's Peter, miss, and he's the colonel's under-coachman.'

'And you're smitten?'

'A bit.' Mary smiled at her in the mirror before going on with her brushing.

Helen closed her eyes as the soft crackling sound filled the room, but at last she opened them again to watch Mary. 'Did you find anything out for me?'

The brush hesitated. 'Yes, Miss Fairmead.'

'And?'

'You won't like it, miss.'

'No, I don't suppose I will, since everyone here seems to think Lord Drummond is the devil incarnate, but I still have to know.'

Mary didn't really want to say what she'd been told about the seemingly dashing and gallant lord, but knew by the look in her mistress's green eyes that she had to. 'Well, miss, Peter told me that Lord Drummond and a gentleman named Mr Ralph St John were very good friends of Colonel and Mrs Bourne, often staying here. Mr St John still does stay here a great deal.'

Helen lowered her glance quickly. Adam had stayed here, in this very house?

'Mr St John is so close a friend, miss, that Peter says he seems like one of the family.'

'Yes, from what I was told at the dinner table last night, that's quite true. I'm expected to like him very much indeed; neither Colonel nor Mrs Bourne think there's any doubt that I will.'

'He's a racing man, miss, like the colonel, and like Lord Drummond was before last year, but he likes to wager on the horses, not own them.'

'I hope you're soon going to get around to telling me what happened last year,' declared Helen with feeling, 'because I think I shall scream if you don't.'

Avoiding her eyes in the mirror, Mary went slowly on with her work, drawing the brush gently through the long honey-colored hair. 'Last year one of the colonel's best racehorses was one called Prince Agamemnon, and it was due to run in the Maisemore Stakes, with odds as short as possible, because it was reckoned a certainty to win. Then, a week before Royal Ascot, the horse ran unexpectedly at an unimportant race at another meeting. The colonel said it was because he wanted to keep it up to the highest pitch, and another race was needed. Well, it ran very badly indeed, and its jockey, a man called Sam Edney, said the horse was off color and wouldn't win the Maisemore. This naturally meant that the odds for the Maisemore lengthened very much indeed, and so there was a great deal of whispering when the horse romped home by a distance. The colonel's honesty was called into question, for it was thought that he'd deliberately tampered with Prince Agamemnon to change the odds and thus make a great deal of money.

There was a Jockey Club inquiry, and while it was actually in progress the truth came out and the colonel's name was cleared. Mr St John had happened to be in Windsor and he saw Sam Edney, Prince Agamemnon's jockey, deep in conversation with Lord Drummond. Money changed hands and in a flash Mr St John realized that the racehorse had indeed been tampered with, and by whom. It seems that Lord Drummond had mysteriously come into quite a large sum of money at the time of Royal Ascot last year, and although he said it was an inheritance, Mr St John now knew it was definitely not, it was money obtained by arranging for Prince Agamemnon's odds to lengthen. Naturally, Mr St John hurried here to Bourne End, where he knew the colonel and Mrs Bourne were very worried indeed about what might come from the Jockey Club inquiry. The colonel could have been forbidden from having anything more to do with racing, Miss Fairmead,' explained the maid.

'I realize that, Mary, please go on,' replied Helen quietly, shocked by the story of trickery she was hearing.

'The colonel sent for Sam Edney, pretending he wished to discuss a forthcoming race with him, but when the jockey arrived he was immediately faced with what Mr St John had seen. At first he denied everything, but at last admitted he'd conspired with Lord Drummond to lengthen Prince Agamemnon's odds. The horse had simply been given a bucket of water before the minor race, it was as easy to do as that.'

'Lord Drummond wouldn't do such a thing, Mary,' declared Helen firmly.

'He didn't deny it when accused, Miss Fairmead, and he did come into a great deal of extra money,' pointed out the maid. 'Naturally, the Jockey Club inquiry was told everything, but before Sam Edney could be barred from riding in this country, he vanished. It seems he went to America, where he's doing very well for himself. Lord Drummond sold his own racehorses and withdrew from the turf, but he'd have been barred anyway for what he did.'

Helen gazed at the clutter on the dressing table. Adam's words sounded clearly in her head. *My name was involved in an unpleas-ant* cause célèbre *last summer, and the experience was enough to persuade me to withdraw. My presence at Royal Ascot this year will undoubtedly raise a great many eyebrows, and if it hadn't been for my sister, I'd have stayed away, but she persuaded me that non-attendance would be construed in some quarters as proof of a guilty conscience.* But if he didn't have a guilty conscience, why hadn't he protested his innocence when accused?

Helen drew a long breath. 'Please continue, Mary. What happened after that?'

'Well, the colonel was anxious to put it all behind him. He felt that his reputation had already been damaged enough, and since the newspapers hadn't printed anything, he thought it best to let the dust settle. He's never forgiven Lord Drummond, though, for not only was his lordship guilty of behaving very dishonorably, he also acted without any thought of the colonel at all. Lord Drummond must have known that any wild differences in the horse's running would inevitably lead to a Jockey Club inquiry for the colonel. It was a very low thing to do, miss.'

'*If* he did it.'

'But, Miss Fairmead, the evidence is all there,' protested the maid.

'I still don't believe it of him.'

'No, miss.'

'Well, you saw him at the Cat and Fiddle, Mary, do *you* think he'd do all that?'

Mary said nothing, but the look on her face spoke volumes of her doubts.

Helen saw the maid's expression and sighed inwardly. Maybe Mary was right to be so mistrusting, maybe it was the height of gullibility to have faith in him simply because his smiles and kisses had kindled a fire within her. She was a green girl, fresh from school and without experience of the world, so how could she expect to judge such a man? Maybe she couldn't, but she had a very firm conviction that he was innocent. She trusted her instinct where he was concerned, and above all, she trusted her heart.

A little later, dressed in a lemon-and-white-striped lawn gown,

Helen went down to join her sister for breakfast. Her hair was dressed in a pretty knot, with ringlets falling to the nape of her neck, and the ribbons of her tiny white lace day bonnet were untied, fluttering as she moved.

Margaret was alone in the sunny peach-colored breakfast room, the French windows of which stood open toward the stables. The view was clear to the archway beneath the clocktower, and Gregory could be seen in the yard beyond, deep in conversation with his head groom. In the room the smell of coffee, warm bread, and bacon hung in the warm air, together with the sweet perfume of carnations from the bowl in the center of the white-clothed table. Margaret was reading the morning newspaper, and there was a silver coffee pot, a blue-and-gold porcelain cup and saucer, and a little jug of cream on the table immediately before her. She wore a coral seersucker wrap trimmed with many little frills, and her hair was brushed loose about her shoulders. She looked pale and fragile, and Helen didn't need to be told she was suffering from the effects of morning sickness.

'Good morning, Margaret, I won't ask you how you feel.'

'Am I that ghastly?'

'Yes.'

'Thank you.' Margaret managed a smile. 'Did you sleep well?'

'Excellently, thank you. Would it be too much for you if I had some bacon?'

'I've managed to watch Gregory devour kedgeree, and if I can do that, I can do anything.'

Helen helped herself from one of the silver-domed dishes on the sideboard, and then sat down as Margaret poured her a cup of coffee. Through the French windows came the sound of hooves, as several racehorses emerged from beneath the clocktower archway. Their jockeys gathered them, and then urged them away across the park. Helen watched them pass from sight. 'Are Gregory's horses all champing at the bit in readiness for the big day?'

'Most of them are.'

'But some aren't?'

'Perhaps I should say they all are, bar one. Musket's giving cause for concern. After running like the wind for months, earning himself a very short price for the Maisemore, he's suddenly losing his edge. The last thing poor Gregory needs is another well-fancied horse suddenly losing form, especially for the Maisemore.'

'After last year, you mean?'

Margaret lowered her cup. 'From which remark I perceive you've been making it your business to find out all you can?'

'In the absence of any explanation from you or Gregory, yes, I have. I've resorted to servants' gossip.'

'Is that what you've been taught over the past five years?' inquired Margaret dryly.

'No, Miss Figgis wouldn't dream of such a thing. You'd better put it down to my prying nature.'

'I already have. So, you now know all about the Prince Agamemnon affair?'

'I know of it, yes.'

'I trust that that means you now accept Adam Drummond's guilt.'

'It means that I now know what he's supposed to have done,' qualified Helen carefully.

'*Supposed* to have done? My dear Helen, he didn't deny it when confronted, and he suddenly acquired an "inheritance," and Sam Edney's evidence was conclusive. Of *course* he's guilty; he's a crimper of the meanest order.'

'Crimper?'

'Someone who deliberately meddles to affect the outcome of a race, or to rearrange the odds. That's what your precious Adam Drummond is, sister mine, and it ill becomes you to question incontrovertible facts, when on your own admission you met him only briefly while your chaise team was changed. Oh, he saved your life, but I doubt if that took him more than a moment, since he's such a valiant hero!' Crossly, Margaret poured herself some more coffee.

'I realize you're angry with me. . . .' began Helen.

'That's putting it mildly.'

'It's just that. . . .'

'It's just that you've gazed into his incredibly blue eyes and been swept off your foolish feet,' interrupted Margaret again. 'Oh, I grant you he's very handsome, and that he could charm the birds down from the trees with one of his engaging smiles, but for all his elegant and attractive exterior, *inside* he's a toad of the first water.'

'Margaret, will you please let me say something?' cried Helen in exasperation. 'All I'm trying to say is that I know you're angry with me, but I can't help being reluctant to believe ill of the man who saved me from a terrible accident. You can understand that, can't you?'

Margaret hesitated, and then nodded unwillingly. 'Yes, I suppose so, but you do seem bent upon whitewashing him, which makes me feel you think Gregory and I are lying.'

'I don't think that at all.'

'I trust so, for the whole business is mortifying enough already, without you adding to it. Adam's diplomatic activities on Lord Liverpool's behalf bring him constantly into the Prince Regent's presence, and the prince thinks highly of him, which has made for some embarrassing moments during the past year.' Margaret glanced at her. 'Perhaps we should change the subject.'

'Yes, perhaps we should.' Feeling disloyal for being totally unable to believe wrong of Adam, Helen prudently started her breakfast. The bacon was already almost cold, and consequently unappetizing, but she applied herself with determination, anxious at all costs not to openly fall out with her sister, whose dark expression spoke eloquently of her deep displeasure.

At last Margaret set her newspaper aside. 'I don't want to quarrel, Helen.'

'I don't, either.'

'But you must understand how dreadful last year was. Horseracing means so much to Gregory, and he's always prided himself on his complete honesty and integrity. The business with Prince Agamemnon called all that into question, and threatened to ruin his name in racing. You have to try to understand that, just as I have to try to understand that you aren't going to accept the truth until it's proved to you beyond any doubt.'

Helen smiled ruefully. 'Are you sorry already that you asked me to live here?'

'Not quite.' Margaret smiled too. 'So, let's to something else, to Ralph St John, for instance; he's a much more agreeable topic of conversation.'

'So you and Gregory kept insisting last night.'

'Ralph's an angel, it's as simple as that.'

'You seem inordinantly fond of him.'

Margaret's smile became a little rueful. 'Well, perhaps that's because he was my first admirer.'

'I thought Gregory was your first,' said Helen in some surprise.

'I thought so too, but it seems that Ralph admired me as well, he just didn't get around to telling me so.'

'Would it have made any difference if he had?'

'Good heavens, no, I adored Gregory from the moment I saw him, but I'm still very fond of Ralph, he's such a darling.'

'Last night you told me he was up to his adorable neck in gambling debts, with the duns positively hammering at his door,' observed Helen.

'It's hardly a heinous crime for a gentleman to find himself in those particular financial straits, Helen. Besides, his father's here at the moment from Jamaica, and Ralph confidently expects to soon be more than solvent again. Did we tell you last night that the St Johns reside in Jamaica? Their plantations are legendary, and one day it will all go to Ralph. He's quite a catch, you know, even if he's a little paupered *à ce moment*.'

'If he was circulating when you first went to London, and if he's considered such a catch, why is he still unattached?'

'Because nothing less than a lovematch will do for him. Oh, I believe he's suffered several unhappy affairs of the heart. . . .'

'Including you?'

Margaret laughed. 'No, not including me. I think he just liked me a great deal, without forming a passionate attachment. I don't know who the ladies in his life have been, I just know there have been one or two.'

Helen put down her knife and fork. 'I can't eat any more of this, it's absolutely cold.'

'That's apt to be the way of it when one chatters instead of getting on with the serious business of eating,' said Margaret, sitting back and taking a deep breath. 'Why, I do believe the wretched queasies have departed for the time being.'

'It's all that talk of the blessed Ralph, it's guaranteed to settle the most lively stomach.'

'Facetiousness was always one of your failings, Helen, but you'll come around quickly enough once you meet him. Gregory and I just *know* you'll take to each other.'

Helen looked sharply at her. 'Do I detect a hint of matchmaking?'

'Why not? You and he would be perfect together.'

'I'd rather decide that for myself, thank you, just as you and Gregory decided for yourselves.'

'And so you shall decide for yourself, truly, but in the meantime there's no reason why Gregory and I shouldn't entertain certain, er, hopes, is there?'

'None at all,' replied Helen slowly, for there was a note in her sister's voice that warned her there was more to this than idle hopes. 'Margaret, you and Gregory wouldn't by any chance have already intimated anything to Mr St John concerning this, would you?'

Margaret shifted a little uncomfortably. 'Well, I. . . .'

Helen stared at her in dismay. 'Oh, Margaret, how could you!'

'Please don't misunderstand. . . .'

'I'm not, I understand perfectly well. You, Gregory, and this Mr St John have been discussing my marriage, and without so much as a word to me. I begin to wonder if the date's set, or even if my passage to Jamaica is booked.'

'Oh, come on, Helen, it isn't like that at all. It's simply a matter of an idea that cropped up during after-dinner conversation a few weeks ago. At first it was just a chance remark, but somehow we began talking about it, and then it seemed such an excellent idea that we, well, we began to hope it might become a reality. Ralph really is a good friend – he's excellent company, kind, thoughtful, generous – and he's an excellent catch. Helen, he's quite perfect, and I know that in the end you'll think so too, just as I know that he'll be bowled over by you when you meet. So don't fly off the handle just yet, give him a chance. Please.'

'I'm not flying off the handle, I'm just incensed.'

'There's a difference?'

'Yes.'

Margaret sighed. 'There really isn't anything to be incensed about.'

'Then we'll have to agree to disagree.'

Margaret glanced at her. 'Yes, and not for the first time since you arrived yesterday,' she observed.

Helen said nothing, for in truth the disagreements were connected. She was irate about Ralph St John as much because he'd been the one to first point a finger at Adam as because she resented discussions about her future taking place without her knowledge or consent. She was predisposed against Ralph St John. Maybe her judgment was flawed where Adam was concerned, but she couldn't help the firm set of her bias against the unknown Mr St John.

Mararet smiled a little sheepishly. 'So, once again we'd better change the subject to something less contentious, the Farrish House ball, for instance.'

Helen smiled too. 'The Farrish House ball it is.'

CHAPTER 7

While Margaret rested that afternoon, Helen went out to the gardens to read *Mansfield Park* for an hour or so. She was still a little displeased to think that discussions had been going on behind her back about a possible match with Ralph St John, but at least the discovery had served to clarify her thoughts, for one thing was now crystal clear: the only man who would ever do for her was Adam, Lord Drummond of Wintervale.

The air was warm and scented in the gardens, for the wallflowers were in full bloom, their rich colors bright and velvety. She sat on a wrought iron bench beneath a laburnum tree, the pendulous golden flowers of which moved gently in the light breeze. Leafy shadows dappled her lemon-and-white-striped lawn gown as she opened the book and removed the embroidered marker, but she hadn't been reading for long when she heard someone hurrying toward her. It was Mary.

'Begging your pardon for disturbing you, miss, but you said if I heard anything more I was to come to you straight away.'

'About Lord Drummond?'

'Yes, miss. It isn't much, but I thought you'd want to know. It's about a lady.'

A lady? Could it be the one whose brief adulterous affair Adam was at pains to protect? The thought flashed instantly into Helen's head.

Mary pursed her lips for a moment. 'Perhaps she wasn't a lady exactly, for she was an actress.'

'Was?'

'Yes, miss – Mrs Maria Tully, who was killed in a carriage overturn early last year.'

Helen knew of Mrs Tully, for she'd been a leading light of the Theater Royal, Drury Lane, and her most famous part had been that of Mistress Fuchsia in *To Find True Love*. Her tragic death had been greeted with the utmost dismay, and the journal to which Helen had subscribed while at Cheltenham had published a likeness of the actress as Mistress Fuchsia. Maria Tully had been very beautiful indeed, and fascinating enough to win the attentions of a man like Adam, but she couldn't possibly have been his unnamed lady, who was still alive and had children, neither of which things could be said of Mrs Tully. Helen looked at the maid. 'Are you about to tell me she was Lord Drummond's mistress?'

'No, miss, although she wanted to be. She pursued him, but she wasn't successful. Mr St John had admired her first, as it happened, but she left him in order to devote her full attention to his lordship.'

Helen slowly closed her book. 'There was bad feeling between Lord Drummond and Mr St John because of it?' she asked.

'I don't think so. Mr St John apparently didn't show any resentment, and anyway, she was being kept by the Marquess of FitzRichard when she was killed.'

'Quite the butterfly, wasn't she?' murmured Helen.

Mary glanced back toward the house, where her duties awaited. 'That was all I had to tell you, miss, except perhaps. . . .'

'Yes?'

'It wasn't about Lord Drummond, but I think you should know anyway. Peter tells me they all know in the servants' wing that you and Mr St John are to be married.'

'I beg your pardon?'

Helen got up angrily. It really was too bad of Margaret and Gregory, who'd obviously discussed the matter far more with Ralph St John than had been indicated at breakfast.

'Everyone thinks it's an excellent match, miss,' ventured Mary, recognizing the flash in her mistress's green eyes.

'It's an odious match as far as I'm concerned.'

'But. . . .'

'Mr Ralph St John could be the finest catch in all the world, but it wouldn't make any difference to me because he's not Lord Drummond.'

'No, miss.'

'I know you think there can't be all that smoke without there being a fire of some sort, but I don't have any doubts. He's all I ever want in this world, Mary Caldwell, and one way or another I intend to have him.'

The maid was taken aback by such a blunt and forward statement. 'Oh, Miss Fairmead, you really shouldn't say things like that.'

'I know, but it happens to be true.'

'But Colonel and Mrs Bourne think him. . . .'

'I know what they think him.' Helen turned away, the hanging blooms of laburnum brushing her shoulder. 'I also know what I think. He's invaded my life, Mary, and I've thought of little else since the moment I met him. I mean to see him again, as soon as I possibly can.'

'I wish you wouldn't even think of seeing him again, miss,' said the maid unhappily. 'You shouldn't, have done all those things at the Cat and Fiddle, and now it's best you put it all behind you. You have your reputation and your future to consider. . . .'

Helen nodded. 'I know, and you're right to try to make me see sense, but I'm afraid I'm already quite beyond redemption where he's concerned. Anyway, there's nothing much I can do for the time being, he's not in Windsor yet, and even if he were, I don't know how I could manage to see him.' She smiled. 'But I *will* see him, Mary, I promise you that. For the moment, however, I have Mr Ralph St John to deal with. I'm not in the least interested in a match with him, but it seems that he's interested in a match with me. I shall be polite, of course, but I shall leave him in no doubt that I'm not the bride for him. I'll make it clear when he escorts me at the Prince Regent's dinner.'

But her first encounter with Ralph St John was destined to take place sooner than she thought; indeed, he called at Bourne End that very afternoon.

Margaret had had her rest, and she and Helen had enjoyed an amiable hour taking tea in the drawing room, discussing the Prince Regent's imminent visit and the very strict etiquette Helen would have to learn in the meantime, for it was unthinkable that she should set a foot wrong during the time he was present. The touchy subject of Ralph St John was left well alone, as was the even thornier topic of Lord Drummond, and in a while the sisters strolled out to the stables, where they were to join Gregory and Helen was to be shown some of the prize thoroughbreds.

After being so wan that morning, Margaret was now much brighter, looking soft and pretty in cherry sarsenet, and she linked her arm through her husband's as they stood in the center of the immense stableyard, watching several fine horses being paraded before the impressive line of white stable doors. Helen looked on in admiration as the gray Musket and the chestnut Lexicon were led back and forth by their proud grooms.

Gregory was pleased enough with Lexicon, but more than a little unhappy about Musket. He ran his fingers through his fair hair, shaking his head slightly as the gray was turned yet again.

Margaret glanced at him. 'Why are you so depressed? He looks in fine fettle to me, and I'm sure he'll come right in time for the Maisemore.'

'He just isn't up to scratch, he wasn't the tippy when he exercised this morning, and when I saw him being stripped and rubbed down in his loose box, he looked quite used up. His jockey on the day is one of the best, but is also a good half stone heavier than the rest, and if Musket is under the weather, that weight will tell. Damn it all, I could do without all this this year.'

'Withdraw him then,' advised Margaret, slipping her hand into his.

'And be accused of being up to something again? Look at him, he seems in perfect condition, so how would it seem if he was pulled out? Besides, the Prince Regent's horse is second favorite, and I don't want any whispers that I'm currying favor by leaving the way clear for him.'

'Gregory, I fail to see how withdrawing Musket because he's unwell is going to lead to such a suggestion,' protested Margaret.

'After last year, I'm prepared to believe they'd say anything of me.' His glance flickered briefly toward Helen, and Adam Drummond's name hung almost audibly in the air.

Margaret hastily drew his attention back. 'I'm sure all will be well in time for the race, and that Musket is only temporarily off color.'

He smiled then, putting his hand to her chin and bending to kiss her swiftly on the lips. 'You're good for me, Mrs Bourne,' he murmured.

'I should hope I am,' she replied. 'Now then, if Musket is worrying you, let's talk about Lexicon instead. He's looking quite magnificent.' She looked toward the gleaming chestnut.

Gregory nodded. 'He is indeed, and he'll leave them all standing in the Odd Cup.' He turned to Helen. 'I paid a paltry thousand guineas for him at Tattersall's, and am flattered that I showed excellent judgment that day.

'How much is he worth now?'

'He's beyond price to a devotee of the turf, especially as he's already proved himself as a sire.'

They watched as Lexicon was paraded up and down a little longer before being led back into his loose box, but then something made Helen glance toward the archway. She was just in time to see a dark blue barouche bowling up the drive toward the house, drawn by a handsome team of roans. As it passed out of sight, she touched her sister's arm. 'Margaret, I think you have a caller, a dark blue barouche has just gone to the house.'

Margaret turned quickly. 'Was it drawn by roans?'

'Yes.'

'It's Ralph St John. Helen, you will give him a chance, won't you?'

'I'll be the soul of politeness,' answered Helen truthfully, seeing no reason to add that she was also going to be discreetly discouraging.

She glanced toward the archway again, waiting for her first glimpse of the man who not only had exposed Adam's apparent guilt in the Prince Agamemnon affair, but who was also prepared to regard her as a prospective bride.

CHAPTER 8

It seemed an age before Ralph St John's fashionable figure appeared beneath the archway. He wore a fawn beaver top hat, a dark brown coat, and white twill trousers. A cane swung nonchalantly in his hand, and he was very modish; indeed, there was a little of the dandy about him, although he was far from being a fop.

As he came closer she saw that he had curly brown hair, long-lashed brown eyes, and was definitely to be described as good-looking, although to her mind his mouth was perhaps just a little too full and sensual. His glance raked her expertly from head to toe in the few seconds before he turned his smile upon Margaret and Gregory, bowing over the former's hand. 'Greetings, *mes enfants*, I trust I find you all in excellent heart.'

'Why, Ralph,' responded Margaret with pleasure, 'what brings you here this afternoon?'

'The delight of your company, of course.'

'Flatterer.'

'Fie, madam, I'm not a flatterer, I'm an ardent admirer.' His glance returned to Helen, resting on her in a warm, appraising way that she didn't entirely like.

Margaret hastened to effect the introduction. 'Ralph, allow me to present my sister, Miss Helen Fairmead. Helen, this is Mr Ralph St John.'

He took Helen's hand and drew it slowly to his lips, his lips touching her skin for a moment. 'I'm honored to make your acquaintance, Miss Fairmead.'

'Sir.'

'The reports preceding you failed to do you justice, Miss Fairmead.'

'My sister is right, sir, you are indeed a flatterer.' Although she smiled, her eyes remained a little cool. She didn't like him, although whether this was an honest and instinctive reaction, or whether it was the result of her feelings for Adam, she really couldn't have said.

Gregory was also pleased to see him. 'And how goes it at the Golden Key with St John *père?*'

'Wretchedly. The old man and I have never seen eye to eye – and never will. Still, needs must when the devil drives, and if I have to toady to him to get what I require, then toady I will.'

Margaret tapped his arm disapprovingly. 'Sirrah, if you hadn't plunged in so deep at the green baize, you wouldn't have to toady to anyone.'

'Point taken. Still, it isn't for long, he's returning to Jamaica soon and I'll be a free spirit again. The Golden Key is handsome enough, I suppose, but not quite up to Bourne End standards.'

'I should think not,' replied Gregory.

'Dear boy, having to sally forth to the races from a mere inn instead of these hallowed surroundings is a positively mortifying prospect.'

Margaret raised a critical eyebrow. 'And is entirely your own fault.'

'*Moi? Mais non, je suis un ange!*'

Margaret smiled. 'Some angel,' she murmured. 'Gabriel, with a pack of cards in his pocket.'

'Come now, blackening my character in front of Miss Fairmead isn't the thing at all.' Ralph smiled at Helen. 'Don't listen to them, for I am indeed an angel of the highest order.'

'I'm sure you are, sir,' she replied, still pondering her first impression of him. He was very charming, amusing, and confident, but it ill became him to speak as he did about the father from whom he required considerable financial assistance to fend off the duns.

Margaret linked her arm in his. 'You still haven't said why you've called, Ralph.'

'It's come to my notice that Hagman's are serving the very first strawberries of the season at the boathouse, and knowing your disgusting appetite for such things, I've hied me here to whisk you and Miss Fairmead to sample the goodies. Gregory isn't invited, I'm of a selfish mind to keep you both to myself.' He grinned. 'And in spite of having the duns at my door, you'll be pleased to know the treat's on me. A modicum of good fortune at the tables last night has put me in Tip Street for the time being, although that's strictly between thee and me.'

'Ralph St John, you're incorrigible,' scolded Margaret. 'I vow you'll plunge in so deep one day you'll never surface again.'

'The old man's worth the ransom of half a dozen kings, so I can consider myself at liberty to continue plunging to my heart's delight,' he replied – rather arrogantly, Helen thought. 'I can certainly consider myself able to entertain you and Miss Fairmead to the first mess of strawberries of the summer. Will you accept my invitation?'

'Of course,' Margaret replied, glancing at Helen. 'You'll come, won't you? You'll love the boathouse.'

'Is it really a boathouse?' Helen asked.

'Oh, most definitely. It's at Eleanor's Lake in Windsor Great Park. The lake is named for Lady Eleanor Parfait, whose unfortunate husband spent his entire fortune damming up a stream to make the lake for her at the beginning of the last century, only to have her promptly run off with his best friend. The boathouse has been there for ages, hiring out pleasure boats to the summer visitors who liked to spend time on the water. About four years ago the present proprietress married a certain Klaus Hagman, a confectioner from Vienna, and it wasn't long before the clients hiring the pleasure boats found themselves lingering over delicious Viennese pastries, creams, and ices, and soon it was all the rage to be seen there. It's a positive crush of Mayfair there all through the summer, especially close to Royal Ascot week, and last year the Earl and Countess of Cardusay actually got married there. It was so romantic, the bride and groom took their vows on a barge so covered with flowers it looked as if it was made of them, and all the guests were on barges too. I wouldn't marry at dull old St George's now, it would be a special license and Hagman's boathouse for me. You'll love it there, Helen, and it's only half an hour away by carriage. Do say you'll come.'

Helen found the thought of Hagman's very pleasing, but not if Ralph St John was issuing the invitation. Nothing that had happened during the past few minutes had shaken her resolve to discourage him from all thought of marrying her, and she knew that her acceptance now might be construed as encouragement. She gave an apologetic smile. 'It's very kind of you to invite me, Mr St John, but. . . .'

'Oh, Helen!' protested Margaret, 'please come, for it really is delightful there, and I *know* you adore strawberries.'

To continue refusing. would look odd, and so Helen gave in reluctantly. 'Very well. Thank you for including me, Mr St John.'

'Not at all, Miss Fairmead.'

Margaret turned to Helen. 'Come on, we must change, for only ladies of great style dare to be seen at Hagman's.' Snatching Helen's hand, she hurried her away toward the archway.

Half an hour later, Ralph's dark blue barouche drove smartly away from Bourne End, its hoods down because the weather was so very warm and fine, Helen was dressed in a bluebell silk gown and matching pelisse, with a gray straw bonnet tied on with wide bluebell ribbons that fluttered in the breeze as the open carriage came up to a smart pace. Opposite her, Margaret wore an orange spencer over a cream muslin gown, and an orange hat from which sprang tall ostrich plumes. Ralph sat next to Margaret, and Helen was conscious of how often his glance, still warm and speculative, moved toward her.

The barouche passed the racecourse, where activity seemed to have increased even since the previous day. The Windsor road led over the open countryside of the heath, and then into a forest where hawthorn bloomed sweetly. Rhododendrons as fine as those at Bourne End began to appear, and then the gates into Windsor Great Park loomed ahead. As the barouche drove through, Helen caught her first glimpse of the town and castle in the distance. The castle looked very white and impressive, framed by a gap in the trees, but then was lost from sight again as the barouche turned sharply northwest along another road.

The two thousand acres of Windsor Great Park were very beautiful indeed, a vista of majestic trees, wide rides, and landscaped perfection. Enjoyed by monarchs throughout many centuries, it now boasted a number of royal residences, including the Prince Regent's fine new *cottage orné*, the Royal Lodge, and it was the delight also of the many ladies and gentlemen who rode or drove through its leafy splendor.

Margaret saw Helen's admiring gaze, and smiled. 'It's very lovely, is it not?'

'Very.'

'But if you look across that way in a moment, you'll see a huge copper beech that marks the way to somewhere less lovely.'

Helen followed her sister's finger and soon perceived the copper beech, and beside it a winding track that swiftly disappeared between rhododendrons. It seemed very innocuous, and she looked inquiringly at her sister. 'Where does it lead?'

'To Herne's Glade. You've heard of Herne the Hunter, of course.'

'Yes. Wasn't he a ranger in Henry VIII's time?'

'A wicked dabbler in things magical, it seems. He is supposed to have hanged himself from an oak in the park, and at times of national danger his ghost appears, complete with antlers, flowing green robes, and an attendant white hart. Our poor King George accidentally ordered an oak tree to be chopped down in 1796, and everyone said it was Herne's oak, but the truth appears to be that the oak in Herne's Glade is the real one. The glade is a rather dark and gloomy place, and so has been the natural choice for many gentlemen wishing to face each other in duels.'

Ralph tipped his hat back, smiling a little. 'It isn't all melancholy, Miss Fairmead, for there's an amusing tale attached to the place as well. You'll no doubt have heard of the letters from Prince Florizel to Perdita?'

'Yes, they were said to be between the Prince of Wales and the actress, Mrs Robinson.'

'Correct. Well, most people know of their romantic assignations on a boat moored on the Thames off Kew, but not so many know they also met at the boathouse on Eleanor's Lake, before it became Hagman's, of course. When returning at dawn in her carriage from such an assignation, they were startled by the pistol shots of a duel taking place in the glade. Thinking he was bound to be discovered, the prince took off on foot like a greyhound into the bushes, leaving poor Mrs Robinson alone in the carriage. She took fright as well, ordering her coachman to drive on, and as she vanished from sight, the prince saw a white hart coming along the track from the glade. Convinced Herne's ghost was close behind, he took off again, and since Mrs Robinson had picked him up in her carriage somewhere in Windsor, he now had to get himself back there on foot, skulking into the castle by a postern gate. The humiliating incident is said to have heralded the end of the love affair.'

The copper beech slipped away behind them as the barouche drove on toward the lake and the boathouse. There were other carriages on the road, and many horsemen and women riding across the park, everyone apparently making for the same exclusive destination, the fashionable boathouse that was threatening to surpass Gunter's of Berkeley Square for excellence.

Hagman's proved to be a very elegant establishment, painted white and backed by gardens and ornamental trees, while to the front there was a long jetty extending into the lake, with pleasure boats and barges moored along it. Tables and chairs had been set out on the jetty and in the gardens, and most had been taken by the considerable gathering of ladies and gentlemen who'd sallied forth on this beautiful late May afternoon. Along the water's edge there was a path, and several nurses were there with their small charges, who were feeding the ducks with crumbs purchased from the boathouse.

The barouche drew to a standstill behind the building, joining the line of waiting vehicles that had collected there. Ralph alighted, assisting Margaret and Helen down. An orchestra was playing somewhere in the gardens, the sound of Vivaldi's 'Four Seasons' drifting in the air to join the murmur of light conversation and laughter from the fashionable crowds. Spying a free table on the jetty, Ralph swiftly escorted his two ladies toward it, and as they sat down he beckoned to a waiter, ordering a bottle of champagne and extremely large helpings of strawberries and cream.

Margaret was as delighted to be at Hagman's as she was to be in Ralph's company, which she made no secret of finding very agreeable indeed. Helen tried not to be drawn into conversation very much, for she wished to keep Ralph as much at arm's length as possible. He was behaving with all outward politeness and gallantry, but there was something about his constant glances that she found disturbing. She avoided looking at him, turning her attention to the arrivals and departures on the road. A young gentleman tooled an alarmingly high phaeton away at speed, the lady beside him clinging on fearfully. A group of army officers, home on leave from Brussels, rode toward the boathouse, looking very splendid in full uniform as they paused to converse with some ladies in an open landau. Two carriages drew up one behind the other, disgorging a number of children and their nurses and nannies. Forming into a neat crocodile, they entered the boathouse to purchase bags of crumbs, emerging in line to walk sedately down to the lakeside to the waiting ducks. A large pleasure barge glided to the jetty, its cargo of elegant passengers disembarking so noisily that for a while their chatter completely drowned the sound of the music, which had now changed from Vivaldi to Haydn.

Helen felt Ralph looking at her again, and suddenly it was too much. She had to escape for a while, and feeding the ducks provided the perfect excuse.

Putting down her glass, she rose determinedly to her feet. 'I fear I cannot resist a moment longer, I simply have to revert to childhood and feed the ducks. I hope you won't mind if I desert you both for a while?'

Ralph got up immediately. 'I'll escort you, Miss Fairmead.'

'There's no need, Mr St John,' she said quickly.

'But. . . .'

'Mr St John, you can't possibly leave poor Margaret to devour all those strawberries on her own, people will talk about her.'

Margaret gave her an indignant look. 'You beast, Helen Fairmead!'

Ralph still wanted to accompany her, however. 'Miss Fairmead, it would ill become me to allow you to walk alone, even at Hagman's.'

'Nonsense, Mr St John, I'm perfectly capable of feeding the ducks without assistance.' Not permitting him another chance to protest, she gathered her silk skirts and hurried away along the jetty toward the boathouse.

A minute or so later she emerged again with some crumbs, walking along the lakeside path in the wake of the crocodile of nurses, nannies, and children, who were now to be seen some distance away, still walking in an orderly line. Helen kept walking too, intending to place some bushes between herself and the jetty, for she knew Ralph could still observe her, and the last thing she wanted was to be constantly under his surveillance.

Some rhododendrons tumbled down to the water's edge in a riot of crimson, mauve, and white, and the path curved between them, sheering from the water for a moment as the land rose slightly. Helen followed the path and glanced back, seeing to her satisfaction that the view from the jetty was cut off by the rhododendrons. Taking a deep breath, she left the path and walked to the side of the lake, beginning to toss the crumbs, which were immediately spied by the watchful ducks. Fluttering and quacking, they milled around on the water, snatching up every morsel.

It was a pleasant pastime, one she hadn't indulged in since a child at home in Worcestershire, and it held her attention so fully that she didn't hear the horseman approaching along the path. She knew nothing as he reined in and looked toward her; indeed, the first intimation she had that she was no longer alone was when he suddenly spoke to her.

'So, we meet again, Mrs Brown.'

With a gasp she whirled about and found herself looking into the inviting blue eyes of Adam, Lord Drummond of Wintervale.

CHAPTER 9

Shocked at seeing him again so unexpectedly, she dropped the bag of crumbs and stared at him.

His large bay horse was restive, but he controlled it with consummate ease. He wore a navy blue riding coat, a silver-gray waistcoat, and beige cord breeches, and there were spurs at the heels of his highly polished riding boots. A gold pin gleamed in the folds of his muslin neckcloth, and a signet ring shone on his finger as he removed his top hat.

Still she stared, so startled she couldn't think of anything to say. After a moment he gave a wry smile, glancing around as if half-expecting to see someone else with her. 'Forgive me if my appearance on the scene has caused you embarrassment. I take it your silence signifies a wish to forget we are known to each other?'

'Oh, no,' she said quickly, 'please don't think that. I was just caught off guard by seeing you again so unexpectedly.'

'That much is obvious,' he murmured, dismounting and leading his horse to one of the rhododendrons, tethering it firmly. Resting his top hat on the pommel of the saddle, he came toward her. 'I'm relieved that we do still know each other, Mrs Brown, for I'd hate to think I was already a thing of your past.'

He'd never be a thing of her past, she thought, conscious of how her heart quickened with each step he took. She had to say something, but what? 'Did – did you keep your London appointment, my lord?'

'I did. War Office affairs can now continue smoothly on their way again.'

'How much worse is the situation in Europe now?'

'Bonaparte's doing his damnedest.'

'I'm sure he is, it's the nature of the beast.'

'He'll come a final cropper very soon, you may be sure.'

'But are *you* sure, my lord?' she asked, endeavoring to hide how much he affected her just by being close, and wondering how best to grasp the nettle of telling him the truth about herself.

He smiled. 'You want my opinion as a denizen of the War Office?'

'Yes.'

'I'm very sure, Mrs Brown. I'm also sure that I don't wish to discuss the Corsican, I'd much prefer to talk about you.'

Color leapt to her cheeks. 'I'm not very interesting, my lord.'

'But I find you fascinating, Mrs Brown, so much so that I've come to Windsor straightaway simply in the hope of meeting you again, and yet I don't even know your first name.'

She could hardly believe what he was saying. 'My name is Helen,' she whispered.

'Fair Helen,' he murmured. 'You already know that mine is Adam.'

'Yes.' She was held captive by his eyes; surely the owner of such eyes couldn't be guilty of dishonesty.

Something must have crossed her face, for his gaze became penetrating. 'You'd make a very poor poker player, Helen Brown, for I can tell that you've been regaled with the whole sorry tale of Prince Agamemnon.'

She looked away. 'Yes, I have heard, but I don't believe it. You wouldn't do anything like that.'

'You hardly know me.'

She found herself smiling at him, drowning in his eyes. 'I know you enough,' she whispered. 'There's something I have to say to you, something very important about me. . . .'

She said nothing more, for at that moment there was a disturbance as a group of small boys ran noisily along the path, startling the horse. Adam turned sharply, leaving her to go and soothe the frightened animal, which was rearing and straining at the reins. Helen watched anxiously, her dismay at having been cut off at the very moment of confession being swiftly replaced by fear for his safety as the horse continued to rear.

Something, she didn't know what, made her suddenly glance in the direction of the jetty. A break in the leaves afforded a perfect view; Ralph was approaching! In a moment or so he'd come around the path and see her with Adam. What could she do? Not only were the men now enemies, but one knew her as Mrs Helen Brown, the other as Miss Helen Fairmead. If only she'd managed to tell Adam the truth, but it was too late now. Panic seized her as she cast desperately around for an escape, but the bushes swept right to the water's edge, and to get away she'd have to pass Adam, and certainly would be seen by Ralph.

Adam's back was still toward her as he soothed the horse, which was quieter now. Her glance suddenly fell on one of the rhodo- dendrons, which was actually one shrub in front of another, and behind it there was a place to hide. Without further ado, she gath- ered her skirts and ran toward it, slipping out of sight just as Adam calmed the horse and turned back to where she'd been.

'It's all right now,' he said. 'What was it you wished to. . . ?' He broke off in surprise, for she was nowhere to be seen.

Gently she held a branch aside, and she saw Ralph appear on the path. Adam turned sharply toward him, and Ralph's steps faltered as he found himself facing not Helen, but the man he'd exposed the year before as a low and shabby cheat.

Adam folded his arms, looking contemptuously at him. 'Well, well, if it isn't my old friend Ralph. How very unfortunate for you that you failed to see me in time, otherwise I've no doubt I'd once again have been treated to a show of your elegant heels.'

'I've never shrunk from facing you, Drummond.'

'Your capacity for glib untruths never ceases to astound me.'

'If anyone should know about shrinking from facing others, Drummond, that person is you.' A sneer crept into Ralph's voice as he began to recover a little from his initial shock.

'Oh, I'm sure you'd like everyone to believe in my guilt, St John, but I'm afraid you haven't succeeded as much as you'd hoped. Your manufactured evidence may have fooled some, the Bournes in particular, but it didn't fool those who really matter to me, the friends I set real store by.'

Helen's lips parted in amazement. Manufactured evidence? *Ralph* had plotted it all, not caring that he'd come close to ruining Gregory's racing interests as well as Adam's honor? But why? *Why* had he done it? She peered from behind the bush, seeing Ralph's face quite clearly, for he was turned toward her. He was a different man now, cold, contemptuous, and full of loathing, and there was no trace at all of his former superficial charm. She'd been so right to dislike him on sight, and she couldn't understand how he'd hoodwinked Margaret and Gregory so completely.

Ralph's lips twisted into a sly smile as he looked at Adam. 'I set out to dishonor your name, Drummond, and I succeeded well enough.'

'At considerable cost to your pocket. Just how much *did* you hand over to that worm Edney to tell his lies? Enough to set him up in America, that's for sure, which fact must be galling you somewhat now the green baize has been so unfriendly.'

'It was worth it, just to see your name denigrated throughout society.'

'Hardly throughout, dear boy.'

'It was also worth it to have you dance to my tune.'

'Ah, yes, the little matter of blackmail. That is the only reason your vile little act has worked, as we both know.'

'Using your sister's infidelity was a stroke of genius, for it meant I had you exactly where I wanted you – under my thumb.'

Helen stared. Adam's *sister* was the lady he'd striven so to protect?

Adam gave a thin, dangerous smile. 'My sister's happiness means a great deal to me, St John, and that is the only reason I've allowed your damned lies about me to go unchallenged. In the end you'll fall into your own mire, vermin always do, and I rather think I'll be there to watch. I neither know nor care why you've felt driven to all this, but if it's to have the likes of the Bournes all to yourself, you're welcome to them, for they've proved as base as you. I wish you well of one another, for if ever insects nested together, it's you three. Or is it four now? I hear you're escorting Bourne's sister-in-law to the dinner tomorrow, in the Prince Regent's presence, no less. I also hear you're expecting to marry her, and I can only conclude that she's as shallow and contemptible as you.'

Helen listened in dismay. Whispers of the match had gone beyond Bourne End's walls and reached Adam himself! Tears filled her eyes at the disdainful way he spoke of Margaret and Gregory, and at the abhorrence he felt for Helen Fairmead. Would she ever be able to confess the truth now?

Ralph was goaded. 'You think you're so superior, don't you? Drummond of Wintervale, the man who has everything – except honor.'

'My, my, how eaten up you are,' murmured Adam coolly.

'Why should I be eaten up about you?'

'I don't know, St John. You tell me. I neither know nor care why you've felt obliged to do all this, but I'm prepared to listen if you wish to explain. Cat got your tongue? Ah, well. . . .'

A thousand expressions fought on Ralph's face, and Helen saw how his fists clenched with hatred as Adam gave a derisive smile, and then went calmly to untether his horse, pausing to tap his top hat lightly into place. Ralph remained where he was as Adam mounted, turning the horse and riding slowly and deliberately toward him: Adam reined in, leaning on the pommel. 'Do step aside, there's a good chap.'

'I don't step aside for you, Drummond,' breathed Ralph furiously.

Adam seemed to find this vaguely amusing, for a faint smile played on his lips as he made the horse walk on, brushing against Ralph's shoulder as he passed. It was a superb display of horsemanship, controlled to the very inch, and calculated to deal as big an insult as possible, but even Adam couldn't have foreseen the crowning moment. Unable to control his anger as the horse nudged him, Ralph whirled around to slap it fiercely on the rump, intending to make it bolt and maybe unseat Adam, but the creature chose that very opportune moment to swish its long tail, slapping him full in the face. Caught off balance, he stumbled and fell, lying there ignominiously as horse and rider vanished slowly and sedately beyond the rhododendrons.

Ralph scrambled to his feet, glancing swiftly around to see if anyone had witnessed his fall; then he brushed his elegant clothes before hurrying away, evidently intent upon continuing his search for her.

She slipped from her hiding place, gathering her skirts to run to the path, peeping along it after Ralph before hurrying in the opposite direction, back toward the jetty and Margaret.

Her thoughts were in turmoil. She'd been right to stand by Adam, for he was completely innocent – Ralph St John was the guilty party. But why had he done it, and how was she going to prove it without harming Adam's sister? And what was Adam going to say when she at last found the moment to tell him the truth about herself, for she now knew he connected her real name very intimately with Ralph. She felt close to tears again, for it was all an impossible tangle, and she didn't know how she was going to even begin to solve it. She didn't even know if in the end Adam would want his name associated with hers; she was too close to Bourne End, and he despised Bourne End.

But as she rejoined Margaret, she hid the tumult within, giving a bright smile. 'I really did enjoy feeding the ducks, it was very agreeable indeed. Where's Mr St John?'

'He went to look for you.'

'Really? I can't imagine how he failed to find me.'

Margaret looked suspiciously at her. 'I trust you weren't hiding from him.'

'Why ever would I do that?' replied Helen, as if hiding from him was the very last thing she'd ever wish to do.

Margaret eyed her for a moment, and then decided she was being honest. 'I knew you'd soon come around,' she said with a smile, 'he's too much of an angel to resist for long, isn't he?'

Too much of an angel? Helen thought of the Ralph she'd just seen and heard; *angelic* was the last word to describe him. For a moment she considered facing her sister with the truth about her precious Ralph, but almost immediately the notion was discarded. Margaret simply wouldn't believe it, and without proof there'd be no gain-saying Ralph's inevitable denial. Besides, there was Adam's sister to consider, and her shameful secret would certainly be in jeopardy if Ralph were to feel threatened. So it was best to leave matters as they were for the moment, but the thought of having him as an escort the following evening was quite horrid.

'Helen? I said I knew you'd come around where Ralph was concerned,' repeated Margaret.

'Mm? Oh, yes. Forgive me, I was daydreaming.'

'Ah, here's Ralph now. We really should be getting back, I've so much to do in readiness for tomorrow, and you and I must have another talk concerning etiquette, for there must not be even a tiny mistake in front of the prince.'

Helen smiled, but said nothing more. She watched Ralph strolling toward them. He looked so much the epitome of masculine excellence and nonchalance that it was impossible to believe he'd taken such an indecorous tumble to the grass a short while ago; it was also impossible to believe how despicable he really was, he looked so charming and amiable. How she loathed him, and how she hoped with all her heart that she'd somehow manage to rout him completely, and win Adam in the process. But it was a very tall order, and she knew it.

There were so many difficulties where Adam was concerned, even without Ralph to consider. She'd lied to him, concealed things, misled him, and now she'd even disappeared into thin air. What he was thinking at this very moment was a matter of complete conjecture, for one second she'd been there with him, the next she'd vanished. And then there was the matter of the rumors he'd heard concerning the imminent betrothal between Ralph St John and Gregory Bourne's sister-in-law; what would his reaction be when he learned that she was that sister-in-law? She lowered her eyes. She'd spoken with such bravado of regarding him as the only man in the world she'd ever love, but she had so much to confess that her path to happiness was so thorny as to be almost impassable.

CHAPTER 10

The dinner party for the Prince Regent was set to commence an hour after dusk, and as darkness fell the guests' carriages began to arrive, each one escorted from the lodge gates by running footmen carrying lighted flambeaux.

In the grounds the trees had been hung with pretty variegated lanterns, and the garden paths were brightly lit with lamps. Every room in the house was illuminated, with the curtains and shutters left open so the brilliance of the occasion could be seen for miles over the Berkshire countryside. On the ground floor the French windows were open too, allowing the distinguished guests to stroll in and out as they chose. An orchestra was playing in the southern conservatory, which led off the beautifully decorated dining room, and the sweet strains of a Mozart serenade carried out into the night, where the scent of wallflowers and honeysuckle was strong and clear.

Margaret had been frantically busy all day, refusing to listen to Gregory and Helen, who implored her to calm down and take things more slowly. She waved their protests aside, pointing out that she had to supervise the preparations, make certain the kitchens had everything properly in hand, *and* deal with the various crises that seemed determined to arise. These crises were particularly vexing, ranging from the nonarrival of the specially ordered Severn salmon to the mislaying of a silver salver the Prince Regent had given to Gregory, which had to be prominently displayed. The flowers, of which there were thousands for such an occasion, required endless arranging and rearranging before she declared herself satisfied with them, although as far as Helen was concerned they'd looked as excellent in the beginning as they had after all the moving around. The despaired-of salmon arrived late in the afternoon, a trundling fishmonger's wagon coming slowly up the drive at what seemed like a snail's pace, and then the silver salver was discovered in a cupboard in the buttery, where it had no business being, and was put in its proper place in the entrance hall so that the Prince Regent would see it as he arrived.

All this had taken up a great deal of Margaret's time, and it was rather late when at last she'd fled to her rooms to begin her lengthy dressing. As the guests arrived below, to be greeted by Gregory, assisted by Ralph, Helen paced nervously up and down outside her sister's door, afraid to go down to her first important social occasion on her own. It would have been bad enough had the dinner party been a small occasion, with only a few distinguished guests, but for it to be graced by the presence of the future king and the cream of London society made her feel quite ill with apprehension. What if, in spite of Margaret's instructions, she still did something embarrassingly gauche? What if she said the wrong thing?

She caught a glimpse of herself in a tall gilt-framed mirror. Was the Tudor gown right after all, or should she have chosen something else? The silver taffeta looked exquisite in the candlelight, and so did the jeweled lace ruff springing so stiffly from the low, square neckline. The little puffed sleeves were slashed to reveal a pale pink lining embroidered with loveknots, and the same pink peeped through the parting at the front of the skirt. Her hair was a froth of Tudor curls, and there was a diamond ornament fixed at the front, glittering against her forehead at the slightest movement. There were more diamonds in her necklace and earrings, and she carried a painted ivory fan, with a silver lace shawl over her arms. A blush of rouge prevented her from looking pale and wan, but had Mary applied a little too much? Did she look bold rather than discreetly healthy?

At last Margaret emerged in a flurry of buttercup silk that shimmered with countless tiny sequins. Plumes streamed from her hair, and a white feather boa dragged on the floor behind her. She wore diamonds as well, for it was well known that the Prince Regent liked to see women in diamonds, and the flush on her cheeks came as much from flusterment as the assistance of rouge.

'Helen, do I look all right? Should I wear the plowman's gauze instead?'

'You look lovely, Margaret, so please slow down a little, you'll make yourself ill.'

Margaret smiled a little ruefully then. 'You're right, of course, just as I'm right to tell you not to worry so about tonight, you'll carry it off in style.'

'I wish I could feel as confident.'

'Besides, you'll have Ralph at your side, and he'll see everything's all right.'

'Yes, I suppose so.'

'Don't look so doubtful, he's going to look after you, believe me. Shall I tell you how I coped with my dreadful nerves when I first came to London? I kept thinking about something nice that was going to happen *after* whatever ordeal I had to face immediately: Tomorrow, you and I are going to Windsor to choose your costume for the Farrish House ball, so you must think of that when your nerves threaten to overwhelm you tonight.' Margaret smiled again, slipping her arm through Helen's. 'But just remember you have Ralph to take care of you, and you won't really worry at all.'

The thought of being taken care of by Ralph St John was enough to fill Helen with trepidation, but she endeavored not to show it as she and Margaret walked toward the balustrade above the entrance hall. The murmur of refined voices grew louder, as did the lilt of Mozart, and Helen paused to look down past the dazzle of chandeliers at the exclusive gathering below. Margaret wanted to hurry on down, but lingered a while too, knowing how nervous her sister was.

'Do be quick, Helen, Gregory will be very cross with me if I take much longer.'

'I know, I just need a final moment to summon up my courage.' Helen drew a long breath to steady herself, still looking down at the guests. Margaret had described them all so well that she had no difficulty identifying them. There was the sensitive but rather deaf young Duke of Devonshire, and with him his widowed stepmother, the still beautiful duchess, shimmering in golden silk and jeweled aigrettes. With them were Lord and Lady Holland, the latter one of London's most celebrated and critical hostesses; Margaret's efforts tonight would be under close scrutiny. Nearby stood the Duke and Duchess of Beaufort, and their nephew the young Duke of Rutland, with his astonishingly beautiful duchess.

Deep in conversation were Lord Palmerston, the Honorable William Lamb, and Count Lieven, the Russian ambassador, but it was the three lady patronesses of Almack's who unnerved her the most, for they looked so very severe and superior, except perhaps Lady Cowper, who had a warmer nature than the others. Lady Jersey was chill, and Countess Lieven positively intimidating, and Helen trembled at the thought of being presented to them more than at the prospect of curtsying to the prince. Still, she could console herself with the knowledge that these three paragons had human weaknesses, for they had all at one time or another taken the charming Lord Palmerston as their lover.

As she took a last look over the balustrade, she couldn't help thinking that the war had never seemed further away, for there was no hint of it in the elegant, relaxed demeanor of tonight's guests.

Margaret could wait no longer. Taking Helen's hand, she virtually dragged her toward the staircase, and then down to where Gregory and Ralph waited at the bottom. Gregory wore a tight-fitting black velvet coat with ruffles at the cuffs and around the collar, a frilled shirt, a white satin waistcoat, silk knee breeches and stockings, and buckled black patent leather shoes. Ralph wore the same, except that his coat was indigo, and he was laughing at something Gregory had said when at last he saw the two ladies descending.

Both men turned, and Gregory gave his wife a slightly reproachful look. 'I was beginning to think you weren't going to come down at all.'

'Oh, don't grumble, for I've had such a lot to do today,' she replied, giving him a disarming smile. 'Besides, am I not worth waiting for?'

His glance moved over her and he gave a sheepish grin. 'As always,' he murmured, taking her hand and kissing the palm.

Ralph turned to Helen, smiling warmly as he drew her hand to his lips. 'You look enchanting, Miss Fairmead. I vow I'm the most fortunate man present tonight.'

It was all she could do not to snatch her hand away. If he was the most fortunate man, she was the most *un*fortunate woman, having such a toad as her escort. He was a low, spiteful, dangerous reptile, as sly as a fox and as untrustworthy as a wrecker's lantern. She found herself wondering suddenly why he was interested in her. On Margaret's admission he would eventually be a very rich man and was already considered a catch, so why was he prepared to consider her as a bride? She was hardly an heiress of any standing; so, why? It was a puzzle to which she saw no satisfactory answer. Surely it wasn't just that he wished to be connected to Bourne End by marriage, as well as just friendship?

Gregory suggested that they mingle with their guests until the prince arrived, and thoughts of Ralph St John and his possible motives slid into the background as Helen steeled herself for the beginning of her ordeal. For the next half an hour she was presented to important person after important person, including the lady patronesses of Almack's, and she emerged at the end in such a daze of nerves that she couldn't remember a word she'd said. She was immeasurably relieved, therefore, when Margaret whispered to her that she was doing very well and hadn't put a toe wrong.

It was ten minutes past the appointed hour when word came that the royal carriages were approaching. Conversation died away immediately as everyone took up positions around the hall, with Gregory and Margaret facing the open doorway. Helen stood just behind them with Ralph, and as she heard the distant sound of carriages on the drive, her heart began to beat more swiftly.

The running footmen's flambeaux smoked and flared as they accompanied the first of the three carriages, a yellow berlin drawn by four superb bays. This was the prince's private carriage, and behind it came the vehicles containing his gentlemen attendants, and his footmen and pages. A detachment of Life Guards rode at the rear, the noise of their horses loud as the procession drew closer. The orchestra in the conservatory ceased playing Mozart and struck up a popular march, for it was well known that the prince liked to think of himself as the commander denied to the army by force of circumstance, since his father the king refused to countenance the heir to the throne taking up military service of any kind.

The berlin stopped before the house, the bays stamping and tossing their fine heads, and Gregory left Margaret to go and greet his royal guest. The berlin's blinds were down, and at first there was no sign of movement. The other carriages drew up as well, and the prince's gentlemen, Lord Lowther, General Turner, and Sir

Carnaby Haggerston, alighted, as did the footmen and pages. At last the berlin's door opened and the prince emerged.

He was nearly fifty-three years old, and immensely fat, his great bulk laced tightly into fashionable evening clothes that did nothing to flatter him. His already highly colored complexion was emphasized by the oils, creams, and other cosmetics he applied too liberally, and his chins rolled in folds above his exceedingly tall neckcloth and stock. His thick brown hair and luxuriant side-whiskers had a suspiciously artificial look, and altogether he was a little grotesque, but such disloyal thoughts didn't linger for long once he smiled, for then he appeared irresistibly charming. Nothing could have been more engaging or gracious than his words of greeting. 'My apologies, Bourne, I know I'm late again. I do hope you forgive me.' His voice was beautifully modulated, carrying quite clearly into the hall above the music from the conservatory.

Gregory bowed low and escorted the prince into the house, followed by the procession of gentlemen and servants. The waiting guests bowed and curtsied, the prince acknowledging them all with elegant nods. He glanced around at the floral decorations and then smiled appreciatively at Margaret. 'My dear Mrs Bourne, I confess I'm instantly delighted with the flowers. So many of them, and all in my honor.'

'Your Royal Highness is too kind,' she murmured, remaining in a low curtsy until he indicated she should rise.

He turned to Gregory. 'Are you all set for the races, Bourne?'

'I am, Your Royal Highness.'

'A little bird tells me Lexicon is expected to waltz off with the Gold Cup, but that Musket ain't up to scratch for the Maisemore. Is this so?'

'Musket's a little under the weather, it's true, but I intend to carry both trophies home, sir.'

'Do you indeed? Well, *I* intend to lay my hands upon the Maisemore this year, for I'm convinced Cherry Brandy is a better nag than Musket, so mark my words, you'll have much to reckon with.'

The prince's glance moved suddenly to Helen, and Gregory immediately hastened to present her.

'Your Royal Highness, may I present my sister-in-law, Miss Fairmead?'

Helen was shaking so much she was sure she'd make a dread-fully clumsy curtsy, but somehow she managed to achieve a certain grace, sinking in a rustle of silver taffeta.

The prince nodded approvingly. 'Please rise, my dear, that I may see you properly.'

She obeyed, hiding her trembling hands in the folds of her skirt.

He nodded again. 'Charming, quite charming. Tell me, my dear, are you a turfite too?'

'I – I'm afraid I know very little about horseracing, Your Royal Highness.'

He chuckled. 'I've no doubt a week or so beneath this roof will soon put a stop to that, and that *The Sporting Magazine* will soon take precedence over Miss Austen. You do read Miss Austen?'

'Oh, yes, sir.'

'Excellent. We must discuss the lady later.' With a gracious nod of his head, he turned to Margaret again. 'Your sister is delightful, my dear, and will be a definite adornment to society. Now then, I'm at your disposal, so lead on to the feast.'

Margart blushed with pleasure, accepting the arm he offered, and they proceeded toward the rose brocade dining room, where snowy cloths covered the gleaming tables, and golden cutlery shone next to glittering crystal. Epergnes tumbling with fruit, flowers, and moss alternated with pink-shaded candlesticks, and the perfume of orange and lemon trees drifted in from the conservatory, where the orchestra was once again playing gentle Mozart.

The other guests formed into a line, strictly in order of precedence, and followed the prince and Margaret into the room. Helen may have just been presented, but she was still socially rather insignificant, which meant that she was one of the last to go in, and that Ralph, as her escort, waited with her until it was her turn.

He drew her hand over his sleeve, smiling. 'I agree with the prince, Miss Fairmead, you will most certainly be an adornment to society.'

'Thank you, Mr St John.'

He hesitated. 'And you will be a credit to me.'

She froze. 'I beg your pardon?'

'I said you will be a credit to me.'

This really was too much. Whatever he may or may not have

understood from Margaret and Gregory, he had absolutely no business speaking to her of the matter without prior arrangement. She could no longer hide her dislike. 'I fail to see in what possible way I could be regarded as a credit to you, sir, since I have absolutely nothing to do with you, beyond the fact that you're a friend of my family.'

'I speak of our marriage, Miss Fairmead,' he explained, not detecting her iciness.

'You presume, sir,' she said coldly.

At last he realized all was not as he thought, and he couldn't hide his surprise. 'My dear Miss Fairmead, as far as I'm concerned it's all settled.'

'It isn't as far as I'm concerned; indeed, it will *never* be as far as I'm concerned.'

'The matter has been discussed and agreed, Miss Fairmead,' he said, becoming cool in turn. 'And may I remind you that such a match is very advantageous for you?'

'That depends by what one measures advantage, sirrah,' she breathed stiffly. How arrogantly sure of himself he was!

His eyes were angry. 'I'm sure you speak in the heat of the moment, Miss Fairmead, for to be sure tonight is an ordeal for you.'

'Maybe this is the heat of the moment, sir, but at such times the truth is apt to come out. I don't intend to ever consent to marry you, Mr St John, and if you require a reason, I'll gladly give one. I don't like you, sirrah, I don't like you at all, and the thought of marrying you fills me with revulsion!'

For a moment his mask slipped and she saw the real Ralph, the unpleasant Ralph who'd faced Adam the day before, but then he dissembled for it was their turn to enter the dining room.

As they moved slowly toward their seats, she knew she'd made a mistake in showing her colors. She wanted to work against him to Adam's benefit, and she'd have had more chance of success if he'd regarded her as a friend. Now he knew she disliked him intensely, and he'd treat her accordingly.

CHAPTER 11

The following morning found Margaret completely exhausted by the effort of entertaining the prince, who hadn't left until after three in the morning. It had all proved much more of a strain than she'd thought, and she woke up feeling totally ragged. Anxious not to make herself ill for the Farrish House ball, or, more importantly, the four days of Royal Ascot, she elected to spend the day in bed, encouraging Helen to take Mary with her for the six mile journey to Windsor to choose a costume for the ball. And so Helen set off in the open landau with only the maid for company, and an opportunity presented itself for furthering her acquaintance with Adam, maybe even for beginning to make her confessions. She intended, most improperly, to call upon him at King Henry Crescent.

Her style that morning, from the black frogging on her powder-blue silk spencer to the tassels and festoons on her matching mock-shako hat, was most definitely military, for she needed to feel as brave as possible. Her gown was made of the softest white silk, while her shoes and gloves were of the same powder blue as her spencer and hat. Mary had combed her hair up into a smooth knot beneath the hat, leaving soft wispy curls to frame her face, and although she looked cool, calm, and collected, she was in a high state of nerves about what might result from any meeting with Adam.

Leaving the bustle of Ascot and the racecourse behind, the landau drove smartly over the heath, where strings of racehorses could be seen exercizing across the open countryside. The landau was driven by Peter, the burly young coachman who'd engaged Mary's affections. He was in his early twenties, with a shock of spiky black hair and shining brown eyes. He smiled easily, and had a lazily good-natured manner that Helen could well understand had attracted Mary's attention.

The maid sat with her mistress, her shy glance resting more on her new sweetheart than on the passing landscape. She wore a straw bonnet over a white mob cap, with a long-sleeved beige linen dress that had a demure white fichu tucked into its low neckline. Her feelings were mixed as the landau drove into the sweet-smelling coolness of the forest, for although she was pleased to be with Peter, she was very anxious indeed about her mistress's rather shocking plan to call upon Lord Drummond.

The forest slipped away behind them and the landau drove through the gates into Windsor Great Park. Ahead the whiteness of Windsor Castle was clearly visible through the trees, and to the northwest led the road to Hagman's boathouse and Eleanor's Lake. Helen glanced along it, just picking out the huge copper beech by the track to the infamous Herne's Glade before the landau came up to a smart pace again and all was swept from her view.

She was so nervous about the prospect of maybe seeing Adam and attempting to confess her past fibs that she knew she had to try to distract herself for a while. She made herself think about the previous, evening, and the honor of being presented to the Prince Regent not once, but twice, for he'd remembered his wish to speak to her again and had particularly requested her company. It had been after the dinner itself, when the ladies had been in the draw-ing room for some time and the gentlemen had at last rejoined them for coffee, tea, and liqueurs. The prince had asked for her, insisting that she sit beside him on a sofa to discuss Miss Austen's books, on which he was very knowledgeable. He'd been very gracious and charming, indicating when the conversation was at an end, and as she'd rejoined Margaret and Gregory, she'd been told that she'd had a very great success, for the prince didn't often sit for so long with some who'd only just been presented to him.

The evening had indeed been a triumph for her; she'd spoken with dukes and duchesses, counts and countesses, lords and ladies, and she'd acquitted herself well. The only blot on the proceedings had been the presence of Ralph St John, who'd remained close at her side throughout, and who'd behaved as if all was perfectly well between them. He hadn't given her another opportunity to speak her mind; indeed, he'd gone out of his way to see they were always in company, and then he'd proceeded to give others the impression that things were coming along very well. She'd been silently furious, but hadn't really been able to do anything about it except be pointedly civil, which attitude she knew was attributed to her inexperience and youth.

It had all been extremely frustrating, the more so since she simply couldn't think why he was so insistent about regarding her as a possible bride. He now knew how totally unsuited they were, and he'd always known she had no financial prospects of importance, so why was he so interested in her? It couldn't simply be that he wished to be allied in marriage to Margaret and Gregory, for no man in his right mind would for such a reason take a bride, who loathed the very sight of him. So what was behind it all? She wondered if Margaret and Gregory knew. She'd have to speak to them about it all, for things couldn't go on as they were, but how was she going to tactfully inform them she despised their beloved Ralph?

With a heavy sigh, she gazed out at the park, where horsemen and women rode between the trees. It was an elegant scene, exclusive and beautiful, and so peaceful that again she found it hard to remember what was happening in Europe.

The landau drove past the Prince Regent's fine new residence, the *cottage orné* known as the Royal Lodge. From the road it was visible only as a number of tall chimneys rising above the trees, but she could tell that it was a large building, probably fully deserving its nickname of 'the thatched palace.'

At last the end of the park was in sight, and beyond it the town of Windsor, sprawling up the chalk outcrop that was dominated by England's largest castle. Helen toyed nervously with the strings of her reticule. Peter had been given instructions to drive to King Henry Crescent, which meant that in a very few minutes now she'd be at Adam's house. She'd screwed up all her courage to go through with her plan, but what if he wasn't in? And what if someone who'd met her last night should see her calling so boldly at his door? What if he *was* in, but threw her out on learning who she really was, and what if she was seen anyway? Then everything would be in ruins. The possibilities were endless, and she hardly dared think about some of them, but she still knew she had to see him and begin to put things on an honest footing. She drew a long, shaking breath, instinctively crossing her fingers as the landau rattled into the town.

King Henry Crescent was in a very fashionable quarter, its curving, elegant façade overlooking the Thames. There were echoes of Bath's Royal Crescent in its perfect lines, and it was evidently a much sought after address, for there were several exceedingly expensive carriages drawn up outside various doors. Almost immediately she realized which house was number five, for the bright red curricle was waiting at the curb, but even as she saw it her hopes were dashed because Adam emerged from his door, tapping on his top hat and pulling on his gloves.

He wore a light-brown coat, a fawn-and-cream-figured waistcoat, and fawn twill trousers, and he didn't glance toward the approaching landau as he climbed quickly into the curricle, turned it around in the street, and drove smartly away in the opposite direction. Helen stared after him in dismay.

Mary could hardly conceal her relief, for in her view her rash mistress had been saved from certain folly. 'It's for the best, miss, truly it is. A lady really shouldn't call alone on a gentleman.'

'I know, but I have to speak to him again. Evidently today is not destined to be the day, however. Peter, will you drive on to the couturière?'

'Yes, madam.' The coachman touched his hat and urged the team on.

Mary looked hesitantly at her. 'Miss Fairmead, perhaps you could write to him, explain it all in a letter?' she suggested wisely.

'I wish I could, but I need to see him face to face to tell him I've been fibbing since the moment we met.'

'But, a letter would. . . .'

Helen thought, but then shook her head regretfully. 'No, Mary, I couldn't do it that way.'

The maid fell silent.

Helen glanced up at the façade of King Henry Crescent as the landau drove past. Maybe Mary was right after all, and a letter was the answer. It was something to consider if she couldn't manage to speak to him soon.

The couturière's premises lay in the very shadow of the castle walls, one of a row of bow-windowed shops of rather exclusive appearance. There was a very superior haberdashery, a milliner, a furniture warehouse, and several other couturières, but it was Madame Blanchet who was the most prosperous.

A bell tinkled in the muffled silence as Helen and Mary entered. Dark oak counters, bolts of costly cloth, and shelves of accessories were all around in the gloom, for little sunlight penetrated. Madame Blanchet, a diminutive Parisienne who proudly wore Bourbon blue and silver, hurried to greet them straightaway, her face breaking into a pleased smile as Margaret's name was mentioned. She led Helen up to the dressing room on the floor above to show her the various costumes she'd set aside in readiness.

It didn't take Helen long to decide, for one costume stood out, a beautiful filmy gown of the most diaphanous ice-blue muslin, stitched all over with fluttering ribbons in the colors of the rainbow. It was meant to represent Iris, goddess of the rainbow, one of the messengers of the gods. The gown was very daring, plunging low over her bosom, but it was exquisitely lovely, and was to be worn with a Grecian stephane headdress, shaped and colored like the rainbow and flashing with jewels. The mask was a domino, the piece covering the eyes again studded with jewels, the veil concealing the lower face shaded in the same rainbow colors as the gown and stephane. Helen thought it quite perfect, and chose it as soon as she saw it.

Several minutes later, she and Mary emerged again, followed by one of Madame Blanchet's footmen, who solemnly loaded the packages containing the purchases into the boot of the waiting landau. Helen was about to climb into the carriage when her attention was drawn up the hill by the approach of a colorful cavalcade of the king's dragoons. They rode splendidly down from the castle, their horses' hooves clattering. As they passed, her gaze returned to the castle turrets. She knew it was very much the thing to stroll on the terraces, especially the north terrace, where the royal apartments were, and suddenly she felt like doing just that.

She turned to Peter. 'Please wait here, I wish to visit the castle.'

'Very well, miss,' he replied, touching his hat. He caught Mary's eye then, and gave her a broad but discreet wink.

The maid blushed, looking quickly away and falling into step just behind Helen, who had immediately begun to walk up the hill. Suddenly the maid halted, glancing across the road at a narrow side street.

Helen paused, looking curiously at her. 'What is it?'

'I – I don't know, miss. I had the strangest feeling someone was watching us, but when I looked, there wasn't anyone there. I'm sure I didn't imagine it.'

Helen glanced across the road as well, but the side street appeared to be empty. 'Oh, come on, I'm longing to see the castle.'

England's largest fortress was very splendid, more than a mile in circumference, and commanding a matchless view over the countryside of Berkshire and neighboring Buckinghamshire. The Thames wound past at the foot of the hill, separating Eton from Windsor, and in the other direction the great park stretched away toward Ascot, the magnificent acres shimmering in the brilliant sunshine. Helen and Mary proceeded into the lower yard, past St George's Chapel, and on toward the gateway into the upper yard, where the famous round tower presided over everything with a mixture of serenity and grimness that sharply evoked the long-lost past.

The north terrace was a place renowned for its breeziness, for it seemed to catch the wind from whichever quarter it blew. The royal apartments faced onto it, and there were many who'd seen the sad face of mad King George III gazing down from one of the windows, for he'd been living there under close watch since succumbing finally to his illness in 1811. There had been royal apartments in this place since the days of Henry I, and in all that time it had been a place to see and be seen in. There were many ladies and gentlemen strolling on the elevated open area, some just talking together, others pausing by the wall to gaze down at the panorama stretching away toward the horizon.

Helen and Mary joined the crowds for a while, but at last stood by the wall. Helen's thoughts weren't on the scenery, they were firmly fixed on Adam Drummond and how she was going to emerge from the tangle her own fibs had caused. She was aroused from her thoughts by the sound of a lazy male guffaw she'd heard rather frequently at dinner the night before. It belonged to William Lamb, whose notorious wife, Lady Caroline, had scandalized society with her outrageous and public affair with Lord Byron. Helen had found him very charming and kindly, and she turned quickly, intending to acknowledge him if their eyes met, but almost immediately she froze with shock, for he wasn't alone, Adam was with him.

The two men were idling along the terrace, in no particular hurry because they were enjoying each other's company. William Lamb laughed again as Adam said something amusing, and they paused about twenty feet away, unaware of her presence. Adam tipped his hat back, and Helen saw his face very clearly.

She had to turn sharply away, her heart pounding. Why had fate always to be so unkind to her? Again she had a chance of speaking to him, but she didn't dare to this time because he was with William Lamb, who knew her as Helen Fairmead of Bourne End.

'What are they doing, Mary?' she whispered.

The maid glanced discreetly toward them. 'The other gentleman's going, miss, he's just taking his leave.'

'And Lord Drummond? Is he going, too?'

'I don't know, miss. No, wait a moment, he's walking to the wall a little farther on. I think he's going to smoke a cigar. Yes, he's lighting it now.' The maid looked quickly at her. 'Please don't do anything you might regret, miss. Think of your reputation.'

'I may not have another chance like this, Mary, I have to speak to him.'

'Miss. . . .'

But Helen had already begun to walk determinedly toward him. He was leaning on the wall, the smoke from his cigar snatched away by the north terrace breeze. Her steps faltered, and she was suddenly less sure of herself. 'Adam?' she ventured nervously.

He straightened immediately, turning to look at her. Surprise shone fleetingly in his blue eyes and for a dreadful moment she thought he was going to cut her. Then he gave a slight smile, but it was definitely on the reserved side. 'Yet another unexpected encounter, fair Helen?'

'If you wish to acknowledge me. I shall quite understand if you don't.'

'How the pendulum swings. I seem to recall that at our last meeting *I* was the one saying something like that.'

'About our last meeting. . . .'

'It came to a somewhat abrupt end, did it not? I did wonder if I'd imagined you. Are you a mirage now? Will you suddenly vanish again?'

She colored. 'I did have a good reason.'

'I hope so, for to do so without good reason would have been contrary in the extreme.'

'I didn't wish to speak to Mr St John. I saw him coming and I hid.'

Slowly he dropped the half-smoked cigar, crushing it with the heel of his Hessian boot before looking at her again. 'Well, I congratulate you on your excellent taste, for only the most discerning manage to view St John with the dislike he so richly deserves. May I ask you where you hid?'

She lowered her eyes in embarrassment. 'In the bushes. I heard everything you and he said to each other.'

'Did you indeed?' he murmured. 'I imagine that what you heard made a great many things clear to you.'

'Yes.'

'I only have one sister, Helen, and her secret is now yours, as well as St John's.'

'I know.'

'Do I need to ask you to be discreet?'

'No, sir, you do not, and you wrong me by asking.'

'Forgive me, but where someone else's happiness and future wellbeing is concerned, it matters too much to allow the possibility of hurt feelings to stand in the way. I've gone through a great deal in order to protect my sister, I've allowed monstrous harm to be done to my reputation and honor, and I've forfeited many friends as a consequence.'

'I know, and I admire you immensely for it. I feel I should remind you that I believed in your innocence, and told you so, *before* I overheard anything at Hagman's.'

A smile played about his lips then. 'So you did,' he said softly.

Her heart quickened. 'I – I've admired everything about you since we met,' she said, color touching her cheeks, 'and if I could prove Mr St John's guilt, believe me, I would. I think he's the most despicable serpent I've ever come across, but even though my feelings are so strong on the matter, I'd never say or do anything that might compromise Lady Bowes-Fenton.'

His smile was warm now. 'If you've admired me, my lovely Helen, let me hasten to say that the feeling is more than mutual, and if I was a little, er, cool when you approached a while ago, it's because I really don't know where I am with you. You're quite the most perplexing creature I've ever met, a lady of true mystery.'

She took a hesitant step closer. 'Adam, there's much I need to say to you.'

'I'm fully aware of that.'

'I just don't know how to begin, or what you'll say when you know.' To her dismay, tears suddenly filled her eyes.

He came to her in quick concern, taking her hands and drawing them both gently to his lips. 'Please don't cry, Helen,' he said softly, looking into her eyes. 'Just answer me this, is there a Mr Brown after all?'

'Oh, no,' she answered quickly.

'Is there a fiancé?'

'No.'

'Is there anyone who has cause to hope?'

'No.'

He smiled a little. 'Have you committed vile murder?'

'No, of course not.'

'Have you stolen the crown jewels?'

She smiled through her tears. 'No.'

'Have you committed any crime at all?'

'No.'

'Then whatever it is that preys on your mind cannot possibly be very important, not to me, anyway. All that matters is that you're a free agent, and you are, aren't you?'

'Yes.' She lowered her eyes again.

He studied her. 'Yes, but?' he urged. 'Tell me, Helen.'

'I – I tried to tell you when last we met, indeed I would have if the horse hadn't distracted you. Then Mr St John arrived, and. . . .'

'I'm listening now, Helen. You have my full attention.' He put a hand to her chin, tilting her lips toward his and kissing her very softly and slowly.

She heard Mary's dismayed gasp, but took no notice, nor did she take any notice that this was a public place, nothing mattered but the ecstasy of kissing him. Her mouth trembled beneath his, and a fire burned through her veins, making her feel weak with sheer joy as his arms moved around her, pulling her close into a full embrace. Warm desire fluttered deep within her, beguiling and irresistible, and she clung to him, returning the kiss. This was what she was meant for, the only reason she existed now; loving him.

Almost overcome by the sheer force of emotion, she drew away, her cheeks flushed and her eyes dark. He put his hand to her cheek, stroking her warm skin with his thumb. 'Now then, what is the dire secret that so weighs upon you?'

She looked away. Suddenly the confession was impossible to make, for she knew that the joy she'd just tasted might never be tasted again if he knew who she really was. She'd have to tell him she was Gregory's sister-in-law, the woman whose name was being so widely connected with that of Ralph St John, and she was terrified that he'd recoil from her forever.

'Helen?'

'I. . . .'

'Yes?' His thumb still moved deliciously against her cheek, distracting, arousing, and so pleasurable that it drove confession further away than ever.

She looked tearfully at him. 'I can't tell you,' she whispered.

'But, if it worries you. . . .'

'I can't tell you, Adam. Please, don't ask me why.'

'If you're sure,' he said slowly, evidently puzzled.

'Quite sure,' she said, feeling utterly wretched, and ashamed of her own faintness of heart. She should tell him the truth, she should get it over with; but that might mean forfeiting so much.

'Will you see me again, Helen?'

She nodded, taking a deep breath to steady herself finally. 'Yes, Adam, I'd like to very much,' she said, her voice much more calm.

'Since I don't know where you live, and since I suspect you're still not yet ready to tell me, perhaps you had better suggest a time and a place.'

The problems crowded in again. She couldn't just slip away from Bourne End whenever she pleased, and she couldn't take a chance that another occasion like today would arise. No, she had to think of something else. Inspiration came from nowhere. 'Are you attending the Farrish House ball?'

'Yes. I believe that this year my valet has decided I am to be a sultan, or some such eastern gentleman, but since I shall be one among at least half a dozen, perhaps you should tell me how to recognize you.'

'I shall be the goddess Iris, but maybe there'll be lots of them too.'

'Possibly, so let's agree to meet at a specific place at a specific time. There's an extremely large long-case clock in the entrance hall of Farrish House, and I promise to be standing by it at exactly midnight. Will that do?'

'It will do very well, sir.'

'But let me warn you that I'm not entirely deceived.'

'Deceived?'

'You've chosen the ball because it means masks, and you will be able to continue concealing your identity, although who from, I'm not quite sure.'

Guilty color touched her cheeks. 'I cannot deny it,' she replied.

'There would be little point,' he said dryly. 'Helen, I can't even begin to guess what secrets you have, but I do know that when you're ready to tell me about them, I'll be ready to listen.'

'I will tell you, but not just yet.'

He smiled, bending his head to kiss her on the lips again. 'That's your privilege,' he said softly. 'But for the moment, I'm afraid I have to bring this sweet encounter to an end. I'm not here at the castle for my own pleasure, I'm here on War Office business. The Prince Regent has been dragged from the Royal Lodge to attend to matters of state, and I'm charged to assist him. Until the night of the ball, *adieu*, my fair Helen.'

'*Adieu*,' she whispered, closing her eyes with a shiver of pleasure as he kissed her again.

Then he'd gone, walking quickly away in the direction of the royal apartments. She gazed after him, her emotions in conflict again. She'd come so much closer to him, but she hadn't seized her chance to tell him who she really was. She'd foolishly and weakly put it off, and thus perpetuated the lies she'd started at the Cat and Fiddle. The longer she delayed, the worse it would become, but nothing could be as bad as actually losing him, and when it came to the point, that was all she could think of. She'd thought herself brave enough for the confession, but she'd proved utterly craven.

Mary came to hesitantly touch her arm. 'We should go, miss.'

'Yes.' Helen glanced at her. 'I don't know what to do, Mary, I just don't know what to do.'

'You have to tell him, miss. If you love him, and wish to be with him in spite of the bad feeling between him and Colonel and Mrs Bourne, then you have no choice but to let him know who you really are.' The maid's reply was blunt and uncompromising.

'And if by confessing, I lose him?'

Mary lowered her eyes. 'Let's go back to the landau, miss, it's a little cold here.'

With a heavy heart, Helen walked with her, back toward the lower ward and the town. From the height of joy, her spirits had plunged into the depths of uncertainty and apprehension. And all because she'd foolishly and misguidedly invented the widowed Mrs Brown; no, that wasn't entirely true, for if she hadn't invented Mrs Brown, she wouldn't have progressed as far as she had. Adam would never have extended warmth to Helen Fairmead.

Now her nerve had deserted her, and she didn't know if it would return. Suddenly Mary's suggestion of writing a letter began to seem the only sensible course, if more than a little unsatisfactory, but in her present timorous mood it offered at least a morsel of hope.

Neither she nor Mary noticed a small, wiry man slipping stealthily along a little distance behind them, watching their every move, as he had since the moment they'd driven out of Bourne End. He followed them down to the waiting landau, and as it drove away, he crossed the road and entered the narrow side street where earlier Mary had quite rightly felt someone watching. He'd left his horse in a livery stable, and he collected it now, riding swiftly out of Windsor and passing the landau as he rode across the park in the direction of Ascot. His destination was Bourne End, where the person who'd engaged his services was waiting.

CHAPTER 12

As the landau turned in through the lodge gates at Bourne End a little later, the horseman was just leaving, urging his tired mount back toward Windsor. Helen hardly glanced at him, she was still taken up with her problems. She was forced to the wry private admission that she wasn't unlike Ralph St John in one way, for if he'd plunged in too deep with his gambling debts, she'd plunged in equally as deeply with her fibs. She didn't want to think about Ralph, but as the landau drew nearer to the house she realized that she wasn't only going to have to think about him, she was going to have to speak to him again, for his dark blue barouche was at the door.

He was the last person she wished to see, and for a moment she considered instructing Peter to drive away again, but she knew the landau would have been observed from the house. There was nothing for it but to grit her teeth and face him.

Morris was waiting in the hall, his face as solemn as ever. 'Welcome back, madam. I trust your expedition to Windsor was successful?'

'Very successful, thank you, Morris. I see Mr St John has called.'

'He has, madam. He wishes to speak to you, and is waiting out on the drawing room veranda.'

Her heart sank. 'To speak to me? He hasn't called on Colonel or Mrs Bourne?'

'No, madam, he's called specifically to see you. Colonel Bourne has been engaged in the stableyard since breakfast, and Mrs Bourne is still resting in her rooms. I informed Mr St John that I didn't know when you would return, but he insisted on waiting.'

She sighed inwardly, for she knew the interview would be very embarrassing. She glanced at Mary, who was waiting discreetly with the two footmen who'd gone out to unload the packages from the landau. 'Please take everything to my rooms, I'll be up directly.'

'Yes, Miss Fairmead.'

Helen watched the little procession mount the staircase, and wished she was accompanying it. But Ralph St John was waiting, and so reluctantly she turned toward the drawing room.

She entered quietly, so much so that he didn't hear her from out on the veranda, where he sat at the white-painted wrought iron table, lounging back with his black patent leather shoes resting on the table itself. Today there was much more of the dandy about him, from his lilac coat and silver satin waistcoat to his extremely full Cossack trousers, made of charcoal-gray wool and gathered at the waist and ankles. His muslin neckcloth was unstarched and voluminous, and there were no fewer than three jeweled pins nestling in its folds. His top hat, gloves, and cane lay on the table, and he remained totally unaware of her presence, for he was absorbed in studying a little gold-framed miniature in his hand.

He was so completely preoccupied that Helen's curiosity was aroused. She paused by the open French window a few feet away from him, one hand resting on Gregory's telescope, which still stood pointing toward the park. A light breeze stirred through the net curtains, obscuring her view, and she moved to hold them slightly aside in order to see the miniature more clearly.

It was of a young woman in the clothes of the previous century, her long chestnut hair curled and frizzed in a cloud of curls around her head and shoulders. Her long-waisted gown appeared to be made of magenta satin of peculiar brilliance, and there was a black velvet ribbon around her throat, with an oval gold locket suspended from it. She was breathtakingly beautiful, and from the way Ralph gazed at her, Helen knew he was in the habit of often looking at her, whoever she was.

Helen's brows drew together thoughtfully, for somehow the woman seemed familiar, although no name came to mind.

The moments passed, and Helen knew she'd have to indicate her presence. She cleared her throat and stepped out onto the veranda. 'Good afternoon, Mr St John, I understand you wish to speak to me.'

Her voice startled him so much that he dropped the miniature. It fell with a clatter on to the stone-tiled floor, and Helen darted forward with a gasp to retrieve it, thinking that it must be damaged, but to her relief it was unharmed.

Ralph had risen hurriedly to his feet, and now immediately held out his hand for the little likeness. There was something oddly hasty about his manner, something of which she could only be very aware as she slowly handed the miniature back to him. 'She's very lovely,' she said.

'Yes,' he replied, pushing the miniature quickly into his pocket and avoiding her eyes.

'Who is she? She looks a little familiar.'

'I really have no idea who she is. I saw her in a Windsor shop this morning and purchased her.'

The answer took Helen aback. She was sure he wasn't telling the truth, and that not only did he know the lady's name, but he'd also possessed the miniature for much longer than a day.

He drew out one of the chairs. 'Please sit down, Miss Fairmead.'

She obeyed, sitting rather stiffly with her hands clasped in her lap, and then he sat down too, toying with his cane on the table for a moment. 'Miss Fairmead, about last night. . . .'

'The matter is forgotten as far as I'm concerned.'

'But not as far as I'm concerned. I've been guilty of a gross error of judgment, for I was vain enough to imagine you were bound to agree to a match with me.' He gave her a disarming smile.

Whatever she'd been expecting, it hadn't been this, and the smile might have taken her in had she not seen and heard the real Ralph St John beside Eleanor's Lake. For whatever devious reason, he was evidently still intent upon her as a bride, and today's smiles and apologetic words were intended to smooth her ruffled feathers and bring her around to what he wanted. He was about to be disappointed. 'I assure you that the incident is entirely forgotten, sir, and I trust that all is now perfectly clear between us.'

'On the contrary, things aren't clear at all, for you are under a severe misapprehension about me.'

'I am?'

'Yes, the foolish *faux pas* I made just before dinner last night was an isolated departure from my usual rule. I was guilty of putting my thoughts into hasty words, words which led me into broaching a subject I had no right to broach. I ask you to forgive me, and allow me to set such a false start aside and begin again.'

'I forgive you, Mr St John,' she fibbed, for she'd never forgive him, 'but there is little point in attempting to start anything again, for you and I are like oil and water, and a match between us would be an absolute disaster.'

'I realize you don't like me, Miss Fairmead,' he persisted, 'but I'm sure it's because I've approached everything badly. I can really be very amiable indeed, and would appreciate the chance to prove it.' He gave another disarming smile.

So, he could be amiable, could he? No doubt he could, if it suited his purposes, but he could also be utterly base. Blackmail was a weapon he didn't shrink from employing, nor did he think it amiss to willfully and despicably manufacture evidence against a friend. If Adam had done something vile, then maybe there could be a modicum of justification for Ralph's actions, but Adam had no idea in what way he'd offended. She gazed at Ralph, her face expressionless as these thoughts followed one after another through her mind.

'Miss Fairmead?'

She looked away from him. 'Will you satisfy my curiosity, sir?' she inquired.

'Your curiosity?'

'Yes. Will you tell me why it is that you think me a suitable bride?' Her green eyes swung toward him again, cool and opaque.

'Perhaps I'm more than a little smitten with you,' he replied easily.

'Really? Then you became so before you even met me. Be honest with me, sir, for your reasons are very important, are they not? No man contemplates marriage without first giving the matter deep and full consideration. I'm not an heiress, so marrying me will not solve your immediate financial problems, which only leaves my family connection. I cannot believe you'd want to marry me simply to become closely related to Gregory and Margaret, and as you are already very much associated with Bourne End, that doesn't seem to offer an answer either. So why are you set on me, Mr St John?'

His brown eyes were veiled, and a faint smile played about his sensuous lips. 'I did not need to meet you, Miss Fairmead, for I'd heard all about you before you left Cheltenham, and as to your not being an heiress, *et cetera, et cetera*, well I think you underestimate your beauty and many sovereign qualities.'

'And you, sir, underestimate my intelligence,' she replied astutely.

'Meaning?'

'Meaning that I don't believe a word.'

He lounged back in his chair, his eyes giving nothing away. 'Miss Fairmead, do I understand that you think I'm acting with foul ulterior motive?'

'With ulterior motive, certainly, but as to the degree of foulness, well, I can only hazard a guess.'

'And given your low opinion of me, I would imagine your guess would credit said motive with a great deal of foulness.'

She remained eloquently silent.

'Very well, Miss Fairmead, I admit to having an ulterior motive, but it isn't foul at all, so would it be at all possible for us to begin again?'

'You may have an ulterior motive for wishing to continue, sir, but I don't have any motive at all for wishing to marry you. On the other hand, I have my reasons for *not* wishing to marry you, so I'm afraid my answer has to be a very definite no.'

For a long moment he said nothing, but his eyes ceased to be veiled and became cold with dislike. 'Then you leave me no choice but to take off the kid gloves. You are a very difficult young woman, Miss Fairmead, given to unbecoming displays of spirit and standing stubbornly between me and what I want. I'm not about to let that continue, my dear. You're going to do my bidding.'

Her breath caught in disbelieving anger, and she began to rise from her chair to leave, but he leaned across to seize her hand, forcing her to remain where she was.

'I don't like you any more than you like me,' he breathed, 'but circumstances have forced me into a corner from which I'm finding it damnably difficult to wriggle free. Your willful intransigence isn't going to hold me down!'

'Let me go, sirrah!'

'When I'm ready, madam. I'm fully aware of why you've formed this aversion for me. It's because of Drummond, isn't it?'

She stared at him. 'I don't know what you're talking about.'

'Don't play games, my dear. I was informed all about your meeting with him on the way from Cheltenham, so it doesn't take a genius to realize that he's regaled you with his whining claims that I'm the villain of the piece, nor does it take great insight to perceive that much more went on at that meeting than you've admitted to your sister.'

For a dreadful moment she thought he'd somehow found out about Mrs Brown, but then she knew he hadn't, he was just surmising. She tried unsuccessfully to wrench her hand away, but he held her too tightly.

'Let me go!' she cried. 'I overheard everything you said by the lake yesterday, that's why I despise you, and why I know you for the louse you are. Now, please let me go, or I'll scream for help!'

'Do that and I shall have no option but to tell Margaret and Gregory all about your romantic and intimate meeting with Drummond today at Windsor Castle. Oh, yes, my dear, I know all about it.' His eyes were ice-bright, and a confident smile curled his full lips.

Shaken, she could only stare at him.

'Ah, I see that we are both a little taken aback to realize how our secrets are found out. I should have known you were somewhere nearby yesterday, you couldn't have vanished like that. And you, my dear, shouldn't have been so indiscreet today, for then my man wouldn't have had anything to see when he followed you, would he?' He pretended to sigh regretfully. 'Forgive me for having stooped to such vulgar levels, but I was curious about the virulence of your dislike for me, and when Margaret mentioned that you'd encountered Drummond, well, I thought it would be worth while seeing if there was more to it than met the eye. My man was so certain I'd be interested in what he'd witnessed – right in front of the royal apartments, too – that he hastened here to tell me straightaway, rather than wait until I returned to the Golden Key and dear papa tonight. He was right, for I was very interested indeed. You aren't the sweet Miss Chastity you're supposed to be, are you, my dear? I wonder what poor Margaret would say if she was regaled with such shocking facts about her little sister?'

From somewhere she found the steel to look him steadily in the eyes. 'If you knew all this, sirrah, I'm more surprised than ever that you persisted, right up to a minute or so ago, in promoting a match between us.'

'Because I needed you to serve a purpose, my dear; indeed, I still need you to serve that purpose. I want your agreement that you will at least consent to a temporary betrothal, one which can be discarded in the very near future.'

Her lips parted in amazement. 'You can't really think I'll agree. I would as soon drink poison.'

'Then I'm afraid I must resort to threats. To refuse this quite reasonable request of mine will lead not only to the exposure of your sordid little affair with Drummond, but also to the ruin of his sister. Oh, yes, my dear, I'll play any trump it pleases me to. And if I blow the gaff on Lady Bowes-Fenton, I'll make damned sure he knows it's your fault. There'll be no more cozy little hugs and kisses then, will there?' Slowly he got up, reaching for his top hat, gloves, and cane. 'All you have to do is be agreeable for a short while, pretend to consent to our marriage, and you have my word that soon there will be no further need for the betrothal.'

She was numb. He had her in a corner and she knew it. He was relying on her love for Adam, and her desire to at all costs protect the welfare of Adam's sister. 'Why – why should I believe in your word, Mr St John?' she whispered.

He smiled a little. 'Oh, my dear, you may be certain that in this particular instance, my word is indeed my bond. I now realize that you are the last woman on earth I really want as my bride, but circumstances have trapped me into needing you, and only you. You'll never be Mrs St John, but it is imperative to me that for the moment society believes that you are going to be. Now then, I've done with this conversation; do you agree to my request, or must I take myself off to Gregory and begin my wearisome task of scandalmongering?'

'I hate you,' she breathed.

'No doubt, but will you temporarily agree to marry me?' he pressed.

'Do I have any choice?'

'Not really, if you want to keep Drummond's – er – love. You do want to keep it, don't you?'

'Yes.'

'Which delightful little word will serve as your consent, I fancy,' he observed smoothly. 'We'll commence our tiresome little charade in public next week, when I escort you to the Farrish House ball, but in the meantime I expect you to let it be discreetly known that you now welcome the match.'

She nodded, trembling so much she couldn't speak, but as he tapped his top hat on and prepared to leave, she turned suddenly to face him. 'Why did you do it to Adam? What had he done to warrant it?'

'Oh, a great deal, believe me.'

'He doesn't know what it is.'

'But I know, and that's what matters.'

'And what of Gregory?' she went on, realizing he wasn't going to be forthcoming about Adam. 'He and Margaret are your friends, they mistakenly believe you to be perfect, and yet you deliberately brought Gregory's integrity into question as far as the Jockey Club is concerned. Racing is his life, he'd have been heart-broken if he'd been banned, but you didn't care at all, did you?'

He smiled a little. 'I'm a cad of the lowest order, am I not?' he murmured. 'Now, I'm afraid I must say *au revoir*. Just remember how disagreeable I can be when I'm crossed. Oh, and remember too to sing my praises from now on. I want Margaret and Gregory to be delighted because our little *tête-à-tête* on the veranda has paid such romantic dividends. Until the ball next week, then.'

With a cool nod of his head he strolled back into the house, his cane swinging idly in his hand. A minute or so later she heard his barouche driving away.

She bowed her head, blinking as the hot tears stung her eyes.

CHAPTER 13

Early the following morning, the sun streamed in through the French windows of the drawing room, the beams falling obliquely across the escritoire where Helen sat trying to compose the most important, and most difficult, letter of her life. A virgin sheet of paper lay before her, as it had for the past half an hour, and she was no nearer commencing her confession to Adam than she had been when she'd first crept secretly down before everyone else was awake. Now she could hear the housemaids moving about their business, and outside in the stableyard the first clatter of hooves signified another day's activity, but her pen had not yet even dipped into the ink.

Her long honey hair was brushed loose, tumbling heavily about the shoulders of her wrap, and her green eyes were tired and sad, for she hadn't slept at all because she was so aware of the extra pressure Ralph St John's demands had placed upon her already difficult situation. The letter she'd decided to write to Adam had been onerous enough anyway, without having to add to the problems by explaining why she'd now agreed, albeit temporarily, to a betrothal with Ralph. Oh, if only she hadn't fluffed her chance at Windsor Castle, when he'd been so prepared to listen. Instead, she'd given in to her chicken heart, and now the price was even higher.

An ironic smile curved her lips for a moment. She'd retreated in disarray, and was now reaping an increasingly bitter harvest. She simply had to write to him, she had no other choice if she was to stop the fibs and wipe the proverbial slate clean; but what could she say? How could she even begin to word it so that he'd not only understand, but forgive as well? More than anything she wanted to go to the Farrish House ball knowing that if he kept the tryst it was because he accepted the truth about her, for from that moment on her love would be completely honest, and thus free. But the sheet of paper remained stubbornly pristine, her nib dry, and her head frustratingly devoid of inspiration. Why was it that when the chips were down and she really needed to acquit herself well, she couldn't even call upon the basic skill of letter writing, which had been drummed into her for five long years?

Slowly she put the pen down, sitting back in the chair and turning her head to gaze out of the French windows. The rhododendrons looked magnificent, as usual, but from this room their splendor was spoiled by having to look past the veranda where Ralph St John had so cruelly and triumphantly imposed his will upon her. Like Adam before her, she'd had no choice at all but to go along with Ralph's demands, and although it had galled her to the very soul to bow to his blackmail, she'd done just that, allowing it to be known at dinner the night before that she thought Ralph was indeed as personable as had been claimed, and that she was now much more amenable to a betrothal. Margaret and Gregory had been delighted, and a bottle of the very best champagne had been broached in celebration of her change of heart. Helen had felt wretched, knowing she was deceiving them, and not only that, she knew she was helping to sustain their misguided faith in a man who was more than just obnoxious, who was downright evil.

With a heartfelt sigh, she returned her attention to the sheet of paper. She had to begin, for soon the housemaids would come into the drawing room and then it would be quite hopeless. Taking up the pen again, she dipped it in the ink.

My dearest Adam,

I don't really know how to begin this letter, except to say that I'm sorry, from the bottom of my heart, that I ever embarked upon a string of untruths that have given you an entirely wrong impression of me, wrong in every way but one, for I do indeed love you with all my soul.

Please read this letter to the very end, don't throw it away in anger, for I'm finding it impossible to choose the right words to explain why I lied.

My name is indeed Helen, but not Brown, and I'm not a widow, indeed I've never been married, because I'm fresh from five years at a seminary for young ladies in Cheltenham. You were right to be curious about my age for if I look young, then it's because I am young; and I'm ashamed to say I've behaved with the appropriate lack of maturity.

When my journey was interrupted by the weather and fears of Lord Swag, my only concern was the protection of my reputation, and that is why I pretended to be a widow. Once I'd embarked upon the masquerade, of course, I became increasingly embroiled in fibs. I shouldn't have dined alone with you, but I couldn't resist, nor should I have succumbed to your kisses, but the temptation was too heady to deny. By the time we parted at the Cat and Fiddle, I was already lost, and I was beset by a problem of which you couldn't be aware. You see, when you told me how bad the feeling was between you and Gregory Bourne, you were telling me how much you disliked my brother-in-law, and how much he disliked you. No, don't tear my letter up now, for I must explain everything, for although my real name is Helen Fairmead, it changes nothing where my feelings for you are concerned. I love you deeply, Adam, and I know you're entirely innocent of all the vile charges laid against you, for Ralph St John is the real villain.

I tried so much to confess my identity when last we met at Windsor Castle, but my courage failed me, and if I told you that I drove to King Henry Crescent to tell you but was forestalled because I saw you leaving in your curricle, would you believe me? It's true, my love, and I wanted desperately to say it all when I had the opportunity, but I was so afraid of losing you, I simply couldn't say a word. Forgive me my weakness, and please try to understand, for the agony I feel is an unbearable torment, especially as I now have much more to confess than I did then.

You've heard whispers connecting my name with Ralph St John's, and when last we met the only substance in those whispers was that Margaret, Gregory, and Ralph, without my knowledge or permission, had discussed and virtually agreed upon a match. For a reason he is not prepared to divulge, Ralph is very set on such a betrothal – indeed, it seems to me that it's betrothal and not marriage itself that concerns him – and when I refused pointblank to even consider him as a future husband, he resorted to the same vile course he used on you, i.e. blackmail. He had me followed to Windsor, and so knows about our meeting, and he's threatening not only to expose it, but also to tell all about the lady whose reputation you've gone to such honorable lengths to protect. His price for silence is my temporary agreement to a betrothal; it's a price I've felt obliged to pay, even though I despise him with every fiber of my being. So when you hear of the match, understand it for what it really is, and understand my reasons for submitting to his will.

It's you that I love, Adam, and you that I believe in. I love my sister and brother-in-law, but I know they're wrong to condemn you, and if it came to a choice between them and you, my darling, there is no choice, for you would come first.

I don't know if I've explained all this well, but I hope I have. I realize you may not be able to find it in your heart to forgive me for all the untruths, but if you do, then I beg you to keep our tryst at the ball.

Know that I love you, and only you.

                                        Helen

With a trembling hand, she put the pen down, reading the letter through very slowly. Was it enough? Did it convey the depth of her love and feeling? With a resigned sigh, she folded it, knowing that she wouldn't be able to manage anything better in her present state of mind. The words had come from her heart, and she'd written them down as they came.

She'd brought her night candle with her, to melt the sealing wax, and her hand shook a little as she held the hard red stick to the flame. The molten drops splashed on to the folded letter, and were still soft as she pressed her signet ring into the seal. H.E.C.F. Helen Elizabeth Caroline Fairmead. Taking up the pen again, she wrote the name and address, then she tucked the letter carefully

into the sleeve of her wrap, intending to ask Mary to give it to
Peter to deliver, for he was due an afternoon off, and intended to
visit his sick mother in Windsor. To risk the royal mail was too
hazardous, for Morris supervised all letters, and one addressed to
Lord Drummond was bound to be brought to Margaret and
Gregory's attention.

Slowly, she rose from the escritoire. She felt drained and in need
of sleep, but knew she was really too wide awake now. Opening
the French windows, she stepped outside. The freshness of the
morning was perfumed and restoring, and in spite of the awful
memory she had of the last occasion she'd been on the veranda,
she sat at the table, leaning her chin in her hands and gazing across
the park. What was Adam doing now? Had he risen from his bed?
Was he thinking about her? Would he ever think of her again once
he'd read the letter? Oh, please let him understand, and forgive
... Tears pricked her eyes, and wearily she rested her arms on the
table, hiding her face, her hair spilling over the white-painted
wrought iron surface.

She must have drifted into sleep after all, for the sound of voices
in the drawing room woke her with a start. It was Margaret and
Gregory, and Margaret seemed upset about something.

'Gregory, I fail to see why I should remain here, when so many
wives have accompanied their husbands to Brussels. There are
even whispers that the Duchess of Richmond wishes to hold a ball,
Caroline Capel told me so in her last letter.'

'Lady Caroline Capel likes to dramatize everything, besides, all
this is pure speculation, Margaret, for there's no reason at all to
suspect that I'm about to be dispatched to Brussels, or anywhere
else for that matter.'

'Isn't there? Louis Whiteman has been called to London and
told just that, so why should this letter summoning you to the War
Office be any different? Come on now, you know as well as I do
that Lord Llancwm has been no friend of yours since you turned
your back on his precious nephew.'

'This has nothing to do with Adam Drummond.'

'No? Is he or is he not Llancwm's great-nephew?'

'Of course he is, but Llancwm wouldn't use his position at the
War Office to be avenged on me.'

'Would that I had such faith. Llancwm made little secret of his displeasure when all that wretched business was in progress last year.'

'Family loyalty, but not enough to make him send for me and dispatch me to Brussels. Be sensible now, my love. If there is any spite in his actions, it will amount to little more than seeing that I miss the Farrish House ball and the first day or so of Royal Ascot.'

'Little more than?' cried Margaret incredulously. 'Gregory, both the Farrish House ball and Royal Ascot are unthinkable without your presence, as unthinkable as Christmas without a yule log, or a coronation without a king!'

'My love, you're exaggerating somewhat,' replied Gregory calmly. 'You're letting this get quite out of hand. All that's happened is that I've received a letter summoning me to the War Office. It's inconvenient, but hardly the end of the world. And I've no reason to believe it will concern anything other than my involvement with the local militia. I'll toddle along. . . .'

'On the very day of the ball,' interposed Margaret.

'On the very day of the ball, and I'll be back as soon as I can, probably before the last race on the opening day. Come now, sweetheart, let's have a smile before we go in for breakfast. We don't want to upset Helen when she's just come around to being happy about Ralph.'

Helen rose from her chair and went to the French windows, brushing past the nets. 'I'm afraid I've been eavesdropping,' she confessed, smiling a little ruefully.

They both turned sharply, and Margaret looked in amazement at her wrap and unpinned hair. 'Helen, you haven't been out like that, have you?'

'I was sitting out there and I just fell asleep. I've only been on the veranda, not to the racecourse and back.' Helen went to them, kissing them both on the cheek. 'I take it there's been a disagreeable letter?'

'There has,' declared Margaret with feeling, 'although my dear husband chooses to remain unruffled by it.'

Gregory drew a weary breath. 'Margaret, I don't intend to argue anymore, I've said all that's necessary. I have to go to the War Office, and that's the end of it.'

Margaret moved crossly away from him. 'It's all petty vindic-tiveness by the Drummond family, and you know it.' She glanced at Helen. 'Since you've been earwigging, you know all about it; you also know now that Adam Drummond is a toad, for it's his hand that lies behind this. I'm so glad you've seen the light, Helen, for it was so unjust that you should stand by him and dislike poor Ralph. Still, it's past now, and you and Ralph are as good as matched.'

'Yes.' Helen managed a smile, but it was like drawing teeth.

'I'm afraid you'll have to share him with me at the ball now.'

'Share him?'

'Gregory intends to ask Ralph to escort me as well – *if* I decide to go.

Gregory groaned. 'Margaret, I swear I'll sink into a sulk with you if you continue on this tack. You're going to the ball, and you're attending the races. I won't hear of anything else.'

'Only on condition that I accompany you to Brussels if you're sent there,' replied his wife stubbornly.

'No.'

'The Duchess of Richmond. . . .'

'Is long since past expecting her first child.'

Margaret's green eyes flashed rebelliously, and Helen went to her. 'Gregory's right, sweeting,' she said gently, 'Brussels is most definitely *out*. I won't countenance any risk to my sister and my first nephew or niece. Come now, even supposing they do intend to send Gregory there, which I don't think they do, you must see that he'll be much more capable of doing his task if he doesn't have your safety and welfare to worry about every minute of the day.'

Margaret didn't want to see sense, but knew she had to. She gave Helen a baleful glance, smiling ruefully. 'I wish you'd stayed in Cheltenham.'

'I'll go back if you want me to.'

'I wouldn't hear of it, especially if I'm to be left all alone while my husband rushes gallantly off to war.'

Gregory breathed out with relief, and then went to hug her fondly. 'That's my girl, but it won't come to that, you know. I'll be back before you know it, with instructions in my capacity as

Colonel of the Berkshire Militia.' He put his hand to her chin, raising her face toward his. 'Now then, can we drop the whole
subject?'

'I suppose so,' she whispered, closing her eyes as his lips
brushed hers.

'Good, so let's to breakfast, mm?' He smiled, and then turned
to Helen, holding out his hand. 'It's my privilege to escort two
ladies to breakfast in their undress.'

Helen smiled too, accepting his hand, but as his fingers closed
warmly around hers, she felt wretchedly guilty. No matter how she
chose to view her actions since meeting Adam Drummond, both
Margaret and Gregory were bound to regard them as the actions
of a snake in the grass if they ever found out. Unless she could
prove Adam's innocence. She lowered her glance to the floor as
they proceeded from the drawing room to the breakfast room. She
wanted so much to clear his name, and yet she didn't even know
if he would ever wish to speak to her again after Peter delivered
her letter.

CHAPTER 14

The week passed, May gave way to June, and Peter didn't have his afternoon off until the day before the ball. When at last he set off on his cob to visit his mother, the letter to Adam was safely in his pocket.

Once he'd gone, Helen simply couldn't relax. Mentally she traveled with him all the way to Windsor, and then to the door in King Henry Crescent. Would Adam's eyes soften and clear when he read what she'd written? Or would they darken with anger at the way he'd been deceived? She wondered if Peter would simply deliver the letter, or if he'd be there when it was opened. She wished he'd return quickly so that she could quiz him, but the hours passed, the afternoon became evening, and then darkness fell with still no sign of him.

At the dinner table her ill-concealed restlessness went unnoticed, for Margaret and Gregory were too taken up with his imminent departure for London. He was set to leave first thing the following morning, and Margaret was still convinced that the War Office letter was pure malice on the part of Adam's vengeful great-uncle. More than once she reiterated quite firmly that far from an intention to discuss militia matters, Lord Llancwm's real purpose was to pack Gregory off to the war, as punishment for the besmirching of Adam Drummond's honor. Helen wisely refrained from participating in the conversation, especially as she was uncomfortably aware that Adam had recently attended a War Office meeting where his great-uncle had also been present, so that at the very least he probably knew of the letter to Gregory. Margaret was upset by the whole business, and the situation wasn't helped by the thought of attending the costume ball without the husband who was the racing world's leading light, and the further prospect of Royal Ascot's opening day without him as well was so awful that her enthusiasm was quite dampened. It took all the ingenuity of both Helen and Gregory to arouse her usual interest in the clothes she planned to wear, so that by the end of the meal she could almost have been described as cheerful, smiling a little as she discussed which of her lovely new outfits she would wear for her first sallying forth to the races.

It had been decided that a reasonably early night was in order, both because of the ball the following night, which would go on until dawn, and because Gregory had to set off very promptly for his War Office appointment. As Helen went to her room, there had still been no sign of Peter, and then there was no sign of Mary either. Half an hour passed, and still there was no tap at the door, and at last Helen became a little concerned. Taking up her shawl, she slipped down through the silent house, and as she reached the entrance hall she encountered a rather anxious footman, who was on his way to see her.

'Miss Fairmead? It's Mary, she's very distressed.'

Helen's eyes widened anxiously. 'Distressed? What's happened?'

'Peter was set upon by the highwayman on his way to Windsor this afternoon. A shot was fired at him, grazing his head, and he lay unconscious in a ditch until a wagoner found him and brought him back here a short while ago. He's conscious now, but Mary's in a terrible state.'

'Take me to her.'

'Yes, miss. This way.'

He led her toward the door opening from the entrance hall into the kitchens, where a number of servants were seated quietly around a wellscrubbed table, evidently discussing what had befallen poor Peter. They rose hastily to their feet, their chairs scraping, but Helen waved them to sit down again, hurrying on after the footman through another door and into the servants' wing extending from the rear of the house.

Mary was in Peter's room, together with Morris and the cook, and her stifled sobs could be heard long before Helen entered. The room was small, but adequate, its walls crisply whitewashed, its chintz-curtained window facing toward the stableblock. There was a small wardrobe, a chest of drawers, a chair, and a narrow bed, upon which Peter lay now, his face wan and his head bandaged. Morris was standing at the bedside, and Mary was weeping on the chair, the plump cook doing her best to offer comfort.

Morris turned the moment Helen appeared. 'I trust it was in order to send for you, miss?'

'Yes, of course. How is Peter?' Helen went to the bed and looked down at the injured coachman.

'The head groom, who has experience of such things, having been a surgeon's man in the same regiment as Colonel Bourne, says that he's only slightly hurt, Miss Fairmead. He says Peter was lucky, the highwayman's shot only scraped him, and apart from a headache tomorrow, he'll be none the worse. I wouldn't have bothered you, miss, but Mary seemed to think you'd be particularly concerned.' The butler couldn't hide his curiosity, for why on earth should a lady be interested in a mishap to an under-coachman?

Concerned? Yes, thought Helen, for if the waylaying took place before Peter had reached Windsor, then the letter hadn't been delivered, and she was no nearer explaining everything to Adam than she had been before putting pen to paper. She sat on the edge of the bed. 'I'm so sorry you've been hurt, Peter.'

'Thank you, miss,' he replied.

'Was it Lord Swag?'

'I – I think so, miss, but I couldn't really say. I thought Lord Swag only came out at night, but this was broad daylight, right in the middle of the great park. He was bold as brass, miss, robbing me of the money I was taking to my mother. She's a widow, miss, she lives alone and needs what help I can give.'

'I'll replace what was stolen, Peter,' Helen reassured him, seeing how anxious he was.

'Oh, no, miss. I couldn't ask that of you.'

'You didn't ask, I offered. Besides, one good turn deserves another, and I can quite well-afford to dip into my purse, so let's not hear any more protests.'

'But, miss, I didn't get to do the good turn. . . .'

'I realize that, but you still meant to help me, and I'm grateful to you.'

'I – I don't know what to say, miss.'

'Then say nothing, just try to sleep; you'll need it if you're going to be nursing a sore head tomorrow.'

'Yes, miss. Miss. . . ?'

'Yes?'

'Please persuade Mary I'll be all right, she's crying fit to burst, and nothing we say will make any difference. I've had a knock, but that's all. Please tell her.'

'I will.' Helen rose to her feet, going around the bed to the chair where poor Mary was in such a flood of sobs that she was hardly aware of her mistress's presence.

'Mary?' Helen put a gentle hand on the maid's shaking shoulder.

The tear-stained eyes were raised immediately, and Mary's breath caught as she found herself looking at Helen. 'Oh, miss, f-forgive me. I – I didn't know y-you were here.' More tears welled from her eyes. 'I should have attended you. . . .'

'I'm not angry with you, Mary, for the circumstances are rather pressing.'

'But your letter, miss. . . .'

'I know.' Helen glanced uncertainly at Morris and the cook, who had been listening to everything. 'Now then, Mary, you're to come with me, and leave poor Peter to try to sleep. He's going to be all right, so you don't need to cry any more. I'm sure the cook will see that some hot drinks are sent up to my room. Then you and I can sit together like we used to at Cheltenham.'

The maid's eyes were grateful. 'Oh, yes, miss. I'd like that.'

'Come on, then.' Helen held out her hand, glancing at the cook. 'Will you do that for me?'

'Oh, yes, Miss Fairmead, I'll attend to it straightaway.' The woman hurried out, her starched brown cotton skirts rustling and the huge mob cap on her graying hair wobbling a little on its pins.

Morris inclined his head to Helen. 'I will remain with Peter until he's asleep, miss. Then I'll see that someone looks in on him through the night.'

'Yes, Morris, that will be excellent. I don't think we need wake the colonel or Mrs Bourne.'

'No, miss.'

'But when the colonel leaves in the morning, I wish you to tell him what's happened, for he shouldn't travel unarmed if Lord Swag has taken to daytime activities.'

'Yes, Miss Fairmead.' The butler bowed gravely.

Helen took Mary's hand and led her up through the quiet house. A few minutes later the cook personally brought a tray on which stood two porcelain cups and a jug.

'I've made bold with a bottle of the colonel's best claret, miss, for I thought you'd like some good cardinal.'

'Cardinal?'

'Yes, miss. Cinnamon, cloves, orange and lemon, sugar, and good hot claret. It's called cardinal, and is just the thing for times like this.'

Helen smiled. 'Thank you, it smells excellent.'

The woman carefully put the tray on the dressing table.

'It'll warm young Mary up a treat, miss, and she'll sleep like a top in spite of her nasty shock.'

'I'm sure it will. I'll dispatch her to her room directly, and no doubt you're eager to retire to yours, so I won't keep you any longer. Oh, and don't concern yourself about having purloined a bottle of the colonel's claret, for I distinctly remember instructing you to make some cardinal.'

The cook smiled. 'Yes, miss. Thank you, miss.' Bobbing a curtsy, she withdrew.

Helen went to pour the spicy drink, pressing a cup into Mary's trembling hands. 'Drink up, it'll do you good.'

'It'll make me tipsy, miss.'

'Then you'll fall asleep immediately when you go to bed, which is what you need tonight.'

'When I saw poor Peter like that, all pale and weak, I just went to pieces. I didn't know I cared so much about him, I didn't think it was possible after knowing him for such a short time.'

Helen smiled wryly. 'Oh, it's possible, Mary. I should know that, should I not?'

'Yes, miss.' The maid looked at her and then put down her cup in order to take a crumpled, mud-stained letter from the pocket of her apron; it was the one Helen had written to Adam. 'It's all spoiled, miss, for Peter fell in a ditch when he was shot, and the water and mud . . .' She held it out. 'The address can still be read, so I suppose the rest can too.'

With a sigh, Helen took it.

'What will you do now, miss? Write it again?'

Helen was silent for a moment. 'No, I think I'll try and screw up the courage to tell him to his face tomorrow night at the ball.'

'Do you think you'll be able to, miss?'

'I really don't know.'

Mary was sipping her cardinal again. 'You could always give him the letter as it is, miss, and explain why it never reached him. If you said all you wanted to say in the letter . . . you did, didn't you?'

'Yes, I think so.'

'Well, then, maybe it will still do.'

Helen smiled. 'I'm supposed to be comforting you at the moment, Mary Caldwell, not the other way around.'

'But you are comforting me, miss, for I feel a lot better now I've been sitting here for a while, just like we did at Cheltenham. You've always been more than just my mistress, Miss Fairmead, you've been my friend, too, and there's not many maids can say that of their ladies. Tonight you've been a friend first and foremost, and I know that Peter will think the world of you from now on. If there's ever anything we can do for you, you know you just have to say.'

'Thank you, Mary. You're a friend to me, too; indeed, you're the only person I've been able to confide in since. . . .'

'Since Lord Drummond?'

'Yes.'

'It'll come all right in the end, miss, I'm sure it will.'

'I hope you're right, but when I think of all the obstacles, difficulties, and downright bad luck that seems to be besetting my every move, I'm afraid I'm not very optimistic.'

'You mustn't lose heart, miss, not if you love him.'

Mary fell silent then, for her mistress's apprehension was well founded. A gulf of mistrust and misunderstanding separated Lord Drummond from his former friends at Bourne End, and it was Helen Fairmead's extreme ill fortune to be caught in the middle.

CHAPTER 15

The following night seemed to come only too quickly, and as it was also the eve of Royal Ascot, Windsor and its environs were filled to overflowing not only with London's *beau monde*, but also the entire world of racing. Constables were out in force on the roads, for it was feared that Lord Swag wouldn't be able to resist so many rich pickings. In the town there wasn't a room to be had anywhere, and every available horse had been hired, as devotees of the turf prepared for one of the highlights of the racing as well as the social calendar; but first there was the costume ball to enjoy, and enjoy it they intended to do, to the best of their considerable ability.

As twilight fell, the great house was ablaze with lights, and a jam of carriages blocked the drive. Farrish House was a formal seventeenth-century mansion with a hipped roof and dormer windows, and had been designed by Robert Hooke for one of Charles II's favorite courtiers. It had large ugly chimneys, but the rooftop was also graced by a balustraded promenade, where an elegant cupola afforded fine views over the town and the Thames. The rectangular windows of the house itself were set out in perfect symmetry on three floors, and the pedimented main entrance was approached up a flight of shallow steps that were strewn with flowers and sweet-smelling herbs for the great occasion.

Music drifted from the glittering ballroom out onto the wide terrace above the water gardens. The strains of a stately minuet soon became lost amid the jingle of harness and rattle of wheels, as the endless procession of carriages made its way toward the house. A thousand lanterns shone in the grounds, bright torches flickered on the tiny island in the center of the ornamental lake,

and all was set for a dazzling night of music, laughter, and dancing.

In the Bourne End landau, the three occupants had very little to
say. Margaret was brought very low again by Gregory's absence,
Helen was nervous about her tryst with Adam, and Ralph seemed
to have something important on his mind.

He was inappropriately attired as Richard Lionheart, for he
wasn't kingly or lion-hearted, and Helen certainly couldn't envis-
age him embarking upon anything as noble and creditable as a
crusade, he was too contemptible and poisonous for that. Tonight
was the first time she'd seen him since their unpleasant confrontation on the veranda, but the moment they'd come face to face
she'd known how smugly confident he was that he had her exactly
where he wanted her.

She surveyed him secretly. He looked splendid enough, wearing
mock chainmail beneath a long white tunic that sported a crimson
cross. There was a splendid golden crown on his head, and his
brown hair looked almost reddish enough to be Plantagenet, but
behind his black velvet mask his eyes were sly, clever, and cold, if
somewhat preoccupied for the moment.

Margaret was a porcelain figurine come to life in a pale-pink
satin shepherdess dress that was all flounces and petticoats. Tight-
waisted, with a very full skirt, the dress came audaciously to just
below her knees, thus revealing her white-stockinged legs and high-
heeled satin shoes. Her honey-colored hair, so like Helen's, was
curled in ringlets to her shoulders, and she wore a wide-brimmed
gypsy hat tied on with wired pink ribbons. A slender little satin
mask hid her eyes but very little else of her face, so that she was
instantly recognizable as Mrs Gregory Bourne, and anyway she
wore around her neck a golden locket on which was engraved the
Bourne family coat-of-arms and the initials G and M, which meant
that it was virtually impossible not to know exactly who she was. A
crook adorned with pink ribbons and a garland of flowers rested
against the seat next to her. On her lap there was a basket containing a very unconvincing lamb that had a peculiar squint, and it was
this lamb that had prompted Ralph to make his only amusing
remark of the evening, when he'd observed rather dryly that the
lamb might benefit more from a mask than the shepherdess.

Helen gazed through the lanternlit night toward the house. Had Adam arrived already? Margaret's lack of real disguise had dismayed her a little, for it could be that Adam would see the goddess of the rainbow in company with Mrs Gregory Bourne; it might be enough for him to decline to keep his assignation at midnight. She glanced in her reticule at her gold fob watch. It was ten o'clock, and she had two more hours to wait; it seemed like a lifetime.

Her hair was dressed up in a classical Grecian style, and the jewels in her stephane headdress flashed, as did those on the mask of her domino. A light night breeze fluttered through the rainbow ribbons adorning her ice-blue gown, touching her bare arms and making her shiver a little. The letter to Adam was in her reticule, to be used as a last resort. So very much depended on tonight, but she knew that her courage was as weak as ever, and having to reveal her wretched secrets was going to be so difficult it was almost impossible. Above all else she was afraid of alienating him, and it was this that colored her entire approach; fear of losing him was so strong it was in danger of once again allowing her heart to overrule her head, and if that happened, she'd leave the ball tonight without a word of confession having passed her foolish lips. How her life had changed since she'd left Cheltenham; then, she hadn't had a care in the world, now, she was beset by problems.

At last the landau reached the flower-strewn steps, and two Farrish House footmen in green and silver livery hastened to open the carriage door and lower the rungs. Ralph alighted, pausing to adjust his crown, then he turned to assist first Margaret, complete with basket, lamb, and crook, and then Helen, who snatched her fingers away from his at the earliest opportunity, recoiling from any physical contact.

There was such a queue of guests waiting to enter the house that for a minute or so it was impossible to move. Helen glanced around at the variety and ingenuity of the costumes, and she immediately perceived another goddess Iris, whose gown may not have been as exquisite, being merely paneled in rainbow colors, but whose hair was a very similar shade of blond to Helen's own.

There was a preponderance of Stuart ladies and gentlemen,

especially Old Rowleys, Prince Ruperts, Duchesses of Cleveland, and Nell Gwynns, for far too many guests had been seized with the inspiration of dressing to suit the period of Farrish House. Apart from them, she saw several Britannias, three Queen Elizabeths, some Indian rajahs, and a sprinkling of pharaohs. Among the more original were a Madame de Pompadour, a Nero complete with fiddle, a Cyrano de Bergerac with the most ridiculously long nose imaginable, and a lady so swathed in flowing sea-green muslin that she could have been just about anything, but was, so Helen was to learn later, the spirit of the ocean.

Another carriage had drawn up behind the landau, and a Russian cossack alighted, turning to assist down a high-ranking naval officer whose hand he tenderly kissed! Helen was taken aback to say the least, but just as she was beginning to think the worst, she realized that the naval officer was a very bold lady.

Margaret perceived the duo as well. 'Good heavens,' she murmured, 'do you see what I see? I vow she'll shock every matron in the house. Look how she swaggers, swinging her hips from side to side like a tar! No wonder she hides her face so well behind that mask, for she'd have no reputation left if her identity were known.'

'Her identity *is* known,' said Ralph. 'It's Caro Lamb, and she has no reputation anyway.'

'That's very true,' agreed Margaret. 'What William Lamb ever saw in her I'll never know.'

'Whatever it is, he still sees it, for if I'm not mistaken he's the cossack. Yes, I'd know that laugh anywhere,' said Ralph as a lazy and very familiar guffaw carried to them.

'I despair of him,' sighed Margaret. 'She's behaved abominably, betraying their marriage vows and making a fool of herself and of him, and yet he still seems to dote on her. Mind you, he isn't a great judge – he remains Adam Drummond's crony. Still, that's his problem, I have enough of my own to worry about, not least of which is having to deal with the endless inquiries I'm going to face concerning Gregory's absence tonight. Everyone will be most put out, for it's quite unheard of for Gregory Bourne to be absent from this occasion. I shall lay the blame for it fairly and squarely at the odious feet of Lord Llancwm.' Adjusting the lamb in its basket, and brandishing her crook, she swept up the steps.

Helen made to follow, but Ralph detained her for a moment. 'Remember what's expected of you tonight, my dear.'

'How could I forget?'

'I don't know, but I'm sure you would if you felt you could. Just behave like my prospective bride, and blush prettily when mention is made of an imminent betrothal, for that is the way to see that Drummond still looks kindly upon you.'

'I despise you,' she breathed. 'How you've managed to fool not only my sister and brother-in-law but a great deal of society as well, I really don't know.'

'It's my irresistible charm,' he replied smoothly, offering her his arm. 'Shall we proceed?'

Reluctantly, she rested her hand on the cool chainmail of his sleeve, but as they ascended toward the brightly lit doorway, she was determined to strike free of him at the first possible opportunity. She had to be completely at liberty when midnight struck.

The crush in the hall was tremendous, a squash to end all squashes, and the babble of voices was amplified so much inside the house that the music from the ballroom was inaudible. Chandeliers of particular brilliance shimmered in the warm air above the distinguished gathering of lavishly costumed guests, and the smoke from the gentlemen's cigars vied with the perfume from the countless flowers brought in for the occasion. From the painted walls, stern-faced figures gazed down a little disapprovingly from between the columns of a classical temple, as if taking exception to such frivolity, which well they might considering the dire situation across the Channel in Europe.

There was an Ionic colonnade at the far end of the hall guarding the entrance to the magnificently gilded ballroom, and to the right swept up a black marble staircase with a golden handrail. Against the wall at the foot of this staircase, passed constantly by a stream of guests, stood the large long-case clock by which she was to meet Adam in two hours' time.

Margaret was standing just inside the entrance, talking with a Boadicea, an exceedingly tall Louis XIV, and an armored knight who was already looking very hot and uncomfortable, for his visor was raised and he constantly mopped his perspiring face with a large handkerchief. Helen soon realized that the Louis XIV and Boadicea were the Earl and Countess of Cardusay, who'd been married so romantically on the lake at Hagman's the year before, for Margaret was exclaiming that she was astonished it was really one whole year since that glorious and memorable day.

'A year? Is it that long already? I can scarce credit it.'

'Well, we felt we should mark the occasion in suitable style,' replied Boadicea, 'and when Henry suggested a water party, well, what could I say but yes? It's a marvelous notion, don't you think? We've invited everyone who came last year, but then were horrified to find that a whole bundle of invitations had been mislaid, so half our friends know nothing of it. You and Gregory will come, won't you? It's to be straight after racing ends tomorrow. We expect everyone to rush from the racecourse straight to Hagman's, where a veritable feast will await.'

'If Gregory's back from London, then we'll be delighted to come, Ann.'

Helen was only half listening, for she was too busy glancing around for Adam. There was one sultan dressed in voluminous cloth-of-gold, but although he was facing directly toward her, he paid scant attention. It couldn't be Adam, for he'd show some reaction at seeing a goddess of the rainbow standing with a shepherdess who was so obviously Mrs Gregory Bourne.

Her attention was drawn back to her immediate circle, for Louis XIV turned as she and Ralph joined the small group. 'St John, is that you?'

'It is. Good evening, Henry.'

The other nodded, raising his mask for a moment to look more closely at Helen. '*Enchanté*, my dear, you must be the delectable Helen.'

'Sir.'

'Fie, madam, your fame preceded you, for even with that wretched domino I'd know you for a beauty. St John's a fortunate fellow, eh?'

She smiled, but didn't respond.

Boadicea chided her husband. 'Henry, you mustn't embarrass her, she's fresh from school.' She put an understanding hand on Helen's arm. 'Take no notice of him, he's being familiar because he has his mask to hide behind, he's a model of civility really. Now then, you do know you're included among the guests for our water party, don't you? We didn't realize you'd be at Bourne End when we originally compiled our list, but if we had, you'd have been on it as a matter of course. By the way, you might care to know that Lady Cowper spoke very highly of you yesterday.'

'She did?' Helen recalled a brief conversation with the prettiest of the lady patronesses of Almack's before the Prince Regent had arrived for dinner.

'Oh, yes, my dear. She said Prinny was very taken with you.'

The subject was suddenly changed, for Louis XIV gave a dismayed groan. 'Don't look now, everyone, but Huff-and-Puff's on his way over. He may be got up like a stag lost in a forest, but I'd know that paunch anywhere.'

Helen glanced in the direction he was looking, and saw an extremely portly Herne the Hunter bearing down on them. He was dressed in green, with a bow and quiver of arrows over his shoulder and the most enormous set of antlers protruding precariously from his hooded head.

She soon understood why he was called Huff-and-Puff, for he spoke as if he was quite out of breath. 'What's all this, huh? Where's Gregory, huh? No, don't tell me, huh, for I've heard. Damned shame, huh? Still, the old wheels keep turnin', huh? Who's the mysterious divine, huh? Your sister? 'Pon me soul, a fair goddess indeed, eh, huh?' Before Helen knew it, he'd seized her hand and was drawing it to his lips. 'This dance, m'dear, huh? Of course you will, no question, huh.' Still holding her hand, he almost dragged her away from the others.

She could have protested, for his conduct was pushy to say the least, but she wanted to escape from Ralph and so allowed herself to be spirited away toward the ballroom.

Huff-and-Puff walked with quick, short steps, and each one jerked another grunt from him. 'Huh, huh, huh.'

The ballroom was a lofty chamber, its walls glittering with mirrors and richly gilded panels of plasterwork. The ceiling was coffered in gold and white, and from it were suspended two rows of priceless chandeliers. A line of French windows stretched down one wall, standing open to the illuminated terrace overlooking the water gardens, and the other walls were tiered with crimson chairs and sofas from which those guests who weren't dancing could survey those who were. A sea of people moved to the slow music of a landler, played by the orchestra high in an apse on the far wall.

The music was just coming to an end and as the dancers left the floor, the master of ceremonies announced a contre danse. This more lively measure was greeted with delight, and a surge of people hurried onto the floor. Huff-and-Puff propelled Helen into the melee. 'Huh, huh, huh,' he grunted, his fat little legs moving at the double as he hastened to take up his position. The orchestra struck a chord, and then launched into a jaunty country tune. The dancers swept happily to and fro, and round and round, and Helen could hear Huff-and-Puff all the time. 'Huh, huh, huh. . . .'

As they danced, Helen glanced constantly around, wondering if at any moment she'd catch a glimpse of Adam. She'd recognize him immediately, she knew she would.

The contre danse ended, and a polonaise began. Huff-and-Puff relinquished her almost gladly to a Roman centurion, for the brisk country dance had quite exhausted him. The centurion was a strutter, putting Helen very much in mind of a chicken as he danced, for not only did he move around like one, he also jutted his head backward and forward like one too. The polonaise gave way to a cotillion, and the centurion to a Falstaff. Then there was another contre danse, a quieter one this time, and she was partnered by the Cyrano de Bergerac she'd noticed on arriving. She still hadn't caught a glimpse of anyone who might be Adam, then while she was glancing around, a hand touched her shoulder.

She whirled around to see Ralph, who drew her angrily from the floor, ignoring her partner's justified protests. 'Madam, it's evidently escaped your memory that I am your escort tonight.'

'Oh, no, sirrah, it hasn't escaped me at all!'

'Good, because I'm about to place a demand upon your acting talents. I'm taking you to meet my father, who believes we are to be betrothed. You'd better make a convincing show of it, my dear.' With a taunting smile, he drew her hand over his sleeve and walked her around the edge of the crowded floor toward the tiers of sofas and chairs facing the French windows.

St John Senior was not what she'd been expecting, for where his son, was tall and well-made, he was small and rather frail. He had a fine head of silver hair, and behind his black satin mask his eyes were as bright as buttons. He was seated alone on a sofa, and made a very unlikely Bacchus. His wine-colored robes hung limply against his slight person, and the wreath of vine leaves around his forehead was a little skew-whiff, as Helen's father had always said of something that wasn't as straight as it might be. He rose as soon as he saw his son.

'Ah, there you are, Ralph, I was beginning to think you'd forgotten me.'

'I'm as ever the dutiful son,' replied Ralph with a convincingly warm smile. 'The delay was solely due to Miss Fairmead's popularity in the dance, but I've secured her person at last, and present her to you now. Helen, my dearest, may I present my father, Mr Richard St John. Father, Miss Helen Fairmead, the lady who has so graciously consented to be my bride.' As he said this last, he drew her hand to his lips, kissing the palm lingeringly.

It was all she could do not to shudder, but somehow she managed to smile, glancing toward his father. 'Sir,' she murmured.

St John Senior stepped quickly forward, taking her hand from Ralph and kissing it in turn. 'My dear, how very glad I am to meet you at last. Ralph has told me so much about you. May I say how very charming you look tonight? I realize your face is hidden, but I do not need to see it to know you're very beautiful indeed.'

'You're too kind, sir.'

The button-bright eyes were very sharp and shrewd behind his mask. 'I shall return to Jamaica happy in the knowledge that Ralph has made a very wise choice, and yet I very nearly didn't make the voyage here.'

Ralph looked at him. 'You didn't have to come at all, you know. I'm quite capable of handling your business affairs.'

'I know, my boy, but one likes to keep one's finger on the pulse of things, and it's been a positive age since I was in England. I've found it all, er, most illuminating.' Again the bright eyes rested on Helen. 'My dear, will you honor an old man with a dance?'

'Why, certainly, sir,' she replied.

He nodded at his son. 'I do believe you can amuse yourself with taking some supper in that room over there,' he said, taking

Helen's hand again and drawing it determinedly through his arm.

A minuet had been announced, and the dancers were taking up their positions. Helen and Mr St John joined them, but she was aware that his attention was not on the imminent dance, it was still on his son. Ralph remained by the sofa, but then glanced toward the supper room. After deliberating for a moment, he made his way toward it.

Mr St John immediately drew a rather startled Helen from the floor again. 'Forgive me, my dear, the dance was but a ruse to get you away from my son, whom I suspect you dislike as much as I do at the moment.'

She stared at him, caught completely off guard.

He smiled a little, patting her hand. 'Don't look so alarmed, Miss Fairmead. It's just that I'm not the fool my son likes to think me. We must speak privately, so I suggest we walk in the gardens for a while. Trust me, my dear, and at least agree to hear me out.'

For a moment she hesitated. Fear of Ralph's reprisals made her reluctant to do anything that might antagonize him, but as she saw how earnest his father's eyes were behind the mask, she nodded.

He glanced again toward the supper room door, but Ralph had gone inside and was nowhere to be seen. 'Come, my dear, we'll toddle outside without delay, for the coast appears to be clear.' Taking her hand, he led her toward the French windows, and then out onto the brightly lit terrace.

CHAPTER 16

Chinese lanterns were suspended above the steps leading down from the rather crowded terrace to the water gardens. A long lily pond extended into the darkness, and on either side of it ran a rose pergola where the way was lit with more lanterns. A large fountain should have been playing halfway along the pond, but something had gone wrong with it, and some estate workers were busily endeavoring to put it right.

Not many people had chosen as yet to stroll outside, and Mr St John steered Helen along one of the pergolas to a quiet alcove directly by the water. 'This will do, my dear, we can be private here.'

The ribbons on her gown fluttered as she sat down. The lily pond was like satin, with reflections shimmering in it, and from time to time a fish rose to the surface, causing ripples to undulate silently toward the alcove. The scent of June roses filled the night, and the distant melody of another landler drifted from the house. She could see the terrace, and the guests moving to and fro, their costumes bright in the lantern light.

Mr St John joined her and removed his mask. 'Miss Fairmead, may I see your face? I much prefer to look into the eyes of the person I'm addressing.'

She removed the domino, and the jeweled mask flashed as she placed it on the seat beside her. For a long moment he studied her, then he smiled. 'I was right, you are beautiful. You are also, I suspect, very honest and proper, and much put out by the situation my son is somehow managing to impose on you. You don't wish to marry him, do you?'

She became a little flustered. 'Sir, I. . . .'

He put his hand reassuringly over hers. 'Whatever you say will
be kept in the strictest confidence, my dear, and if you wonder
how on earth I've guessed your secret, let me explain that from my
place in the ballroom, I could see you quite clearly when my son
dragged you from the dance. Your manner spoke volumes to me,
Miss Fairmead, and confirmed what I already suspected anyway.
I'm afraid I know Ralph rather better than he realizes, for he was
spiteful and conniving as a child, and I've no reason to think he's
changed. But for all his sins, he's still my son, and although I may
not like him very much, I love him a great deal. It's my duty to
correct his faults before it's too late, for I made a grave mistake in
letting him come here from Jamaica, with a Mayfair allowance and
no parental hand to curb his excesses. He regarded himself as free
to do as he pleased, living a very wild life while all the time writing glibly proper and untruthful letters to me. He was too clever
by far, and my suspicions were raised, the more so when he
suddenly began to mention a possible betrothal and suggested a
large sum of money would be necessary in order to purchase the
matrimonial home. I decided it was time to put in an appearance
here, and my sudden arrival rattled him, for it meant he had to
produce the intended bride. Until then, I believe his conversations
with your family concerning you had been merely idle exercises,
but he quickly realized he was in a fix and needed the firm suggestion of a match with you. I think he was confident you'd accept
the proposition – forgive me, my dear, but I gather you're not a
great heiress.'

'That is correct, sir.' She'd listened with great interest to every
word, for his explanation clarified so much.

'It didn't take me long on my return to sniff the truth out about
Ralph's life here. The whispers were strong, concerning huge
gambling debts, expensive affairs with actresses, and so on, matters
of which he's still confident I remain ignorant. The duns are upon
him, and he needs desperately to convince me the betrothal is
genuine so that I'll come across with the necessary lifesaving cash,
Am I right, Miss Fairmead?'

'I – I think you probably are, sir.'

He seemed surprised. 'Don't you know?'

She hesitated. 'Sir, I don't wish to say anything that. . . .'

'That might reach Ralph's ears? Don't worry on that score, my dear, for he will never learn a word.'

She drew a long breath. 'I can't tell you why he wishes to pretend that we're to be betrothed, Mr St John, because he's never told me why. I do know that it's only to be temporary.'

He nodded. 'Until I've handed over the cash and toddled conveniently back across the Atlantic.'

'Probably. I really don't know his reasons, sir, for I am definitely not in his confidence.'

'Why have you consented to his wishes?'

She lowered her eyes. 'I'd rather not say.'

'Because you will compromise yourself?' He smiled, patting her hand again. 'Please tell me, my dear, for it will help me greatly if I know exactly what my son is prepared to do in order to have his own way.'

Reluctantly she looked at him again. 'He knows that I've been meeting a gentleman who is more than a little *persona non grata* with my sister and brother-in-law.'

'Lord Drummond?'

Her eyes widened. 'Yes. How. . . ?'

'I've made it my business to find out all I can about the circle in which my son moves, and naturally the Prince Agamemnon affair came to my attention. Lord Drummond is the only man I know of who could be described as more than a little *persona non grata* at Bourne End, and since I happen to have had him pointed out to me, I know that he is the sort of gentleman a young lady like you might be persuaded to meet.' He smiled at her.

She colored a little. 'I love him very much, Mr St John.' For a moment she was tempted to tell him the complete truth about the previous year's racing scandal, but then she drew back from it. He was disillusioned about Ralph, but still loved him, and to shatter what was left of his affection seemed somehow to smack of a spitefulness worthy of Ralph himself. Surely it was sufficient that he knew what Ralph was doing to her personally, without revealing the extent of his malice toward Adam as well, including the threat to expose Lady Bowes-Fenton's affair.

Mr St John was looking sadly at her. 'So, my son says he will tell of your liaison with Lord Drummond unless you agree to this temporary betrothal?'

'Yes.'

He sighed unhappily. 'He's a grave disappointment to me, my dear. I had such high hopes when he was born, I wanted him to grow up into a man I could be proud of, and to whom I could safely relinquish my vast fortune. Instead, it seems he's a conniving coxcomb, intent upon furthering his own selfish pleasures and desires at the expense of anyone who stands in his way.'

She didn't reply, for Ralph merited such a description.

He gazed at the men working on the fountain. 'Well, my son is about to have the tables turned on him, for I have the ultimate ace up my sleeve, which is rather appropriate since he appears to have been dealing from the bottom of the pack. At the correct moment, I will face him with my knowledge concerning his pressing debts, and I will offer to settle them for him on condition that he return immediately to Jamaica with me. He will not like that one little bit, for he loathes it out there, and if he refuses, as I fancy he will, then I will threaten to disinherit him.'

'You – you'd go that far?'

'Oh, yes, my dear, for he needs more than a mere rap over the knuckles. I'll threaten to disinherit him, *and* leave him to stew in debtor's jail. I fancy he'll come around rather quickly to viewing Jamaica with an almost fond eye. It's time to crack down on him, and to do it with a vengeance, for he has much to do if he's ever to redeem himself in my eyes. I shall make immediate plans to leave, and I promise you he'll be out of your life in a very short time.'

'I don't know what to say.' She could hardly believe the complete turnabout. When she'd arrived at the ball she'd been under Ralph's thumb, but now she was being freed, and instead it was Ralph himself who was going to be under a thumb.

Mr St John smiled a little. 'Don't say anything, my dear, for I'm only sorry you've been hurt by my son's gross misconduct. I tell you this, if I hear of anything else he's done, I'll disinherit him anyway, for I cannot and will not endure behavior as disgraceful as his. You must realize that it will be a little difficult for me to say anything to him tonight, but the moment we return to the Golden Key I'll confront him.

'Now then, enough of my unpleasant offspring; let's talk of you instead. I may have spent many years in Caribbean oblivion, but I still remember that masked balls serve a very sovereign purpose, for they make possible forbidden meetings right under the noses of those who would forbid them. I cannot believe that you and Lord Drummond do not have such a meeting planned tonight.'

She colored a little. 'At midnight,' she admitted.

'Then I wish you well, my dear, and I trust that only happiness lies ahead for you. I'm sure that if you love him, then he cannot possibly be guilty of misdeed, certainly not of an act that threatened to do such damage to Colonel Bourne.'

She glanced away for a moment, for although she now knew why Ralph had been so set upon a betrothal with her – he'd already told his father of a fictitious betrothal in order to gain sufficient money to ward off the duns – she still didn't know why he'd turned so vindictively against Adam, or why he'd shown so little consideration for Gregory, who certainly had never harmed him, and who even now remained a loyal, if misguided, friend.

Mr St John took out his fob watch, which was concealed in his wine-red robe. 'My dear, did you say your assignation with Lord Drummond was at midnight?'

'Yes. Why?'

'I rather fear it's already five past midnight.'

'Oh, no!' With a gasp, she looked at her watch in her reticule. It said only a quarter to twelve. Dismayed, she rose to her feet, snatching up her domino and putting it on. Her watch, her wretched watch! When it was in need of winding it lost time, twenty minutes to be precise! Maybe Adam had already given up on her!

Mr St John caught her hand for a moment more. 'No doubt we'll meet again later, my dear, and when we do, rest assured that not by so much as a flicker of the eye will I reveal what has passed between us. Ralph will never know that I interrogated you, or that you conceded certain snippets of information. Good-bye for the moment, Miss Fairmead, I wish our acquaintance had taken place under more pleasant circumstances.'

'I do too, sir.'

'And I wish you every good fortune in your love for Lord Drummond.'

'I will need every good fortune, sir, for although I love him, and I think he loves me, he doesn't actually know who I am.'

Mr St John blinked with surprise. 'Then your problems are far from over, my dear.'

'I know.'

Gathering her skirts, she hastened back toward the terrace steps, leaving him sitting to reflect sadly on the unpleasant facts he'd unearthed about his son.

She paused on the terrace, glancing back toward the pergola and lily pond. Should she have told Ralph's father absolutely everything? She lowered her eyes then, remembering the unhappiness in his eyes. No, she couldn't have told him any more, it would have broken his heart completely.

Wending her way around the ballroom, she emerged at last in the entrance hall. Her heart was pounding, and she hardly dared look toward the clock, for fear he wouldn't be there. Maybe he'd never kept the tryst, maybe he'd somehow stumbled upon her real identity and decided not to have anything more to do with her! Apprehension and doubt filled her in those few moments, but then she saw him.

He was dressed in a long white robe, with a wide crimson sash around his slender waist. There was a dagger and scimitar thrust into the sash, and on his head there was a crimson turban adorned by a glittering jeweled brooch. His unruly hair was completely concealed, and little of his face was visible because of a golden mask, but she knew him immediately.

A flood of joy washed gladdeningly over her, but the apprehension and doubt lingered on, for what would be the outcome of this fateful meeting?

CHAPTER 17

He wasn't aware of her, for as she saw him he turned to look up at the clock. There was something restless and almost uneasy in the way he glanced at it and then turned again to search over the sea of people crowding the hall. Then he seemed to suddenly sense her presence, his gaze moving unerringly toward her. His mask didn't conceal his lips, and she saw him smile as he held out his hands to her.

She hurried to him, her fingers curling around his. He drew her close, holding her for a moment without speaking. She could feel his heart against hers, and she closed her eyes. Dear God, how she loved him.

He pulled back a little. 'I was beginning to think you'd changed your mind.'

'My watch was wrong,' she confessed ruefully. 'I put it in my reticule but forgot to wind it up! I'm always doing it, I just don't seem able to remember.'

'I'm afraid I have to leave at half past twelve, I've been called urgently to London.'

'The situation in Europe?'

'I fear so. Wellington expects to come to grips with Bonaparte any day now.'

Her thoughts turned instinctively toward Gregory. 'Is – is that why Colonel Bourne has been sent for? I've heard everyone commenting on his absence,' she added quickly.

He smiled a little wryly. 'And no doubt you've also heard comment that he's been recalled because of Drummond family spite. It's true that my uncle Llancwm wrote to him; it's also true – as you already know – that I attended a War Office meeting chaired by my uncle; but it's *not* true that vengeance was the motive for Bourne's recall. He's been sent for because of his involvement with the Berkshire Militia, and he's not alone, because every officer in command of militia has been sent for. I'm not party to every War Office decision, and so have no positive knowledge of what's intended, but I'd be very surprised indeed if Mrs Bourne's loudly expressed fears concerning her husband's imminent dispatch to Brussels have any foundation at all. Bourne, and those like him, are of prime importance on the home front should the enemy invade, and it's my guess that the powers that be merely wish to confirm contingency plans should such an invasion take place.'

She took a long, steadying breath. 'I think you should know that Ralph St John may not be in a position to continue his vendetta for much longer.'

His blue eyes sharpened. 'Why do you say that?'

She glanced around. 'It's too public here. Can't we go somewhere more quiet? The gardens, maybe? I have so much to tell you, so much I should already have confessed. . . .'

'Is tonight the right time? I have to leave for London in only a few minutes now.'

'I must say it all, Adam. I can't bear things to go on as they are. Please, can we go out to the gardens?'

'Of course.' His fingers were warm and firm around hers as he led her back into the ballroom, and then out onto the terrace.

At the foot of the steps, in case Mr St John was still there, she made him take her down the other side of the lily pond to a similar alcove with the same degree of privacy, opposite the former.

The sound of the ball faded behind them, drowned by the rush and splash of the fountain, which had been repaired at last. The satin surface of the water had been broken into countless shining spangles, and the fountain played with such height and vigor that she could feel the spray on her skin as they reached the alcove. She glanced through the dancing water at the alcove on the other side, but it was empty now; Mr St John had gone.

Adam reached up to remove her domino, putting it on the bench, then he took off his own mask before facing her. 'Don't say a word, not yet,' he murmured, drawing her close and bending his head to kiss her on the lips. He took his time, and her senses stirred to move in time with his. She felt the same tempting warmth as before; it stole richly over her, enticing and irresistible. Her body ached with love and desire, and she slipped her arms around his neck, pressing against him. There was a shameless surrender in her response, but she was a victim of her own heart, incapable of denying the passion she felt for this one man.

He drew gently back, his eyes dark as he smiled. 'I'm in danger of giving in right here to certain base notions where you're concerned, and that wouldn't do at all,' he said softly. 'I'm afraid you bring out the beastly male in me.'

'I like the beastly male in you.'

'That's a most improper admission,' he said with a low laugh.

'I feel very improper when I'm with you, and that's an even more improper admission,' she whispered. 'I've broken so many rules in order to be with you that I vow the doors of Almack's would be slammed in my face if the truth was known.'

He became more serious. 'Tell me the truth then.'

Tears filled her eyes and she tried desperately to blink them back. 'I'm so afraid you won't understand, that you'll hate me for what I've done.'

'Hate you? I could never hate you.' He put his hand to her cheek. 'Please tell me, for I can't bear to see you so unhappy.'

She tried to meet his eyes, but was so miserable now the moment was upon her that she had to look tearfully away again. She strove for the right words, but they simply wouldn't come. Suddenly she remembered the letter. Maybe it was better if he read it after all, for at least the written word didn't break down in helpless tears. She fumbled in her reticule, but as she took the crumpled letter out it somehow slipped from her trembling fingers, floating inexorably on an invisible draft to fall onto the surface of the lily pond, where the splashing of the fountain swiftly dashed it out of sight beneath the lilypads.

Numb with disbelief, Helen could only stare at the water. How could fate continually play such cruel tricks on her? Each time she tried to put things right, something happened to prevent her. It was almost as if she wasn't meant to be honest with him. More hot tears stung her eyes, her lips quivered, and she turned away, trying desperately to compose herself.

He came closer, resting his hands gently on her shaking shoulders. 'Don't cry,' he said softly, his voice almost inaudible above the splash of the fountain. 'Whatever was written in that letter, you can tell me to my face.' Slowly he turned her toward him again.

For a moment she strove to regain her self-possession, then she swallowed and made herself look at him, but even as her lips parted to say it all at last, a tinkle of laughter drifted along the pergola, and with a gasp she turned to see Margaret's pink shepherdess dress shining beneath the lanterns as she strolled in company with the Cardusays and Huff-and-Puff.

Helen froze. No, not again, *please*, not again. Not another perverse stroke of fate! But Margaret was coming relentlessly closer and at any moment might glance directly at the alcove. What little was left of Helen's failing nerve disintegrated into complete confusion, and with a panic-stricken sob she pulled from Adam's startled arms, snatched up her domino, and fled along the pergola away from Margaret. The ribbons on her gown fluttered wildly, and her hair was shaken loose from its neat pins, but she reached the far end without her sister's seeing anything, and in a moment had disappeared into the anonymity of the gardens.

Behind her, Adam was riveted by the suddenness of her flight. He glanced in the other direction to see what had frightened her, but Margaret and her companions had turned back again and were ascending the terrace steps again, intent upon raiding the supper room, and Adam didn't recognize them. Taking up his mask, for a moment he considered pursuing Helen, but the gardens were vast, and his chances of finding her very slender indeed. Time wasn't on the side of love, it was pressing him hard to set off for London, and affairs of state had to take precedence over affairs of the heart.

With a sigh he glanced in the direction she'd fled, and then slowly walked back toward the house, beckoning to a footman as he reached the top of the terrace steps.

In the welcome darkness of the gardens, Helen's distress knew few bounds. Casting around for somewhere to hide away from everyone, her glance fell on the line of waiting carriages, drawn up two abreast along the drive. By pure chance she saw the Bourne

End landau, its hoods raised now against the cooler night air. The coachman was with some of his fellows, standing around intently watching a game of dice, and no one saw her hurrying toward the vehicle, or heard the door open and close as she crept inside.

She flung herself onto the seat, giving way to a flood of bitter tears. Her whole body shook with wretchedness. What had she done to deserve all this bad luck? It just wasn't fair. She wanted so much to wipe her foolish slate clean, but each time she tried to do so something happened to stop her. She'd tried to tell him on the terrace at Windsor, but her courage had failed her, and before that she'd been about to tell him by the lake, when Ralph's approach had interrupted. She'd fretted long and hard over writing an explanatory letter, only to have Lord Swag intervene, and now she'd failed again, suffering the twin blows of watching that same letter sink beneath the surface of the lily pond and then having the confession frozen on her lips by the sound of her sister's laughter.

The sobs continued to rack her unhappy body, and she lay with her face hidden against the velvet upholstery. Her eyes were red-rimmed from the tears, and she felt as if her heart was breaking.

It was a long time before the weeping subsided and she became aware of sounds, from the carriage drawn up alongside, a rather grand coach with gleaming black panels. Kittenish laughter carried into the landau, and Helen sat up slowly, realizing that two lovers were meeting. Taking a handkerchief from her reticule, she wiped her eyes and peeped out. The blinds were down on the other carriage, but the window glass was lowered just a little, and she could hear voices.

The woman was in a teasing mood. 'Come now, Ferdy, are you going to tell me you don't *like* what I'm almost wearing? Perhaps you'd have preferred all the hooks and eyes of the costume I nearly decided to choose tonight? They would certainly have hampered your, er, progress.'

'And what costume was that?' The man's voice was good-humored.

'Mistress Fuchsia, and you should just see how many wicked hooks and eyes there are on that dress.'

In the darkness of the landau, Helen gasped. Mistress Fuchsia. Of course! *That* was why Ralph's miniature had seemed so familiar, it was a likeness of Mrs Tully in her most famous role! He'd claimed to have purchased the miniature that day, and he'd said he had no idea who the lady was, but both claims were patently untrue.

Helen sat back, the realization suddenly so clear it was like being told aloud. She'd felt at the time that he'd been in the habit of gazing at the little portrait, and now it was quite obvious that he had. It was also quite obvious that his feelings for the actress had always run far deeper than he'd revealed. He'd pretended not to mind when Mrs Tully deserted him in order to pursue Adam, but in fact he'd minded very much indeed. Enough to want revenge? Was it as simple as that? Had the whole Prince Agamemnon business been contrived solely in order to punish Adam for wounding Ralph St John's male vanity?

She exhaled slowly, knowing that she was right, but then her breath caught again as she remembered something Margaret had said. She'd revealed that Ralph had been her first admirer, but that she had fallen for Gregory. If Ralph could turn on Adam because of Mrs Tully, then surely he was equally capable of punishing Gregory because of Margaret, maybe not as much, because he hadn't felt as much for Margaret, but enough to make Gregory suffer a little.

Helen twisted the strings of her reticule, oblivious now to the sounds from the adjoining coach. The final two pieces of the puzzle had quite suddenly and unexpectedly fallen into place, and now she knew exactly why Ralph St John had done everything. He was governed by injured pride. How a kindly, considerate man like his father had ever produced such a son she couldn't even begin to know.

There were more sounds from the other carriage, and she looked out in time to see the lovers slipping out and back toward the house. It was time she returned as well, or Margaret might wonder where she was.

Composing herself, she pinned up her hair as best she could, and then put on her domino again, thinking that at least it would serve to hide her tear-stained face. Opening the landau door, she alighted in a rustle of muslin and ribbons, breathing deeply of the cool night air before retracing her steps toward the house.

The fountain still splashed noisily as she walked beneath the pergola, and she paused for a moment where only a short while before she'd been in Adam's arms, then she hurried on to the terrace steps.

As she reached the top, a footman suddenly approached her. 'Madam?'

'Yes?'

'Begging your pardon, but is your name Mrs Helen Brown?'

She stared at him. 'Yes, it is,' she replied hesitantly.

'Then I'm charged to give you this, madam. The gentleman told me he had to leave, and that I was to watch for a lady answering your description returning from the gardens.' He pressed a note into her hand and then walked away.

Slowly she opened the note, and read.

My darling,

Your poor little confession seems doomed, but all is not yet lost. I will be back from London in time to attend the Cardusays' party at Hagman's tomorrow night after the races, and at eight o'clock will wait for you by the lake where we met.

Adam

Tears pricked her eyes again, but this time they were tears of happiness. She had another chance.

CHAPTER 18

It was twelve noon exactly as the Bourne End landau, its hoods down, bowled out of the lodge gates and turned west toward the heath and the racecourse, where society was converging in strength for the commencement of the turf's most fashionable occasion.

Helen and Margaret sat together, Margaret's parasol twirling gaily beneath the brilliant June sun. They were both in a buoyant mood, although for entirely different reasons.

Margaret was on top of the world, for she'd heard from Gregory that morning and knew not only that his recall had been entirely due to militia matters but that he'd be home that very evening, missing only this first day of the races. The fact that it was the day of the Maisemore Stakes and Musket's much-heralded run against the Prince Regent's well-fancied Cherry Brandy was a disappointment more than compensated for by the good news in the letter. Margaret paid scant attention to the rest of the letter, which spoke of disquiet in the streets of London because of the situation across the Channel; she was concerned only that now Gregory might return in time to escort her and Helen to the Cardusays' anniversary water party

She looked very lovely in her Royal Ascot togs, soft white plumes curling down from her cerise silk hat. She wore cerise from head to toe, and it suited her very well. Her corded silk pelisse was trimmed with velour embroidery on the cuffs, collar, and hem, and her gown was of delicate, rather paler silk, its neckline low and square, its hem delightfully stiffened with rich rouleaux so that her neat ankles and little cerise patent leather shoes were shown off to excellent advantage. The fringed parasol that went with the outfit cast only a delicate shadow over her face, and she was so bright and fresh that it was hard to believe she hadn't gone to her bed until dawn after the ball.

Helen wore lime-green frilled muslin, and the color brought out the green of her eyes as well as making her hair shine like warm gold. Her sleeveless full-length pelisse was fitted lightly at the high waist by a wide gold-buckled belt, and the hem was stiffened by frills and by the almost mandatory rouleaux. Beneath the pelisse, she wore a long-sleeved gown, the cuffs gathered in a frill to match the one on the wide collar spilling out over the shoulders of the pelisse. Her hair was dressed in a knot from which fell a single heavy ringlet, and her wide-brimmed lime-green hat was held on by a dainty muslin scarf that was tied in a huge bow beneath her chin. She looked good, and knew it.

However, vanity and pride had little to do with her confidence today; she felt good because she'd come to terms with herself. This evening she had another opportunity to clear the air and let Adam know everything he should know, and after so many failures and disappointments, she didn't intend to let this chance pass her by. The debacle by the Farrish House fountain the night before had taught her a salutary lesson, for as she'd wept in the landau she'd thought she'd ruined everything once and for all; his note had changed all that, and this time she knew she had the courage to finally say all she should. That was why she felt so buoyant now; she'd summoned up the inner strength that was necessary and she knew her nerve wouldn't fail her again. Maybe it would all be in vain, maybe he'd spurn her once he knew who she was, but at least she'd have done the right thing.

As the landau drove smartly along the road to Ascot, she wondered if Mr St John had confronted Ralph. At the ball nothing more had been said, and when Ralph had escorted her and Margaret back to Bourne End, his manner indicated that he was still confident of having his own. way. Helen was glad he was to be taught a singular lesson, but her silent delight had been more than tempered by a deep regret that that lesson was being administered too late to undo the damage to Adam's honor, and thus to her prospect of complete happiness. More than anything in the world she wanted to be with him, and she wanted him to be reconciled with Margaret and Gregory, but after all that had happened she doubted if that would ever be possible. She could either be with him, or with her sister and brother-in-law, but not with both; and if he spurned her tonight anyway, then the decision was made for her.

The nearer they drove to the racecourse, the more the traffic and the landau's speed was reduced to a mere crawl as it joined a crush of carriages, gigs, chaises, curricles, cabriolets, phaetons, and wagons. There were horsemen too, weaving swiftly in and out of the jam, or riding directly across country toward the heath.

As the racecourse loomed ahead, Helen's thoughts returned to Adam again. He was in London now, expecting to return in time for the water party, but what if he returned earlier than that? What if he came to the racecourse and saw her in the Bourne box with Margaret? Suddenly she wished she'd worn a hat with a veil, but it was too late now.

Ascot racecourse could have been the camp of Wellington's army, for there were horses and tents everywhere, to say nothing of countless battalions of people, both elegant and not so elegant; it was as if Bonaparte himself must also be camped somewhere nearby, maybe in Windsor Great Park, and that soon the long-expected battle would commence. The noise was tremendous, and clouds of dust rose from the road as the vast concourse of vehicles and riders came together. The jam was made worse than ever as the Bourne End landau halted in the middle of the highway, the coachman alighting to solemnly raise the hoods in order to protect the occupants from the unpleasantness of the dust and noise. Other travelers were less than amused by this additonal delay to progress, and made their feelings known volubly, but the coach-man returned impassively to his seat, driving on without giving anyone else the satisfaction of so much as a glance.

Behind the racecourse, the mushrooming of tents was now complete, and the city of canvas seemed to stretch for a half a mile or more over the heath. Along the white posted course, the two permanent stands had now been joined by a variety of temporary ones, including the one belonging to Bourne End. Close to the royal stand were those of the Jockey Club and the Master of the Buckhounds, the Marquess of Cornwallis. Next came the Bourne stand, then a number of lesser boxes, before the rows of fine carriages drawn up behind the fence. From these carriages, the wealthy and privileged would watch the day's racing, and during luncheon partake of their sumptuous picnics of cold viands, salad, fresh-baked white bread, and champagne. A military band was playing near the royal stand, the brisk notes of a march just audible above the general hubbub of the meeting.

The landau left the crowded road and made its exceedingly slow way toward the Bourne box, and Helen gazed out at the colorful scene. In the tents and booths, the vendors of spruce beer were doing a roaring trade on such a hot day, and the rigged gaming tables had already succeeded in relieving the unwise of their money. Every vice could apparently be indulged in, for there weren't only alcohol and gambling tents, there were tents outside which paraded ladies of very dubious virtue, with painted faces and brazenly low-cut dresses. Helen stared at them for a moment, and then hastily averted her eyes, looking instead at some of the traveling entertainers without whom race-meetings were incomplete. There were some young women on stilts, some dancing dogs, numerous jugglers and dwarfs, and a giantess from Prussia, or so the gaily clothed showman on the raised stage proclaimed. Next she saw a hunch-backed ballad singer from the Low Countries, and a Bohemian who balanced coach wheels on his chin, much to the marvel of the onlooking crowds.

She lowered the window and the noise and excitement seemed to leap into the landau, a mixture of voices, music, and smells, the latter ranging from the odor of hundreds of horses to the appetizing aroma of hot pies. Helen's gaze moved over the tumultuous scene. There were knowing ones and insiders everywhere, and bookmakers, or blacklegs and pencilers, as Margaret called them. Such an occasion as this attracted the shadier characters, and she knew there'd be a very liberal sprinkling of thieves and rogues. A large contingent of Bow Street Runners and constables had been drafted in to cope, and as she looked there was a disturbance as a pickpocket was caught in the very act of relieving a gentleman of his purse. Ladies in the crowd cried out in alarm as several burly runners pounced on the culprit, ignoring his vain protestations of innocence as they dragged him away to the pound.

The landau reached the Bourne box at last, and the footmen who'd been dispatched there not long after dawn with the copious supply of iced champagne and Fortnum and Mason hampers, hastened to open the carriage doors and assist the two ladies down. The select party of distinguished guests who were always invited to view the races from the box had already gathered inside and turned gladly to greet Margaret and Helen as they climbed the wooden steps and entered the luxuriously appointed room inside.

There were velvet-upholstered chairs and sofas, a table laden to groaning point with superior refreshments, and a matchless view over the racecourse itself. The grass where soon the horses would gallop was for the moment crowded with strolling people, but when the marshals cleared them all away, the winning post would be clearly visible.

Helen knew all the guests, having met them either at the dinner party or the ball, and she was no longer beset by nerves at the thought of conversing with a countess or a duke. Nor was she intimidated by the lady patronesses of Almack's, for Lady Cowper and Countess Lieven were among the party, and both spoke graciously to her. One face was, for Helen, glaringly absent from the proceedings, for although Ralph St John had been invited, there was as yet no sign of him.

Sipping champagne, she moved among the guests, who were primarily interested today in Musket's prospects in the Maisemore. As with Prince Agamemnon the year before, a great deal of money was resting on the outcome of the race, and everyone was impatient to see if the Prince Regent's horse was going to be seen off. Musket's performance had improved at his last gallop, and before leaving for London Gregory had expressed himself much happier with the horse, so that today's race promised to be very close indeed, although there were some reservations about the jockey's weight. While discussing the race, it was inevitable that Prince Agamemnon should be mentioned, although clearly no one relished doing so, for it wasn't at all the thing to speak of an event that had almost resulted in the permanent banning of their host from all races run under Jockey Club rules. One thing became clear to Helen, however, and that was that although the evidence against Adam seemed conclusive, many of the guests thronging the elegant Bourne box harbored grave doubts about his guilt. Helen actually heard the Duke of Rutland murmur in an undertone to his uncle, the Duke of Beaufort, that he was dashed if he could believe Adam Drummond would ever do such a thing, not even to an enemy, and certainly not to a friend.

At last the prerace period came to an end, and the band by the royal stand broke off in mid-note to change from a march to the national anthem. It was the signal that the royal procession of carriages had arrived from Windsor, and the marshals immediately came out to clear the course. The great crowd began to cheer, pressing eagerly forward to watch as the first open carriage appeared, drawn by a team of cream horses. The Prince Regent was seated inside with his mother and sisters, waving graciously in acknowledgement. The cheering reached a crescendo, however, when the second carriage came into sight, for it contained the prince's brother, the Duke of York, who was the racing fraternity's darling.

As the prince's carriage drove slowly past the Bourne box, he smiled charmingly at Margaret, who stood looking down at him, then he smiled at Helen too. Her heart almost stopped with pleased surprise. He'd actually remembered her!

Margaret waited until the royal procession had all passed, then came to speak to her. 'How honored you are, sister mine.'

'I can hardly believe he remembers me.'

'He always remembers a pretty face, and you, you wretch, are very pretty indeed.' Margaret glanced at Helen's watch, which was pinned to the bodice of her lime-green pelisse. 'I wonder where Ralph can have got to? He's never late, especially not for Royal Ascot.'

'Perhaps he's had to change his plans.'

'No one, but no one, changes plans for today,' declared Margaret firmly. 'I hope he hasn't met with a mishap. The Windsor road is so busy today, maybe his carriage has overturned!'

'Don't overdramatize, Margaret. I'm sure he's quite all right.' To herself she added, He's probably just nursing his furious disbelief that the tables have been turned on him.

But even as this uncharitable thought entered her head, the door of the box opened and Ralph came in. He was dressed very elegantly in a dark gray coat and cream cord trousers, with a gray beaver top hat pulled forward on his head. A diamond pin glittered in the excellent folds of his starched neckcloth, and a silver-handled cane was held lightly in one gloved hand. He looked the picture of nonchalant sartorial excellence, but Helen could see by his eyes that his father had carried out the threat.

'Greetings, *mes enfants*,' he murmured, removing his hat and bowing over Margaret's hand. 'Forgive me for being late, but it was just one dashed thing after another.'

Margaret smiled, reaching up to kiss his cheek. 'Well, you're here now, and that's all that matters. Isn't it, Helen?'

'Yes, of course.'

His eyes slid to Helen's. 'How kind of you to say so,' he said softly.

She met his gaze squarely. 'Not at all.'

For a long moment he continued to look at her, but then returned his attention to Margaret. 'I'm afraid I have some very disagreeable news. I have to return to Jamaica immediately with my father.'

Margaret stared at him. 'Oh, no, surely not. Whatever's happened?'

'My father had word this morning that there's been a terrible fire on the plantation, and much of the house has been gutted. He has to go back immediately, he has no choice, and under the circumstances I can hardly permit him to go alone. It's my duty to accompany him.'

Helen lowered her eyes. How very noble of you, Ralph, she thought wryly.

Margaret was upset. 'Oh, Ralph, how dreadful. And how caring you are to go as well.'

'I'm rather afraid that being caring where my father is concerned has brought about a situation that might appear *un*caring where Miss Fairmead is concerned.' He looked at Helen again, his brown eyes cool and veiled.

Margaret was puzzled. 'Uncaring? Whatever do you mean, Ralph?'

'Simply that I cannot possibly say how long I'll be away, but it's bound to be some considerable time, which means that I cannot with any degree of justification or honor expect her to wait.'

Helen's face was expressionless, but Margaret was dismayed. 'Oh, Ralph. . . .'

'You must understand my predicament, Miss Fairmead. I trust you will find it in your heart to forgive me for failing you.'

Before Helen could reply, Margaret spoke for her, 'Failing her? Oh, Ralph, my dear, how can you possibly speak like that of what you're doing? Of course you haven't failed her, and of course she forgives you. Why, she might even wish to wait, no matter how long it takes.'

He smiled a little, his eyes searching Helen's face in a way that told her he suspected her of having been indiscreet in her conversation with his father. 'I couldn't possibly expect her to wait,' he murmured.

Helen gave a slight smile. 'And I couldn't possibly place the responsibility for such a wait upon your shoulders, Mr St John. You're already enduring problems enough without having me to concern yourself with as well.'

'You're far too kind, Miss Fairmead,' he replied.

Margaret was close to tears. 'Oh, dear, this is such a disappointment, and to think I was so pleased with today so far. Tell me, Ralph, when exactly will you be leaving? I must arrange a farewell party. . . .'

'There isn't time, I'm afraid; we're setting off before dawn tomorrow morning.'

Her eyes widened with still more dismay. 'Oh, no, surely you don't have to leave as quickly as that.'

'My father wishes to return with as much haste as possible. There's a ship sailing from Falmouth the day after tomorrow, and we expect to be on board.'

Margaret blinked back the tears. 'Oh, Ralph, we'll all miss you more than you'll ever know. Society will simply never be the same again.'

No, it will be much improved, thought Helen, looking away.

A footman was hovering nearby with a tray of champagne, and Margaret quickly took a glass, pressing it into Ralph's hand. 'You will at least remain with us for the racing, won't you? And you'll be at the Cardusays' do tonight?'

'I'll gladly remain with you for the races, but alas, the water party has to manage without me.'

Margaret slipped her hand through his arm. 'Ralph, I simply cannot believe you're leaving us, it's too awful for words.' She glanced around the box. No one else had heard Ralph's news, they were all too intent on watching the runners for the first race. 'Listen, everyone,' she cried, causing them all to turn, 'I'm afraid I have something very sad to tell you. Dear Ralph is leaving us to rush off across the Atlantic to Jamaica, we only have him for today.'

There were general murmurs of astonishment, and as they all came to express their regret, Helen moved away, watching Ralph as he smoothly acted his sad role. If she hadn't known the truth behind his abrupt departure, she would have found him very convincing indeed – she could almost see the gutted plantation house and smell the smoke, so eloquently did he describe it.

The first race commenced, providing little real excitement as the Duke of York's well-fancied colt Hippocampus romped home virtually unchallenged. As was the custom, an hour's break for luncheon followed immediately, and then came the Maisemore. An air of great excitement pervaded the scene as the horses went down to the start, led by the Prince Regent's Cherry Brandy. Musket danced past on his toes, his jockey's purple and silver silks gleaming in the sunlight.

Margaret pressed anxiously to the front of the box, watching the horse. 'What do you think, Helen? Is he up to the mark?'

'I'm sure he is.'

Ralph came to stand next to them. 'The nag's looking well enough to run around the course twice and still win,' he declared.

'I do trust you're right,' murmured Margaret, bending her head to look at the start through Gregory's spyglass, which had been brought from the house. 'They're lining up. Cherry Brandy's not coming around . . . now he's there. They're off!'

A great roar of excitement went up from the crowd, and Helen watched nervously as the field of five came thundering along the course. She could see Musket quite clearly, for he was second, but the horse in front of him was the prince's distinctive white-faced bay, Cherry Brandy.

The thunder of hooves filled the air as they came at full stretch toward the finish, and Margaret was almost hopping up and down with excitement as inch by inch Musket came up on the leader. It was a hard race, both horses neck-and-neck for the final furlong, but Musket was under pressure first, his jockey forced to be severe. Musket was game to the last, but his recent ill health, and the fact that his jockey was heavier than his rival's told on him in the end. At the post Cherry Brandy had him beaten by a head.

A groan of disappointment passed through the Bourne box, and Margaret watched in dismay as the horses slowed to a canter and then turned to come back. There were as many boos as cheers from the great crowd, for the two horses had started as joint favorites at three to one, and for every man who'd backed the winner, there was one who'd gone for Musket.

Gregory's fears of the accusations of the previous year being resurrected were very swiftly proved unfounded, however, for it was soon being generally agreed that the best horse had won on the day, for no one could possibly have claimed that Musket hadn't been game. It was the weight that did it, it was said, and but for that the prince's nag wouldn't have come within a tail of him. Margaret's disappointment in the race being lost was soon replaced by relief that the past was evidently going to be left alone, and she was smiling and cheerful when word was brought from the royal box that the Prince Regent would be honored if she and Miss Fairmead would join him for a few minutes.

Helen was very nervous as she accompanied her sister to the royal box, for not only would she be meeting the Prince Regent again, she would also be presented to the other members of the royal family, including the rather formidable queen.

The royal box was crowded, so much so that Helen's presentation to more royalty passed without remark, either to herself or, she suspected, to those to whom she'd curtsied. The princesses were all more interested in the scene outside than what was happening inside, the Duke of York hardly glanced at her because he was deep in conversation with an equerry about the next race, and the queen cast a baleful eye upon the figure in lime-green, saying that she was much pleased to see Mrs Fairford among them again after so long.

The Prince Regent, however, was well aware of Helen's identity, and in a very good humor after Cherry Brandy's success. Already rosy from a number of glasses of champagne, he positively glowed with delight as he sat in an adjoining room on a large gilded chair by the window. He waved them closer.

'M'dears, may I say how pleased I am to have trounced that wretch Bourne at last? He's come to regard the Maisemore as his personal preserve, and we can't have that, eh?' He beamed, pressing a glass of champagne into Margaret's hand. 'Your health, m'dear, and just let your odious husband attempt to steal, the race back from me next year – I'll give him a run for his money.'

He was just about to hold a glass out to Helen when someone pushed discreetly through the crush behind her, making the prince look up in some surprise. 'Good heavens. Drummond, what can I do for you?'

Helen froze. Oh, please let it be another Drummond . . . But she knew it wouldn't be.

'Forgive the intrusion, Your Royal Highness, but it's important that I speak to you.' It was Adam.

'Speak away.'

'In private, sir.'

'Drummond, I'm enjoying the races, and I don't really relish the notion of government business right now. It is government business, isn't it?'

'Yes, sir.'

Helen managed to look surreptitiously at him, hiding most of her face with the wide brim of her hat. He was dressed in a wine-red coat and pale-gray trousers with Hessian boots. The frill of his lawn shirt protruded from his partially buttoned gray silk waistooat, and there was a ruby pin in the knot of his starched cravat. He'd removed his top hat, and his dark hair was a little tousled, as if he had but a moment before run his fingers through it. His eyes were as blue as forget-me-nots, and so intent upon the prince that they didn't flicker even momentarily toward her. Her heart was thundering, and all she could do was stand there, so close she could have reached out to touch him. Please, don't let him look at her, don't let him know she was there. One word now from Margaret, or even from the prince, would see all her good intentions dashed.

The prince was surveying him a little irritably. 'I have no wish to budge from this seat, my lord, so I suggest you spit out whatever it is that Lord Liverpool has sent you to say.'

'As you wish, sir. The situation in London is becoming hourly more uneasy. Every packet arriving in Dover brings more unsettling news from Brussels, and the newspapers have become a little, er, hysterical. In Lord Liverpool's opinion, and the opinion of most of his ministers, the situation would be improved by your presence.'

'To give heart?'

'Yes, sir.'

There was an increasing stir in the box, and nervous glances were being exchanged.

The prince sat forward. 'I take it Boney ain't at the door?'

'No, sir, nor likely to be, Wellington will see to that, it's just that Lord Liverpool believes your presence in the capital would be the, er, music to soothe the savage beast.'

'I've never thought of myself as soothing music. You've got a way with you, Drummond, damn your diplomatic soul. Very well, I'll return to the capital. When does Lord Liverpool think I should make my gesture?'

'After racing today, sir.'

The prince sighed. 'I will do as he wishes, but I don't want to, no, I don't want to at all. Take yourself off, then; the hospitality of the royal box is at your disposal.'

'Your Royal Highness.' Adam bowed and began to withdraw, still without realizing Helen was standing so close to him.

But just as relief was beginning to slip through her veins, the prince returned his attention to her, pressing the glass into her hand as he'd been about to do when Adam had appeared. 'Even princes must give up their pleasures in the national interest, my dear, *mais c'est la vie, n'est-ce pas?* Well, it may be life, but it ain't fair, is it, Miss Fairmead?'

Her heart sank, for she knew she had to reply, and that the moment she did Adam would hear and recognize her voice, for he was still only a few yards away, answering the discreetly whispered questions of several concerned gentlemen, for everyone was a little disturbed to know the situation in London had changed so sharply.

She summoned up the willpower to smile at the prince. 'It isn't fair at all, Your Royal Highness.'

Adam's reaction was clear. He broke off in mid-sentence to turn sharply in her direction. For a moment he seemed stunned, then a deep disappointment showed in his eyes as he realized that beyond a doubt that his Helen and Miss Helen Fairmead were one and the same.

The prince, who'd been uncomfortably aware of Margaret's reaction the moment Adam had appeared, now thought it would be wiser to dismiss the sisters. Clearing his throat, he smiled charmingly. 'I won't keep you any longer, dear ladies, for I'm sure you have guests you should return to. Mrs Bourne, you must be sure to convey my condolences to the colonel, and tell him that I don't intend to let him get his grasping mawlers on the Maisemore again, eh?' He gave a throaty chuckle, inclining his head to signify the ending of the audience.

Margaret sank into a curtsy, and then moved away; brushing past Adam without so much as a glance. As Helen rose from her curtsy, she turned to look directly at him, wanting to say something, anything, but his manner froze the words on her lips.

The deep disappointment was still in his eyes as without acknowledging her at all, he turned on his heel and walked away, pushing through the crush and out of the royal box, where Margaret had gone only seconds before.

For a moment Helen was too stricken to move, then impulsively she hurried after him, catching him just as he was reaching the bottom of the steps. She ignored Margaret, who was waiting a little further on. 'Adam, I must speak to you.'

He turned reluctantly. 'I don't think we have anything to say to each other.'

'Adam, I must see you again. Please be where you said you'd meet me tonight.' Her eyes fled to Margaret, who couldn't hear anything but was looking curiously.

'I rather think our friendship has to be at an end,' he replied.

Margaret took a step nearer. 'Helen?'

Helen looked urgently at him. 'Be there, I *beg* you.'

Desperately, she spoke again. 'If you've ever felt anything for me, you'll grant me this one request. Please say you'll be there at eight!'

He relented a little. 'Very well, but I warn you, I'm in no mood to be sympathetic, not now I know who you really are.' With a decidedly cool nod, he walked on.

Margaret came up to her. 'Helen, what was all that about? I really think you might show a little more loyalty and consideration than to speak to that man!'

'I do still owe him my life,' Helen reminded her, watching him until he vanished among the crowds.

'Well, he as good as cut you, which will perhaps teach you a sovereign lesson about his real character,' replied Margaret. 'Now, come on, the prince was right, we do have guests to attend to.'

Helen allowed herself to be steered back toward the Bourne box. She was horridly close to tears, but somehow in complete control. The worst had happened, he'd found out the truth and turned from her. Somehow she had to find the right words tonight; she had to reach out to his heart and win it back.

CHAPTER 19

So far, fate hadn't been at all lenient with Helen in her attempts to set the record straight with Adam, and it wasn't about to start now. While she was preoccupied for the rest of the afternoon with how she was going to convince him she was in earnest where he was concerned, it didn't occur to her that there'd be any difficulty in actually reaching the lake in order to speak to him. But difficulty there would be, so much so that for a time it would seem that she wouldn't be able to get there at all, let alone on time.

It was all due to Margaret, whose day had commenced so brightly, but who became increasingly unhappy as the afternoon wore on. She was deeply upset by the suddenness of Ralph's departure, and by the ending of the match with Helen before it had really begun. She was also disappointed by Musket's failure, a failure that had somehow been emphasized by having come face-to-face with Adam. As the afternoon races continued, they ran later and later, and with the sun beating relentlessly down from a clear blue sky, it wasn't long before Margaret was suffering from a vile headache.

At last the final race was run, and at seven o'clock the royal procession had made its elegant way back up the course and onto the Windsor road. Soon, the stream of vehicles that had descended upon the racecourse and heath earlier in the day were reversing the process, choking the roads in the opposite direction, and the guests who'd been invited to the Cardusays' famous water party were caught up in the jam, their progress to the lake conducted at little more than walking pace.

Margaret and Helen had to remain in the Bourne box until the last of their guests had left, and Ralph stayed with them. Soon only Lady Cowper was left, chattering brightly about a forthcoming ball at Almack's to raise money for the poor soldiers who would be wounded at any conflict with Bonaparte.

As Lady Cowper rattled on, Ralph suddenly drew Helen aside. 'It's time for a final word, I fancy,' he murmured, allowing her no opportunity to protest as he steered her out of the box and down the steps to the waiting landau.

At the bottom, out of earshot of the coachman, he turned her to face him. 'So, you're off the proverbial hook rather sooner than you expected.'

She looked at him with loathing. 'Yes, I'm glad to say.'

'No doubt, but I doubt if you have any more cause to rejoice than I have. I gather Drummond cut you.'

She flushed. 'Are you still, having me followed, sirrah?'

'When I have dear Margaret to report on your activities? Hardly.' He gave a sleek smile. 'So, the path of forbidden love isn't running smoothly. How sad.'

'It would run smoothly if you were gentleman enough to do the decent thing.'

'Clear his precious name? Now, why on earth should I be so obliging? No, my dear, I intend to depart for Jamaica without doing a thing to assist you.' His brown eyes were suddenly malevolent. 'I don't know what passed between you and my father last night, but I know you had something to do with his actions.'

'I don't know what you're talking about. Are you telling me there hasn't been a fire at the plantation?' She was all wide-eyed innocence.

He studied her. 'There's no point in playing games, my dear, for I think you and I know each other rather too well, even on so short an acquaintance. You may have succeeded in having me removed from the stage, but you can't erase my role completely. I'm going to leave a lasting mark on the lives of both you and Drummond, because nothing you do can make me tell the truth about what happened last year. I'm going to quit these shores without uttering a word, and he'll carry the blame forever, just as I've always intended.' He suddenly put his hand to her cheek in a horrible parody of a loving caress. 'You shouldn't have spoken to my father, my dear, for by doing so you offended me very deeply, more deeply even than when you were obstinate enough to refuse me. I don't intend to let you get away with it, and I promise you that if things are awkward between you and Drummond right now, they're about to become downright impossible.'

She felt cold. 'What do you mean?'

'That I'm going to see to it that he believes there's been a great deal more to our association than you've seen fit to tell him.'

The coldness intensified. 'You're going to tell him lies about me?'

He smiled. 'When I return to the Golden Key now, I'm going to send him a little *billet-doux*, explaining that you and I have been much more intimate than you'd like him to know.'

She stared at him. 'You wouldn't be so foul!'

'Wouldn't I? I think he'd be most enlightened to know exactly how much of your sweet self you've surrendered to my embraces. You'll protest your innocence, of course, but he'll think there can't be all that smoke without fire.'

'Smoke?'

'Yes, my dear.' His glance moved beyond her to the top of the box steps, where Lady Cowper and Margaret had at last emerged. 'This is what I've been waiting for,' he murmured, suddenly drawing Helen close and kissing her on the lips.

She was caught unawares, remaining rigid with shock for a moment before striving to pull free, but he used all his strength to keep her still, and she knew that the kiss gave every impression of a tender farewell.

He released her at last, turning as the two other ladies descended the steps.

Lady Cowper's knowing eyes took in Helen's flushed face for a moment, then she reached up to kiss Ralph's cheek. 'Good-bye, Ralph, I do hope it will not be long before you return to us. And I'd hazard a guess that Miss Fairmead will join me in the sentiment.' Smiling at Helen, she moved away to her carriage, which was waiting nearby.

Margaret looked sadly at Ralph. 'Is there no way you can delay leaving?'

'None at all.'

'Gregory will be devastated that you've gone without saying good-bye to him.'

'It can't be helped.' He leaned forward, kissing her. 'Off you go now. Enjoy the Cardusays' little splash, and be sure to write to me every single day.'

'I'm a dreadful letter writer.'

'A word or two will keep me happy.' He turned to Helen, his face the picture of charming regret. 'I'm so sorry for all that's happened, Helen, for I know you and I could have made a very good go of it. I trust you'll think kindly of me.'

Words fought for precedence on her lips, but in his eyes she could see the threats. No matter how much she wanted to expose him for the rat he was, the trump, Lady Bowes-Fenton's guilty secret, was still in his hand, and he wouldn't hesitate to put it on the table.

He smiled, reading her thoughts. 'You will think kindly of me, won't you?' he said again.

'I will endeavor to,' she replied at last, managing to quell a shudder of revulsion as he bent to kiss her cheek as well. She glanced up, just in time to see Lady Cowper watching as her carriage drew away.

'I'll bid you both farewell, then,' Ralph murmured, lingering for a moment, as if too upset to tear himself away, then he turned and walked off into the thinning crowds.

Margaret stared tearfully after him. 'I just can't believe he's going. I've known him ever since I came to London, and now he's just leaving. Oh, Helen, you and he would indeed have been happy together. I had such hopes, I could see us all together, the happiest foursome on earth.' She gave a tremulous sigh. 'Today has simply been too much for me. I was so happy when we left the house, but now I feel totally wretched, with one of the worst headaches ever. You'll have to forgive me, Helen, but I really can't attend the party.'

Helen was alarmed. They *had* to go! 'But, Margaret. . . .'

'It's out of the question. I'll have to go home and lie down, and since you can't go alone, you'll have to stay away as well. I'm truly sorry, for I can see how disappointed you are, but I really do feel very unwell.'

'Yes, of course.' There was nothing more Helen could say, for it was obvious that Margaret was indeed feeling ill. She tried to conceal her dismay as they entered the landau, setting off back toward Bourne End instead of over the heath toward Windsor Great Park.

Helpless against this latest intervention by fate, she glanced at her little watch. It was half past seven, and if Adam kept his word, he'd be waiting at the lakeside in another half an hour. He'd wait in vain.

She stared out of the carriage window, hardly able to believe that bad luck was dogging her yet again. The dice were unfairly loaded, and each time they fell, they allotted her more misfortune. Things had been bad enough when Adam had stumbled upon her real identity only hours before, but now she had Ralph's promise of further vengeance to contend with. Adam would eventually return to King Henry Crescent that night without hearing a word of explanation from her; he'd think the very worst of her actions all along, and then he'd receive Ralph's *billet-doux*. She lowered her gaze, toying miserably with the frill at her cuff. If only she could keep the appointment. . . .

She looked up again suddenly. Did she really have to remain unwillingly at Bourne End because Margaret was unwell? It was still very sunny, and sunset wouldn't be for several hours yet; no one would think anything of it if she elected to go for a ride in the park! And no one would know if she rode out of the park and then on to Eleanor's Lake! She wouldn't be able to reach Adam in time for eight, but she wouldn't be as late as all that. Maybe he'd still be waiting. It was a chance she was willing to take; indeed, she had to take it.

At last the landau reached the door of Bourne End, and Margaret delayed only long enough to ascertain that Gregory still hadn't returned before going up to her room. Helen waited until she'd vanished from sight before requesting Morris to have a horse saddled and brought around to the door, then she too hurried up the staircase.

Mary was waiting in her room. 'Did you have a good day, miss?'

'No, I had a horrible day.'

'Whatever happened?' inquired the maid, hurrying to assist her to undress.

Helen explained everything. 'So, you see,' she finished, 'I have to see him somehow, so I've instructed Morris to have a horse brought around. Will you take out my riding habit?'

'But, miss. . . .'

'Don't try to reason with me, Mary, I'm just not in the mood. Time's ticking by and I must try to meet him.'

'Yes, miss.' The maid hurried to the relevant wardrobe, lifting down the mustard riding habit Madame Rosalie had created for fashionable rides in Hyde Park. 'Miss Fairmead, you mustn't go alone, it's not right and it's too dangerous. Please let me tell Peter, he's well enough to accompany you now.'

'Mary. . . .'

'Please, miss.'

Helen hesitated. 'Oh, very well, but tell him to hurry. Go on, I can finish dressing on my own.'

The maid hurried out, and Helen stepped into the tight-fitting habit. She was just fixing the little black beaver hat in place when Mary returned.

'Peter's gone out to saddle his cob right now, miss. Your horse is ready and waiting.'

'Thank you, Mary.'

The maid went to find the gloves that went with the habit, and then the riding crop.

Watching her searching through a chest of drawers, Helen became impatient. 'Oh, do hurry!'

'Here they are, miss.' The maid brought them, and then gave her another anxious look. 'I don't think Lord Drummond is going to understand, not after all you've told me,' she said a little gloomily.

'I love Adam Drummond, Mary, and nothing's going to stop me trying to win him.'

Unknown to them both, Margaret had come to the door in her wrap, wanting to talk some more about Ralph's sudden departure. The door was slightly ajar still after Mary's return, and Helen's last words carried out quite clearly. Margaret halted in shocked dismay. Her sister was in love with Adam Drummond? But how could that possibly be so? Helen had quite definitely indicated an interest in a match with Ralph!

In the room, Mary continued to watch her mistress, who was teasing on the tight gloves. 'Maybe it's just not meant to be, miss.'

'It is, I know it is. I'll do anything I have to keep him, anything at all. Propriety has had very little to do with my conduct since I met him, and I'm not about to shrink from things now.'

Margaret leaned weakly against the wall, her eyes closed for a moment. Anything to keep him? Anything at all? Conduct without propriety? Oh, please, don't let that mean what it seemed to mean! Had Adam seduced Helen? The thought was so appalling in its implications that Margaret almost went straight into the room to face her sister, but then discretion took a hand. Helen's whole future was at risk, and so solving the problem had to be tackled with a cool mind, not one that was hot and upset with outrage. Gregory should be here, it was something that had to be approached together. Maybe it was already too late to save Helen's virtue, but even so something had to be done to separate her forever from Adam Drummond's vile influence. Oh, was there no end to the blows they had to suffer at his hands? Trembling, Margaret smoothed her hands against the folds of her wrap. Helen was green, she knew nothing of the world; at least, she hadn't when she'd left Miss Figgis's seminary; what had happened since then was a matter of awful conjecture.

In the room, Helen was ready now. She took a final look at herself in one of the wall mirrors. 'There, I'm ready for my ride.' She walked toward the door, her riding habit rustling.

Margaret's breath caught, and she fled back along the passage to her own room, slipping inside just as Helen emerged. Leaning back against the closed door, Margaret listened to the light footsteps hurry by, then she went out again, following her sister to the top of the staircase, and peeping cautiously over the balustrade to watch as Helen was escorted to the door by Morris.

The butler bowed as she went out. 'I trust you enjoy your ride, Miss Fairmead.'

'I'm sure I will, I have Peter to show me all over the park. Oh,' she paused, 'if Mrs Bourne should inquire after me, please tell her where I am, and that I won't be very late.'

'Yes, miss.'

The door was closed, and a moment later Margaret heard two

horses moving away from the house. Turning, she went slowly back to her own room. What could she and Gregory sensibly do about this? How on earth were they going to rescue Helen, when she quite patently didn't want to be rescued? How she wished Gregory would return, for she needed to talk to him.

She lay wearily on the bed in her room, closing her eyes. The clock began to chime eight almost straightaway, and as the mellow sound died away, she heard a carriage approaching. With a glad cry, she hurried to the window, holding the delicate net aside to look out. Gregory's carriage was coming toward the house.

Gathering her skirts, she hurried from the room, down to the entrance hall, and out beneath the front balcony just as the coach drew to a standstill.

Gregory alighted, looking at her in great concern as he saw how upset she was. 'What is it, my darling?'

'Oh, Gregory!' She flung herself into his arms, bursting into tears.

Gently he embraced her, smiling fondly. 'I didn't expect quite such torrents because Musket failed,' he murmured.

'It isn't M-musket, it's H-Helen. Sh-she's been seeing Adam D-Drummond, and I fear she m-may already be r-ruined!'

He drew back in amazement, gazing earnestly into her tear-filled eyes. 'What are you saying?'

'It's t-true!'

'Where is she now?'

'Out r-riding in the p-park, with Peter, the undercoachman.'

'I think we'd better go inside, my love. Then you can tell me all about it,' he said, his eyes dark with bitter anger.

CHAPTER 20

The Windsor road was still crowded as Helen rode swiftly past the racecourse and then on over the heath toward the great park. Peter rode just behind her, his stout cob working hard to keep up with her dun hunter.

Windsor Castle flashed momentarily between the trees as they passed through the gates into the park, and then the main highway was left behind as they turned to the northwest along the narrower way toward the lake, and Hagman's. It was some time since Helen had ridden fast. At Miss Figgis's she'd been accustomed to sedate trotting along the Cheltenham streets, with an occasional slow canter through the park, but as a child she'd ridden like the wind across the Worcestershire countryside, and now she was doing so again, the single long ringlet of hair fluttering behind her.

Most of the guests had already gone on to the water party, and there was much less traffic on the road now; indeed, from time to time it seemed she and Peter were alone. The great tree marking the track to Herne's Glade loomed ahead, and as she reached it, she reined in because her horse was in a lather and needed a slight rest. She glanced at her fob watch. It was twenty past eight! She gathered the reins to urge her mount on, but then something made her glance along the track to the glade. Slow hoofbeats were approaching. She stared nervously in the direction of the sound. The trees moved quietly in the light evening breeze, folding over the track in a secret way that made her thoughts turn instinctively to Lord Swag. Even as his name entered her head, a horseman appeared, riding very slowly. He was slightly built, wore a dark cloak, and his hat was pulled forward to put his face in shadow.

Peter had reined in beside her, and now she heard his dismayed gasp. 'It's him, miss, it's Lord Swag, I'd know him anywhere!'

Alarmed, she urged her sweating horse on toward the lake, and Peter did the same. 'We should have gone back, miss,' he cried, his voice jerky from the jolting motion of his horse. 'Now we'll have to return later, and we know he's around!'

It was something she didn't want to think about. He was right, but her reaction had been instinctive. She glanced fearfully back over her shoulder, but the curve of the track now obscured the view, although she could still see the tall branches of the tree towering above everything else. Of the lone horseman, there was no sign.

Only when Hagman's boathouse appeared through the trees ahead did she slow her tired mount from a headlong gallop to a mere canter. The sound of the water party carried clearly, for there was an orchestra playing and a large number of people were enjoying themselves, She could hear laughter and conversation, and as she and Peter reached the boathouse, she saw that the jetty was crowded with elegant people still in their Royal Ascot finery. Out on the water, the pleasure boats moved gently in the lengthening evening shadows, and the Cardusays' flower-garlanded barge was moored at the end of the jetty, its gilded awning gleaming in the warm rays of the sun as it began its long descent toward the western horizon.

Helen's heart was thundering with awful trepidation as she rode slowly along the path by the edge of the lake. The rhododendrons were still magnificent, their heavy crimson, mauve, and white blooms brilliant against the dark foliage. It was half past eight as she reined in just before the small clearing. Would he still be there? Had he been there at all?

Slowly she dismounted, handing the reins to Peter. 'Wait for me.'

'But, miss. . . .'

'I'll only be just beyond those bushes. Please wait here.'

Reluctantly he nodded. 'Yes, miss. But if you need me. . . .'

'I'll call.' She gave a sadly wry smile. 'I rather think I'll be coming straight back, though, for he won't be there.'

She could hear her heartbeats as she walked the final few yards along the path and around the edge of the rhododendrons. The grass swept down to the lakeshore, and her initial reaction was of intense dismay, for there was no sign of his horse, but then her eyes fled to the edge of the water, where one of the small pleasure boats was moored. Its prow was carved like a dolphin, and its awning was brightly striped in red and white. There were no seats inside, just velvet cushions, and a gentleman was lounging on them, a slow curl of smoke rising from his Spanish cigar. He sat up as she appeared, and she knew it was Adam.

Slowly he tossed the cigar into the water, and then rose to his feet. The boat swayed as he stepped ashore, waiting as she went quickly toward him.

She'd been filled with gladness when she saw him, but as she came closer and recognized the coldness on his face, the gladness died away into emptiness. 'I – I'm sorry I'm so late. I couldn't help it. Margaret felt unwell and decided not to attend the party.'

His glance flickered cynically. 'I've had no better diversion for the past three-quarters of an hour, besides, I'm sure it wasn't your fault, Miss Fairmead; indeed, I'm sure you're going to tell me that nothing has been your fault since the moment we met.'

The past three-quarters of an hour? But she was only half an hour late. 'No, I'm not going to say that, because I know it is.'

'Well, that's something, I suppose.'

She felt a telltale trembling inside that warned her it would be only too easy to break down in tears, and she steeled herself to overcome the weakness. He was justified in feeling the way he did, and it was up to her to convince him she hadn't meant to mislead him. 'Adam. . . .'

'Miss Fairmead,' he interrupted, 'I think such intimacy as the use of first names should cease forthwith.'

She tried not to show how deep the hurt went at this. 'Very well, my lord. I was going to say that I didn't set out to deceive you.'

'So, now you're saying you really are the widowed Mrs Brown?' he remarked dryly.

'No. . . .'

'Then you did set out to deceive, didn't you?' he pointed out.

She swallowed unhappily. 'Yes, I suppose in one way, I did. I was on my way from Cheltenham, where I'd been at a seminary for young ladies for five years. During those five years I was drilled over and over as to what proper young ladies did and did not do. One thing they did not do was stay unescorted at an inn, but circumstances forced just that situation on me. I was also taught during those five years that widows are allowed a little more latitude than any other ladies, and so I decided to protect my reputation by pretending to be Mrs Brown. That was all it was, my lord, a foolish pretence because I was afraid for my good name. But I confess to a little willfull determination to enjoy my newfound freedom to the full, and when you invited me to dine with you, I gladly accepted. I was inexperienced, and I really didn't think it all through, which is why I made such a mess of it all when you asked innocent questions. I told one fib, it led to another, and so on, and then when you revealed that there was such bad feelings between you and my family at Bourne End, well, I was shaken. I couldn't believe that my silly fibs had all been uttered to a man who had no reason to care much if such a scandalous tale concerning Gregory Bourne's sister-in-law got out over town. But by the time we finally parted at the Cat and Fiddle, my feelings were such that everything about you mattered very much indeed. I'd never been kissed before, and never wanted so very much to be kissed.'

'I'm flattered, Miss Fairmead, but confess that your display of ardor seemed very far from a first awakening.'

Her eyes sought his. 'Please, don't say that.'

'I was merely observing fact. I believed you were a widow, and nothing in your manner gave me any cause to think otherwise. Now you tell me that it was your first kiss, and so I tell you that there was nothing of the shrinking, virginal innocent in the way you responded to my advances.'

'My responses were very honest, sir. Would you rather I played the coquette?'

'I would rather you had displayed honesty throughout, madam, instead of just claiming it when your story requires it.'

'You're deliberately misinterpreting.'

'Am I? Please proceed, Miss Fairmead, I'm all interest and attention.'

She turned away a little, gazing at the pleasure boat as it rocked gently on the water. 'When I reached Bourne End, I was dismayed to find out what you were supposed to have done last year. You may not believe it, sir, but my determination to support you caused more than a little bad feeling with Margaret and Gregory. I could not, and would not, believe you guilty, and when I told you that, I wasn't being deceitful at all.'

'Maybe not, for your deceit was more concerned with perpetuating the myth of Mrs Brown.'

'I tried to tell you. We were standing right here in this place, and then the horse was frightened, and when I looked back toward the jetty I saw Ralph St John approaching.' She hesitated. 'But then, you know this already, don't you?'

'Yes, you told me on the terrace at the castle.'

'What I didn't tell you was that I'd set out that day to call on you at King Henry Crescent, but that as my carriage approached the house, you emerged and drove off in your curricle. I was going to tell you the truth about myself, but chance stepped in for the second time and prevented me. It prevented me for a third time on the castle terrace when I simply couldn't find the courage to tell you. I was suddenly so afraid that you'd despise me that I couldn't utter a single word. I took refuge in telling myself I'd confess everything at our next meeting, which would be at the Farrish House ball. But something happened when I returned to Bourne End, something that made my confession all the more difficult. Ralph St John was waiting for me, he'd had me followed and he knew all about our meeting. For reasons which I'll explain in a moment, he was determined to make me agree to the betrothal I'd refused to even begin to countenance until then. Oh, yes, my lord, the betrothal you'd heard rumored was based on nothing more than discussions between Ralph St John, Margaret, and Gregory; I'd had no part in them at all, I hadn't even been consulted. Anyway, he forced me to consent to a temporary betrothal, and he used the same means on me that he'd used on you. He threatened not only to ruin me and alienate my family from me, he also promised to use your sister's affair to cause an irreparable rift between you and me. He swore he'd make sure you were told that the exposure of Lady Bowes-Fenton's secret was entirely due to my deliberate interference. I had no choice but to do as he wished, my lord, for to refuse would have brought about the very thing you'd been at such pains to prevent – the destruction of your sister's life and happiness. In the circumstances, I agreed to his demands.'

'Do go on, Miss Fairmead, for you tell a fascinating tale.'

She felt as if he'd struck her, but although she flinched, she gave no other sign of the pain that lanced through her. 'I now had even more to confess than before, and I thought perhaps it would be better if I wrote to you. I labored a long time over that letter, and I dispatched it to you with one of the Bourne End coachmen, a young man who was more than willing to help, because he is my maid's sweetheart. He was set upon in broad daylight by Lord Swag, and the letter came back to me unread. So I took it with me to Farrish House, determined to achieve my long-overdue confession. Before I kept my tryst with you, however, I made the acquaintance of Ralph St John's father, a gentleman who is as unlike his odious son as chalk is from cheese. He's not the fool Ralph believes him to be; indeed, he saw through the false betrothal, which I then found out was needed in order to persuade Mr St John Senior to part with a large sum of money. Ralph had written to him in Jamaica about a forthcoming betrothal and the need to purchase a suitable property ready for married life, but the truth was that the money was for Ralph's huge gambling debts. Mr St John came back here to investigate what was going on, and it didn't take him long to realize that Ralph had lighted on me because he had to produce a bride from somewhere. Ralph had been confident I'd leap at the prospect of a match with him, and he'd had a shock when I turned him down. He was in a corner by then, however, and so used force to bring me around.

'Knowing I could trust Mr St John, I told him about my love for you, going only so far as to tell him Ralph was using that love to make me do his will. I didn't mention your sister, nor did I tell him that Ralph had been the real villain with Prince Agamemnon. I liked Mr St John, my lord, and I didn't want him to be hurt any more than necessary by awful revelations about the depths to which his loathsome son had sunk, and was still prepared to sink. Mr St John had heard enough; he decided that Ralph had to have the tables turned on him. I knew when I met you last night that Ralph was going to have to leave England very shortly, otherwise he was going to languish in jail and be disinherited.'

'I take it that's what you meant when you said something about Ralph not being in a position to continue his vendetta for much longer?'

'Yes. Then I asked you to take me outside so that we could talk. I truly meant then to tell you everything; indeed, I was just about to start when I heard Margaret approaching.' Helen gave an ironic laugh. 'She was walking toward us, in company with the Cardusays. It was too much for me, and I ran away.' She paused for a long moment, aware of the gentle lapping of the lake against the shore. She gazed at the boat, taking a long breath before continuing. 'When I returned to the ball after you'd gone, I was given your message by the footman. I can't tell you how glad I was that you'd give me another chance.'

She turned to face him, but his expression offered no heart, it remained cold. She breathed out tremulously, turning away again. 'When I ran away from you at the ball, I hid in the landau. I was absolutely distraught, and had to hide because I was in tears. I happened to overhear two lovers in the next carriage – I don't know who they were, and it really doesn't matter. What does matter is that something the woman said made me realize why Ralph had turned upon you. It was because of Mrs Tully.'

Adam gave a coolly incredulous laugh. 'She meant nothing to me, and I certainly didn't accept what she offered me. Besides, she didn't hold that special a place in Ralph's heart.'

'She held place enough for him to still carry a miniature of her around with him. I saw him at Bourne End, gazing at it without knowing I was there. I could tell that he often looked at it like that, but he denied even knowing who the woman in the miniature was. I knew the miniature seemed familiar, but I couldn't place it. Then the woman in the next carriage at Farrish House said something about nearly having come to the ball as Mistress Fuchsia. That's when I knew why the miniature had seemed familiar – it was a portrait of Mrs Tully in her most famous role. It was because she spurned him in favor of you that he hates you, my lord.'

'Has he admitted it?'

'I haven't faced him with it, I just know I'm right. I also think I know why he chose a way of hurting you that would also hurt Gregory. Margaret once told me that before she'd fallen in love with Gregory, Ralph had been her admirer, although she hadn't known it. Losing her to Gregory probably meant that in Ralph's warped view Gregory merited a little punishment, although perhaps not as much punishment as you, because Margaret hadn't meant as much to him as Mrs Tully.' She glanced at him. 'That *is* why he did it, he had no more reason than wounded male vanity, but the damage is done, and he doesn't intend to undo it before he leaves at dawn for Falmouth. His threat to Lady Bowes-Fenton is as potent as ever, my lord, and any attempt to force him to confess to everything would certainly still result in your sister's ruin. Our hands are tied, and have to remain tied.'

For a long moment he looked at her, his eyes piercingly blue. 'You are an excellent storyteller, Miss Fairmead, and I've no doubt that a great deal of it is true,'

'It's all true!'

'Perhaps I should rephrase it – it's what you've *omitted* to tell me that makes me doubt your complete veracity, Miss Fairmead.'

'I haven't omitted anything, I've told you the absolute truth. I love you, I've loved you from the first day we met, and if you asked me to go with you now, I'd go. I'm prepared to throw my reputation to the winds for you, I'm prepared to turn my back on my family. . . .'

'But you're not prepared to tell me everything. Oh, if only you knew how much I want to believe in you, for I admit that I've felt for you everything you've claimed to feel for me, and if I could look into your eyes at this moment and see the innocence and honesty I so dearly wish to see, then I'd gladly open my arms to you again.'

'You *do* see that innocence and honesty!' she cried. 'Everything I've told you this evening is the truth, I haven't told a single untruth.'

'As I said,' he responded softly, 'it's what you've omitted to tell me that gives the lie to your fulsome claims to thwarted innocence. I believe your story about the stay at the inn, and I believe what you've told me about Ralph St John's motives for everything, but what I don't believe, and cannot believe, is that you were unwilling to enter into a betrothal with him.'

Stunned, she stared at him. 'That isn't so,' she whispered. 'I loathe him, I turned him down, and only entered into a betrothal because I was forced!'

'I have just cause to think you're lying, Miss Fairmead, three just causes, as it happens.'

'I – I don't know what you mean.' Her voice caught helplessly, a thousand thoughts swirling confusingly in her bead. What was he talking about? What three just causes?

'I'm talking about two tender kisses, outside the Bourne box today when you said farewell to him. I'm also talking about this.' He took a letter from inside his coat, holding it out to her.

Her hand shook as she took it. Fragments of broken seal fell to the grass as she opened the letter to read.

Drummond,

There is unfortunately too much between us for friendship ever to exist again, but that does not mean I wish to inflict a lifetime of unhappiness and disillusionment upon you. I am sure that my departure will delight you, but I am equally sure that it will bring Helen finally to your side. You see, the lady has been playing a double game, keeping you on the sidelines while all the time she hoped to snap me up. She's a tempting morsel, as you no doubt know, and she's more than prepared to surrender her delightful charms in the furtherance of her ambitions. When I found out about her liaison with you, I decided to play her at her own deceitful game. I took all she had to offer, I enjoyed her to the full, and then after kissing her farewell today, I told her I was leaving without giving her the ring she so dearly wanted on her scheming little finger. If you believe her beguiling act, you're a fool, Drummond, and if you're inclined to think I'm acting out of spite by writing this letter, let me advise you to speak to Lady Cowper, who witnessed two tender kisses outside the royal box at the end of today's races before she drove away. What she did not witness was Helen's furious disbelief when she realized I was saying farewell forever. You're better off without the lady, Drummond, although the choice is, of course, entirely up to you.

St John

Helen stared at the signature. This was Ralph's vengeance, his promised *billet-doux*, and oh, how effective it was. Slowly she folded the paper, her hand shaking as she handed it back to him. 'Since you speak so firmly of having three just reasons to disbelieve me, I can only think that you've spoken to Lady Cowper.' Her heart was breaking.

'Naturally.'

'Oh, naturally,' she whispered, blinking back the tears. 'Every word he's written is a lie, except that there *were* two kisses, but I didn't invite them, he knew that I wouldn't dare to do anything about them. Throughout all this I've been mindful of your desire to protect the sister you love, and if I feel obliged to remind you of the fact, then you must forgive me, sir, but I think that under the circumstances such a reminder is in order. He told me today that he was going to send this to you, and he said he was doing it because he guessed I'd said a little too much to his father. He doesn't want to go to Jamaica, but his father is forcing it upon him; this letter, this *billet-doux*, as he was amused to call it, is my punishmnent.' Tears were stinging her eyes, refusing to be denied any longer.

'You're right, of course, my sin is one of omission, for I should have told you that that is what he intended to do, but I didn't and now you've fallen neatly into his trap. Think what you will of me, Adam, there's obviously nothing I can do about it; but there's nothing you can do about the way I feel about you. I love you, and I always will. I wanted to tell you everything from the outset, but it's taken until now, and if there's still something I've failed to confess, well, I don't know what it could be. Put the omission down to weariness, rather than guile. Good-bye, Adam.' Choking back a sob, she hurried away from him.

Tears blinded her. The heartbreak was a burning pain that seemed to shriek right through her. Everything was over, and he thought more ill of her than she'd ever dreamed he would. Distraught with emotion, she stumbled a little as she fled back to the horses, where a startled Peter took an anxious step toward her.

'Miss Fairmead?'

'I'm all right, Peter, I just want to go home.' She almost snatched the reins from him, fumbling as she mounted.

Peter caught her horse's bridle. 'Don't go just yet, miss, there's a large party of gentlemen leaving in a minute or so, I can see them getting ready. There's safety in numbers when Lord Swag's about!'

But she was too upset to listen, urging her horse away so that Peter had to let go, He was in a quandary for a moment, wanting more than anything to travel safely back to Bourne End, but she was riding away at speed, and she was his responsibility. Resignedly, he began to mount his cob to pursue her, but as he did so, a hand restrained him. He turned sharply to find himself looking into Adam's quick eyes. 'S-sir?'

'Did I hear you mention Lord Swag a moment ago?'

'Yes, sir. We saw him when we were coming here.'

'Then get after her, I'll be following!'

Without waiting a moment more, Adam ran toward the jetty. Peter urged his cob away in Helen's wake, and he glanced back in time to see Adam hurry up to a guards officer friend, demand his pistol, and then dash away with it in the direction of his waiting horse.

Peter brought his cob up to the fastest pace it could manage, but already Helen had vanished from sight along the road, where evening shadows were now very long indeed as sunset approached.

Helen was so upset she hardly knew what she was doing. Tears blurred her vision, and sobs racked her body as she urged her nervous horse toward the great copper beech by the track to Herne's Glade. She was devastated that Adam could so totally spurn her, and the misery folded over her so numbingly that she didn't at first see the motionless mounted figure barring the track ahead. Realization swept icily over her as her horse's headlong gallop checked sharply, and its head came up uneasily. She reined in, confused at first, but then her frightened gaze picked out the silent still figure in front of her.

Terrified, she stared at him, her heart almost stopping as she saw the glint of fading sunlight on the barrel of his pistol. Other hoofbeats drummed along the road behind her, and she turned, hoping to see the company of gentlemen, but it was only Peter. The dismayed coachman reined in as well, maneuvering his cob alongside her as the highwayman silently motioned him to do so.

Helen glanced tearfully at him. 'I'm so sorry, Peter, this is all my fault.'

Lord Swag moved his horse toward them, the slow clip-clop ominously threatening. His face was concealed by the shadow from his hat, and by a scarf tied around his nose and mouth. He wore no gloves, and Helen could see how dirty and rough his hands were; he may have been known as Lord Swag, but there was nothing lordly about him at all.

He reined in in front of them, jerking the pistol toward Peter. When he spoke, his voice was thin and nasal. 'Reck'n I knows you my laddo; reck'n I left you in a ditch a while back. You'll be poor pickin' this time, but this fine bit o' muslin, she's more promisin'.' The pistol moved back toward Helen, indicating her watch. 'That's a pretty trinket, my lovely, so why don't you 'and it over, like a good girly.'

Her hands were shaking so much she could barely handle the watch, let alone unpin it, but even as she struggled with it, a single pistol shot rang out and Lord Swag gave a sharp cry of pain, his pistol clattering to the ground.

Helen screamed, and the horses were startled, but then a new sound filled the air, the thunder of many hooves as the party of gentlemen appeared at last Lord Swag was wounded in his right hand, but seeing retribution bearing down on him in force, he somehow found the strength to turn his frightened horse, urging it away along the track in the direction of the main highway.

Adam's voice rang out to the gentlemen from the bushes where he'd managed to hide long enough to take aim. 'After him, it's Lord Swag!'

They needed no further urging. With excited and angry cries, they made off in pursuit, their horses kicking up a cloud of choking dust.

Helen's hunter was thoroughly upset, capering nervously around and threatening to unseat her. Peter tried to grab the reins, but each time the frightened horse moved just out of reach and it was Adam who caught it at last, riding from the bushes and reaching over deftly to seize the bridle. Then he looked at her pale face. 'Are you all right?'

'Yes.' His face was still cold, and she knew there was no hope he'd changed his mind about her. She found the strength to meet his eyes steadily. 'It seems I owe my safety to you yet again, my lord.'

'I, on the other hand, owe you nothing at all,' he replied, glancing at Peter. 'I'll escort you to the gates of Bourne End.'

'Yes, sir.' The coachman looked unhappily at Helen, but she'd averted her face from them both, trying to hide her misery.

Adam dismounted to retrieve Lord Swag's fallen pistol, then he mounted again and they rode on.

The sun was setting fast now, and the shadows were merging. Soon it would be dark. The horses' hooves echoed as they passed through the gates out of the great park, and the scent of elder blossom was heady in the forest before they emerged onto the twilit heath. Fires flickered on the open ground, as the grooms and stableboys in charge of the many racehorses sat around enjoying the evening.

A strange calm descended over Helen, and when Adam left them at the gates of Bourne End, riding away without another word to her, she didn't turn to watch him, even though she wanted to with all her heart. He'd severed all friendship, and now she had to continue with her shattered life.

But it wasn't over yet, and if she thought what had happened so far was bad enough, it was as nothing to the developments that were already in progress.

CHAPTER 21

She dismounted at the house, giving the reins of her tired hunter to Peter. 'I'm sorry for everything, Peter.'

'That's all right, miss, for I understand. I'm only sorry it didn't go as you hoped.'

'I'm sorry about that, too,' she replied, turning to go wearily into the house. She still felt imbued with an odd calm, but perhaps it was just that she felt absolutely drained. Her emotions had been sorely tested over the past week or more, and tonight's denouement had been too much; she'd slipped from living on nervous energy to a dull resignation that all her dreams had been dashed forever.

As she stepped into the chandelier-lit hall, however, she was jolted from her listlessness by the sudden appearance of a desperately anxious Morris. 'Oh, you're home at last, Miss Fairmead! Please come quickly, the mistress is very upset indeed, and I'm afraid she'll make herself ill.'

Helen looked at him in astonishment, and then alarm. 'What's wrong? Has something happened to the colonel?'

'The colonel came home earlier, miss, and then he ordered his horse, riding off with considerable haste to Windsor.'

'Windsor? But what on earth for?'

'I don't know, miss, but I do know that the mistress was close to hysteria when he rode off. Her maid managed to calm her a little, but she's still weeping and distressed.'

Helen unpinned her hat and tossed it onto a table. 'Where is she?'

'In the drawing room, miss. She won't retire to her bed, no matter how much we try to persuade her.'

Pulling off her gloves as well, Helen laid them beside the hat and then hurried to the drawing room. What on earth could have happened? She could hear Margaret's unconsolable sobs before she opened the door, and as she entered, Margaret's maid looked up from where she was kneeling by a sofa. Margaret was lying face down, her face hidden in the sofa cushions, and her whole body was racked with shuddering sobs. The maid got up and stepped aside as Helen hurried across the candlelit room.

'Margaret? Margaret, what's wrong? Please tell me what's happened.' She knelt in concern, putting a hand on her sister's shaking shoulders.

The sobs stopped abruptly, and for a long moment Margaret lay without moving, then slowly she sat up, turning her tear-stained face toward Helen and brushing her hand away. Her eyes were angry, and there was a bitter twist on her lips. 'How can *you* ask me that? How can you possibly pretend you don't know what's wrong?'

Helen stared uncomprehendingly at her. 'I – I don't understand.'

'I know all about your sordid liaison with Adam Drummond. I heard you talking to your maid just before you rode off to meet him. Oh, yes, I know that's where you've been now – Gregory got it out of the maid. How could you do it, Helen? How could you slyly meet that man while living under this roof? Have you no shame? No sense of loyalty and honor? What did they teach you in Cheltenham? How to be little better than a demimondaine? How swiftly did you surrender to his advances, Helen? At the first approach? Or was it the second? One thing's certain, it didn't take him long to make a wanton of you!'

Numb, Helen drew back in dismay. The accusing words beat against her like blows, and the scathing resentment in her sister's tone cut into her like a knife.

Margaret's eyes flickered toward the hovering maid. 'Leave us.'

'But, madam. . . .'

'I said leave us!' cried Margaret, her voice rising.

'Yes, madam.' The maid scuttled out, closing the door softly behind her.

Margaret's furiously reproachful gaze swung back to Helen.

'You've been a snake in our bosom, a viper, enjoying our love and hospitality, then betraying us with *him*! Are you so besotted with him that you enjoy making us the objects of derision throughout society?'

'It – it hasn't been like that at all. . . .' began Helen, struggling to steady herself.

'Hasn't it? How else can it be interpreted?' snapped Margaret, getting agitatedly to her feet, her coral wrap hissing angrily, like the snake she'd just likened Helen to. 'When I first realized what you were up to, I couldn't believe it. Oh, I was angry, but I just wanted to save you from yourself, and from him! Now I've had time to think about it, and I see you for what you really are – a sly, deceitful, disloyal *chienne*, undeserving of any sympathy or love!'

'Please, Margaret, if you'll only let me explain. . . .'

'Let you try to talk yourself out of it, you mean,' replied Margaret, whirling about to face her. 'Very well, let's hear your excuses, I'm sure they'll be enterprising.'

Helen closed her eyes for a moment, for that was the second time this evening she'd been accused of lying cleverly.

'Well? I'm listening.'

'I haven't been disloyal to you by meeting Adam, because he didn't do what you accuse him of.'

'My, my, either he's gulled you completely or you think me addlebrained.'

'He *didn't* do it, Margaret!' cried Helen, rising to her feet from where she was kneeling by the sofa. 'He didn't do anything to harm you and Gregory last year. Ralph St John was the real villain.'

Margaret stared at her, and then gave a derisive laugh. 'Oh, I might have *known* you'd turn on poor Ralph! It's the obvious thing to do in your position, for he won't be here to defend himself, will he? I didn't think you'd sink so low, Helen, but on reflection, I suppose you're running true to form. You were low enough to pretend to invite his attentions when all the time you were seeing Adam, so why should you not try to heap the blame for your lover's sins on to him as well?'

'You're wrong about Ralph St John, Margaret.'

'I don't want to hear any more.'

'Ralph is so sunk in vice that there's nothing he wouldn't do to have his own way, and to punish those who offend him!'

'Enough! I won't hear any more from you!'

'Margaret. . . .'

'I said enough!' Margaret's control snapped, and she struck Helen sharply across the cheek, her fingers leaving angry marks.

Helen's head snapped back and her breath caught. Rubbing her stinging skin, she backed away a little. 'I don't deserve this,' she whispered, 'and no matter what you think, Adam is innocent of everything.'

Margaret was a little shaken at what she'd done. She pressed her trembling hands against the folds of her wrap, her tongue passing over her dry lips. 'Innocent? That's not how his seduction of your innocence should be described,' she said quietly.

'He hasn't seduced me.'

'I suppose you're bound to say that.'

'It happens to be true. Margaret, if anyone has set out to seduce, it's me. I wanted him so much I was prepared to set all propriety aside in order to pursue him.'

Margaret drew a long, shuddering breath. 'Do you honestly expect me to believe that? He's a man of the world – experienced, attractive, sure of himself – and you are a green girl, just out of school. Have done with all this foolishness, Helen; admit that he's far from the knight in shining armor you're pretending he is. He embarked upon your seduction, and you succumbed. That's all there is to it, and nothing you say now will change my mind on it. Why should it, when you've proven yourself a liar of the highest order?'

'Oh, Margaret, you're so very wrong,' whispered Helen. 'Please believe me, for I'm telling the truth. Let me explain about Ralph, and why he did all those things, let me tell you the real reason why he's being forced to return to Jamaica immediately with his father. . . .'

'And let me explain where Gregory has gone now,' interrupted Margaret, her voice thick with emotion. 'He's gone to seek out your precious Adam, to call him out for what he's done to you.'

Stunned, Helen stared disbelievingly at her. 'No. No, that can't be so, it *mustn't* be so!'

'It *is* so. Your deceit and selfishness have brought us to this, Helen Fairmead, and I hope you're proud of yourself.' Margaret turned and went to the bellpull, tugging it.

Helen was still standing dazedly where she was as Morris hurried in. 'Madam?'

Margaret didn't turn to face him. 'Escort Miss Fairmead to her room, Morris, and post a footman at her door to see that she doesn't leave.'

The butler gaped. 'M-Madam?'

'I believe I spoke clearly enough, Morris. It is the colonel's wish that my sister is kept under strict guard, so I would be obliged if you would do as you are instructed.'

'Yes, madam.' Hesitantly, the butler turned toward Helen, who had recovered a little from her initial shock and looked imploringly at Margaret. 'You cannot mean to lock me up!'

'Oh, I mean to, Helen, for how else can we be sure you aren't slipping away to your lover? Morris, take her to her room, if you please.'

The unhappy butler came to take Helen's arm. 'Begging your pardon, miss, but I must do as I'm commanded.'

There was nothing she could do but allow him to remove her from the room. As they reached the door, Margaret spoke again. 'I shall never forgive you for this, Helen. Never.'

Helen didn't say anything; indeed, what was there for her to say? Margaret wouldn't believe a word of the truth, and with Gregory bent upon challenging Adam to a duel, what point was there in trying to explain that all their conclusions were the wrong ones? She could only hope that when Gregory came face to face with Adam, and learned Adam's side of it, he wouldn't feel there was any point in fighting for the nonexistent honor and reputation of his wayward sister-in-law. Adam was bound to repeat his version of her conduct, and that would certainly leave Gregory without any just cause to throw down the gauntlet on her behalf.

Morris lit the candles in her room before withdrawing and carefully locking the door on the outside. Still shaken to the very core by all that had happened in so very short and bitter a space of time, she went slowly out onto the balcony, looking out over the dark park. The scent of summer flowers was sweet in the air, and the remnants of the sunset stained the western sky a dull crimson. She heard the footman taking up his position outside her door, and she lowered her eyes sadly, knowing that Margaret had indeed meant every word she'd said.

Taking a deep breath, she went back into the room, looking at her disheveled reflection in the wall mirrors. Her likeness seemed to gaze forlornly back from all sides, a crumpled, disheartened figure in a mustard riding habit she'd never want to wear again. Suddenly she despised the beautiful garment, knowing that the very sight of it would always bring back the memory of this awful day. She began to undo the buttons, stepping out of the habit and then tossing it aside, for the very touch of the fine cloth offended her now. Hurrying to the wardrobe, she selected a simple white muslin chemise gown, and in a short while had changed her riding boots for little satin bottines and was seated before the dressing table, dragging her brush through her hair as if with every stroke she eliminated one of the many problems besetting her; except that she wasn't eliminating anything at all, her problems were such that they'd remain with her for the rest of her life. And all because of one man's singular and perverse spite.

How long she'd sat there alone before the dressing table, she didn't really know, but at last she heard hoofbeats approaching the house. Hurrying to the balcony, she was just in time to see Gregory riding along the drive. What time was it? She turned, going swiftly to the riding habit to remove her watch. It was gone midnight. Slowly she pinned the watch to the bodice of her gown, moving to sit on the edge of her bed. Would anyone come to tell her what had happened?

The minutes seemed to tick endlessly by, but at last she heard Gregory's step at the door. The key turned and he came in. He looked tired and drawn, and there was the same bitterness in his eyes that she'd seen earlier in Margaret's.

She rose hesitantly to her feet. 'Gregory?'

'I trust you're well pleased with yourself, madam.'

'Please don't think badly of me, Gregory.'

'I know of precious little to commend you.'

She swallowed. 'I – I know what Adam believes of me, but I swear it isn't true.'

'I have no idea what he believes of you, for he didn't express an opinion.'

She looked quickly at him. 'I don't understand.'

'I waited for him at his address in King Henry Crescent, and when he eventually arrived, I faced him with his despicable advances toward you.'

'But, he didn't,' she whispered brokenly. 'He didn't do anything to me.'

'On the contrary, he gave me to believe that he had indeed been set on seducing you.'

She stared at him, taken completely by surprise. 'That can't be so,' she said haltingly.

'It's very much so. He then said that he had no wish to accept my challenge, but I naturally gave him no choice. You are my sister-in-law, Helen, you're just nineteen years old, and until you met him, you were completely innocent and unversed in the ways of the world. By his actions, he set out to ruin you, and for that he must face the consequences. A duel will take place at dawn. We meet with pistols at five o'clock in Herne's Glade.'

Weakly, she put out a hand to steady herself on the post of the bed. 'Gregory, this is all madness. He's lying; he didn't set out to seduce me.' She was so upset, her voice was shaking. Tears filled her eyes, and confused disbelief numbed her thoughts.

'I know you're lying to try to save him, Helen.'

She rounded on him then. 'Save *him*? I want to save you *both*, you're *both* dear to me! I know that your army training has made an excellent shot of you, Gregory, but I also know that he is very accurate indeed, for he saved my life again this evening, this time from Lord Swag. Oh, I'm not going to try to explain it all now, I just want you to know that this duel cannot be allowed to go ahead, because your opinion of him, and your interpretation of his actions, are based on Ralph St John's lies! Adam hasn't done anything to damage your honor, Gregory, nor has he attempted to ruin me. You *must* believe me, for I'm telling the truth!'

'Margaret told me you were attempting to shift the blame onto Ralph.'

'Because the blame *is* Ralph's!' she cried, her fists clenching with helpless frustration. The tears were wet on her cheeks now.

'Please, Gregory, look at me and know I'm not lying!'

'I look at you, and see a woman who's desperate to spare her lover.'

'No!'

'I'm not prepared to argue, Helen, my mind is made up on the matter. Drummond and I will face each other at dawn, and in the meantime you will remain in this room. It is my intention to remove you from the gossip that's bound to result from the duel, whatever its outcome, and to that end I have already written to my aunt in Northumberland. You will be sent there within the week, and you'll remain there until she judges you to be fit to try and salvage what's left of your foolish life. By permitting him such liberties, Helen, you've brought ruin upon yourself, and shame upon this house.' Turning on his heel, he walked from the room. The key turned once more, and she heard his limping steps moving away along the passage.

She sank weakly to her knees, hiding her face in her hands. This couldn't be happening, it just couldn't. How was it possible that her harmless decision to masquerade as the widowed Mrs Brown had led to a duel at dawn between the two men she loved best in all the world?

CHAPTER 22

It was one o'clock by her watch, and Helen paced restlessly up and down in her room, trying to think of a solution to this most dire of problems yet. She had only four hours in which to somehow stop the duel; but how? If only she could think of something, but she was so distracted she couldn't even think why Adam had virtually invited the duel. He had only to have shown Gregory the letter Ralph had written to him for all thought of fighting over her honor to be dropped. Gregory could hardly have pressed for a meeting at dawn over a woman who'd apparently forfeited all claim to any honor. Instead, Adam had allowed Gregory to think she'd been seduced, or was in the process of being seduced, and that had been the signal for the duel to become a certainty. She'd like to have thought Adam's action had been a gentlemanly gesture in order to salvage what remained of her good name, but as she continued to pace up and down, she began to realize that that wasn't the case at all; the cause of this duel went beyond anything to do with her, it went back to the business of Prince Agamemnon the year before. The simmering bitterness of the past twelve months lay behind this confrontation, not the question of her virtue.

Her pacing halted suddenly. Yes, this was all really to do with what had been done to Prince Agamemnon, and if it could only be proved that Adam had had nothing to do with it, then surely Gregory would retract, especially if she told the whole truth about how she'd conducted herself since the moment she left Cheltenham. There was no point in attempting to carry out the second item if the first hadn't been accomplished, for unless Margaret and Gregory understood and accepted that Adam's conduct had been exemplary during the racing scandal, then they wouldn't be prepared to believe his behavior had been similarly exemplary where she was concerned. *She* was the one whose conduct was questionable, and now the onus was on her to do all she possibly could to stop a duel that had been brought about by misunderstanding.

She began to pace again. She bore a share of the guilt, for she'd lied to Adam, but by far the greatest responsibility for all that had happened lay with Ralph St John. If anyone should pay a price, it should be he! Oh, if only she had a trump as compelling and sure as his father had had, something that would force Ralph to confess his many sins.

For the second time her agitated pacing stopped, for suddenly the solution was crystal clear in her mind; she did have a trump, she had the very same trump! St John Senior's words came back to her. *'If I hear of anything else he's done, I'll disinherit him anyway, for I cannot and will not endure behavior as disgraceful as his. . . .'* At the ball, she'd declined to tell Ralph's father everything because she'd wanted to spare the old man's feelings, but lives were at stake now, and such fine sentiments had to be discarded. The threat of disinheritance had proved more than a little effective when first applied, and she saw no reason why it shouldn't prove equally effective a second time. She could threaten to tell poor Mr St John everything his son had done, and was continuing to do, and she had no doubt that such revelations would cause Ralph to be cut off without a penny. He still had Lady Bowes-Fenton's secret to barter with; Helen thought for a long moment and then knew that Adam's sister would have to suffer any consequences, for it was the lesser of two evils, the other evil being the possibility of Adam's death, or Gregory's, or both. But maybe it wouldn't come to that, for hopefully Ralph would prefer not to risk disinheritance.

Helen's mind raced as she tried to consider the matter from every angle. Ralph was hardly going to confess to everything if his father was likely to find out anyway because of the instant furore, so there had to be a safeguard. Ralph and his father were departing before dawn for Falmouth, and so would soon be out of England, very far away from the stir that would inevitably result from the real truth coming out, which meant as far as she was concerned that the obvious thing to demand of him was a letter, something she could take to Adam or Gregory once the journey to Falmouth had commenced, but *before* the time set for the duel. Time was of the essence in all this, for the St Johns' departure, and the hour for the meeting in Herne's Glade, were horridly close. She had to get to Ralph as quickly as possible, demand the letter, and, if she succeeded, get to Adam at King Henry Crescent before he set out for the dawn appointment.

She drew a long breath, exhaling very slowly as she tried to think if there was any other way of stopping the duel. There was the possibility of reporting it to the authorities, but that would merely postpone the matter, for the challenge would remain, and the two men would merely meet at another time and place, and by then Ralph would be well gone. No, she had to get to Ralph now. If she could pull it off, it would be poetic justice, with a vengeance. But how was she going to accomplish it? She was locked up here in her room at Bourne End, and he was six miles away at the Golden Key in Windsor. She glanced at her watch again. Time was ticking inexorably away. She had to get out of here, get to Windsor, and confront Ralph; six miles, but it might as well have been six hundred.

She hurried out onto the balcony, peering over the edge. Everything was very dark, for the moon was behind clouds. A light breeze stirred the leaves of the climbing plants twining up the columns supporting the balcony, but as she looked hopefully at them, she knew straightaway that the branches weren't sturdy enough to hold her. Her glance moved toward the end of the house, and the way to the stables. Even if she got down from the balcony, she had to saddle a horse and ride away, something she could hardly hope to do without detection. Her eyes brightened then, for although *she* couldn't saddle a horse or take a carriage, Peter could!

Gathering her skirts, Helen hurried back into the room, crossing to the door and knocking urgently on it. 'Is anyone there?'

The footman outside shifted his position. 'Er, yes, miss, it's Luke.'

'Luke, I need my maid.'

'I don't know, miss. . . .' he began doubtfully.

'Surely I'm not to be denied my maid as well as my freedom? Send her to me at once, Luke.' She spoke authoritatively, but her fingers were crossed.

For a moment there was silence, then the footman cleared his throat. 'Very well, miss, I'll go directly.'

'Thank you.'

She breathed out with relief as she heard him hurrying away. A glance at her watch showed that the time had moved on to half past one. Oh, hurry, Mary, please hurry! It seemed an age before she heard the maid's light footsteps hurrying toward the door. The key turned in the lock, and Luke's voice spoke warningly. 'I don't know if I'm supposed to do this, Mary Caldwell, so just you see you don't do anything we might both regret.'

'All right, Luke Harding, don't be such a misery.' Mary came in a little crossly, darting a dark glance back at the footman before the door closed again and the key turned.

Turing to her mistress, Mary's face changed to one of shamefaced regret. 'I'm so sorry, miss, I didn't mean to tell on you, but the master was so angry, I got frightened and. . . .'

Helen went to her, taking her hands. 'It's all right, Mary, I don't blame you.'

Tears filled the maid's eyes. 'Oh, thank you, miss.'

'Mary, I have something very important to ask of you.'

'Miss?'

'I have to get out of here, and somehow reach Windsor. I need to see Mr St John.'

The maid stared at her. 'Oh, no, miss, please don't! You're in trouble enough. . . .'

'Do you know there's to be a duel, at dawn between Colonel Bourne and Lord Drummond?' interrupted Helen.

'Yes, miss. The master told Mr Morris.'

'I must do something to stop the duel, Mary. It's imperative that I see Mr St John before he and his father set out for Falmouth, and I need you to go to Peter and ask him to saddle a horse for me, or maybe harness a coach and drive me there himself. I know it's asking a great deal of you both, but the alternative really doesn't bear thinking about. I promise that it won't put your positions in jeopardy, for whatever the differences between myself and Mrs Bourne, she will not dismiss either of you if she knows you acted in an attempt to save the colonel's life. Please, Mary, will you help me?' She looked urgently into the maid's unhappy eyes.

'I – I don't know, miss, Peter may not feel he can. . . .'

'Will you at least ask him?'

Mary was in a quandary, wanting so much to help but beset by the fear that by doing so, she might do her mistress more harm than good. At last she nodded. 'I'll go to him, miss.'

'Oh, thank you, Mary! I'll be forever grateful. But do hurry, there's no time to waste if he's willing to help. I have to reach Mr St John as quickly as possible, and then, if I'm successful in what I plan to do, get to Lord Drummond before be leaves for the duel.'

'I'll tell him, miss.' The maid went back to the door, knocking on it. 'Luke? I have to get a fresh pillow, Miss Fairmead has spilled water on hers.'

The key turned in the lock, and the door opened. Mary slipped quickly out, and the door closed again. The turning of the key was a horrid sound, for it brought the feeling of helplessness back.

The minutes ticked relentlessly by, and there was no sign of Mary's return. Helen resumed her frustrated pacing. It was a quarter to two, then ten to, but at last she heard the maid's footsteps.

Luke was disgruntled. 'What took you so long?'

'I couldn't find the right pillow. Oh, I pity the girl you marry, Luke Harding, for you're the most complaining ferret it's ever been my misfortune to meet. Now open that door and let me get on with my tasks.'

The key turned again, and Mary slipped in with the fresh pillow. She waited until the door closed again before coming close to whisper. 'It's all planned, miss, Peter will gladly help. He says it's safe on the roads now for Lord Swag was caught by all those gentlemen and flung into Windsor jail. Cook heard all about it tonight from a peddler.'

Relief flooded weakeningly through Helen. 'Oh, thank God,' she whispered.

'Peter's gone directly to the stables to harness up the small carriage. He says it's too risky taking three horses. . . .'

'Three?'

'I'm coming too, miss, I won't hear of anything else. Anyway, he says the saddle horses are too close to the grooms' quarters, but the coach horses are further from them and therefore easier to take. The small carriage is kept right at the far end of the coach house, and he'll wait there until we arrive.'

'But how am I going to get out?'

'Down over the balcony. Peter says if we knot your bedsheets together. . . .'

'Of course, why didn't I think of that?' It was so simple.

Mary glanced back at the door. 'I'll go back out in a moment, making as if you're going to sleep, and then I'll come around beneath the balcony. When you climb down, I'll take you to Peter.'

'Mary, I don't think you'll ever know how grateful I am to you, and to Peter. I know I've no right to involve you both, but I couldn't think of any other way.'

''We want to help, miss. I'd stand by you, no matter what, and there's nothing Peter wouldn't do for you, or for the colonel and Mrs Bourne. If I seemed reluctant, it was because I'm anxious for you.'

Impulsively, Helen hugged her. 'I know, Mary. I don't deserve an angel like you.'

Mary hesitated, and then returned the hug. 'I could say the same, miss,' she replied, blinking back tears and then drawing away, afraid she'd start to cry. 'I'll help you knot the sheets together, and then tie them firmly to the balcony rail.'

Together they dragged the sheets from the bed, attaching them with knots as firm as they could manage. Then they carried it all out onto the balcony, tying one end tightly to the wrought iron railing.

Mary straightened. 'Don't lower it over the edge until I come outside, miss, for someone might see it and raise the alarm. I'll go now.' The maid went to the door. 'Luke? Let me out now.'

Again the key turned, and the door opened. Mary paused, looking back at Helen. 'Good night, miss. Please try to sleep.'

'I'll do my best.'

The maid went out, and the door closed yet again.

Helen hurried to a wardrobe and took out a warm shawl. Did she need anything else? She glanced at her reflection. Her hair was brushed loose, tumbling about her shoulders in a way that wasn't at all proper for leaving the house, but apart from tying it back with a ribbon, there wasn't much else she could do. It would take time to pin it up into a creditable knot, and time was the one thing she didn't have. Searching in a drawer, she found a white ribbon, and dragging the brush through her hair once more, she tied the heavy tresses back, fluffing out the bow at the nape of her neck. Then she pulled the shawl around her shoulders, and stepped out onto the balcony.

A minute or so more passed before Mary's shadowy figure appeared below. Helen lifted the tied sheets, lowering them carefully over the edge. Suddenly the drop seemed further than ever, and her heart began to beat more swiftly at the thought of entrusting herself to those hastily tied knots. Her tongue passed nervously over her dry lips, but she made herself climb onto the railing. Closing her eyes, she slowly lowered herself into the darkness, every muscle in her body trembling as she began to climb down.

It seemed a lifetime before she reached the bottom. Mary whispered urgently, 'Come on, miss, someone might come at any moment.' Catching her mistress's hand, she moved swiftly away past the front of the house.

Their steps crunched lightly on the wide gravel area before the entrance to the stable yard, but instead of taking Helen beneath the clocktower, Mary led her on around the outside, where the perimeter wall seemed impregnable, but at last they came to a wicket gate which creaked a little as it was opened.

As they stepped through the gate and into the shadowy coach house beyond, the moon came out, throwing a clear silvery light over the house and park, and illuminating the straw-strewn cobbles on the floor.

Horses tossed their heads nervously as the two stealthy figures slipped inside, and then Helen made out the shape of the coach, a two-seater berlin of an indeterminate dark color, but she thought it was green. Peter was crouching by the forelegs of one of the two chestnuts he'd harnessed, and she saw that he was tying cloth on to muffle the clatter of the hooves.

He straightened as they approached. 'It's all ready, miss. I can't do anything about the wheels, but without the hooves there won't be that much noise. No one goes around the back way, at least not often, and I reckon we can get across the park and into the boundary woods without being seen.'

'I'm truly grateful to you, Peter.'

He grinned. 'I owe you a favor, miss,' he reminded her. 'What Lord Swag took away, you replaced, and that means a lot.' He went to open the berlin's door, assisting them both inside, then closed the door very softly, not wanting to make any unnecessary sound that might raise the alarm. Next, he opened the doors of the coach house, peering out into the yard beyond before returning to lead the horses forward.

It seemed to Helen that the carriage wheels made a very loud noise on the cobbles, and she found she was holding her breath as Peter led the team across the shadowy, deserted yard and out past several outhouses to a track leading along behind the walled kitchen gardens.

Helen gazed back toward the house, listening for anything that might tell their escape had been discovered, but all was quiet, she could even hear an owl hooting somewhere. Turning to look ahead, she could see the open park, moonlit and exposed, and beyond it the dark silhouette of the boundary woods.

Reaching the end of the kitchen garden wall, Peter climbed onto the carriage box, taking up the reins. The berlin seemed to jolt forward as he urged the team into action again, taking the risk of making too much noise by bringing them up to a fast trot, rather than dawdle quietly along and be visible for too long from the house.

Helen crossed her fingers tightly, her eyes closed. The berlin swayed and bumped on the little-used track, the wheels rattling loudly, but the horses made hardly a sound. At last the trees enveloped them, shutting off the view, and she knew their escape was almost complete. The track was more rutted than ever in the woods, and the berlin lurched alarmingly from side to side, but the weather had been fine and there was no mud to bog it down.

There were gates ahead, set in the perimeter wall surrounding the estate, and because they were never used, there was no occupant in the silent lodge. Peter reined the team in, climbing quickly down to remove the muffles from the horses' hooves and then go to open the gates. He'd somehow procured the padlock key, but the lock was so rusty it was some time before he persuaded it to turn. At last it gave way, and he began to haul the heavy gates open. The hinges creaked and groaned, the sound seeming to echo through the trees as if wanting to arouse the distant house. Peter led the team through, and then closed the gates again, locking the padlock and pocketing the key safely before resuming his place on the box. Then, taking his whip, he galvanized the team into action. The berlin flew forward, the horses coming swiftly up to a smart canter on the road that led toward Windsor, six miles away to the north.

Helen glanced at her watch. It was almost twenty to three, there were well over two hours to the allotted dawn time for the duel. Surely that was time enough for all she needed to do?

But although she didn't know it, she only had just two hours, because she'd failed to wind her watch that day. It was a careless omission, and one she couldn't know about, for although the watch was running slower and slower, it was still ticking reassuringly.

If she'd only realized at the time, Adam's remark by the lake had been significant. He'd told her he hadn't had anything more diverting to do than wait for her for the past three-quarters of an hour, but she'd been under the belief that she'd only been half an hour late. Her watch had been running fifteen minutes behind then; now it was running twenty minutes behind. . . .

The berlin drove urgently through the night, but the time set for the duel, and for the St Johns' departure, was closer than Helen knew.

CHAPTER 23

Windsor was quiet. The sound of the speeding berlin echoed loudly along the empty streets as the foam-flecked horses flung themselves into their collars, negotiating a sharp hill before turning at last into the main thoroughfare where the Golden Key inn occupied a prime site on the road to Oxford.

Street lamps threw a pale light over cobbles and pavements, and the bow-windowed shops were illuminated, showing off fine displays of wares. The officers of the watch stood idly in a corner, enjoying an illicit pipe of tobacco. One of them held a lantern, while the others had rested their staves against a wall. They straightened hastily as the berlin drove swiftly by, but then lounged again, determined to finish their smoke at their leisure.

The only other vehicle Helen saw was a bright-red 'Planet' stagecoach, bound for Maidenhead and High Wycombe, and it had evidently pulled out of the Golden Key yard only a minute before, for the coachman was urging the fresh team up to a smart pace, his whip cracking like a pistol shot over the otherwise peaceful street.

Peter began to rein the berlin team in, slowing to a trot as the brightly-lit inn loomed ahead. The Golden Key was a posting house, one of the best, and as a consequence was always a hive of activity. It was a splendid half-timbered building, with origins in the fifteenth century, and its many upper story windows looked toward the castle. Another stagecoach emerged from the low way into the galleried courtyard, a light-blue one this time, and as it turned away in the opposite direction, Helen caught a glimpse of the words on its panels. *Express. London. Windsor.* Its lamps shone in an arc against the road ahead as it set off on its short journey to the capital.

Helen's watch pointed to half past three as the berlin negotiated the entrance to the courtyard, the hooves and wheels making a din in the narrow way before emerging into the lamp-lit courtyard, where an ancient vine climbed high around three stories of wooden galleries. The inn was busy enough at all times to warrant two ticket offices, each one occupied by a meticulous clerk, and a number of passengers were waiting to be attended to at the glass windows of each.

There were two other stagecoaches in the yard, one waiting to depart, the other having arrived only a short time before, and with them was a third vehicle, one of the inn's own fine post chaises. The chaise was black-paneled, its doors adorned with a distinctive painted golden key, and from the demeanor of its postboy and the attention being given to its team of four well-matched bays, it was preparing for a long journey. As the berlin halted and Peter came to open the door for Helen and Mary to alight, Helen distinctly heard the postboy grumble to an ostler that he hoped the coves he was taking to Falmouth weren't scaly ones, as a thing he couldn't stand at any price was a bad tipper.

Helen stepped down from the berlin, looking in alarm at the chaise. Falmouth? Surely there couldn't be anyone else traveling to that destination from this inn? It had to be Ralph and his father, and if the chaise was anything to go by, she was only just in time!

Insisting on Mary's staying with Peter, she hurried into the inn, pushing through the crowded coffee room toward the counter, where she saw a large man in an innkeeper's crisp white apron. 'Sir? Are you the landlord?'

He turned, his practiced glance sweeping, over her. Perceiving that she was definitely a lady, he was pleased to give her a gracious smile. 'I am, madam. May I be of assistance? Do you require accommodation? Or maybe a chaise?'

'I wish to see one of your guests, a Mr Ralph St John.'

He cleared his throat uncertainly. 'This is, er, a little irregular, madam. It isn't the custom of this house to disturb guests. . . .'

'I doubt very much if he's still in his bed, sir, since I think the chaise waiting in the yard is the one taking him to Falmouth with his father. It *is* their chaise, isn't it?'

'Yes, madam.'

'Then would you please inform him that Miss Fairmead wishes to see him urgently?'

Again his glance moved over her, but more speculatively this time, for it was usually only a certain type of female that called on gentlemen guests in the middle of the night.

She colored, guessing his thoughts. 'You're entirely wrong about me, sirrah, so please do as I ask.'

He nodded then, deciding there was more to her than met the eye. 'Very well, miss.'

'Is there a private room where we can talk? Somewhere where there is writing equipment?'

'Such things cost, miss.'

'Mr St John will be pleased to recompense you in full, sir.'

'Yes, miss. Please follow me. I'll show you to a room and then inform Mr St John that you're here.'

He conducted her out of the coffee room, along a red-tiled passage, and into a small room lit only from the street. Pausing to light the candles with one he'd brought with him, he then withdrew.

The new light shivered over the room, revealing a low-beamed chamber with paneled walls. The intricately carved fireplace yawned black and empty, and on either side of it were two high-backed settles. The only other furniture was a comfortable chair and a writing desk with all she required for the letter she hoped to coerce Ralph into writing.

The stagecoach that had been on the point of departure, now made a noisy exit from the inn, sweeping out onto the road and then turning toward London. For a bright moment its lamps flooded the room with light, but then it was gone.

A wry thought struck her. This was the second time she'd flouted the cardinal rule about ladies not going unescorted into inns, and on this occasion she was doing it under her real name.

It seemed that minutes, were ticking by. She looked a little anxiously at her watch. It was only twenty-five to four.

Footsteps sounded in the passage. The door opened and Ralph came in. He was very much the gentleman of fashion, clad in an emerald-green coat, cream cossacks, and black patent leather shoes. The cossacks were gathered at his ankles by golden ribbons, matching exactly the hue of his silk waistcoat. His shirt sported a fine starched frill, and he wore two neckcloths, one black and one white. He looked relaxed and unconcerned, but his brown eyes were sharp and wary, and a guarded smile played about his sensuous lips.

He closed the door softly and then faced her, folding his arms. 'Well, well, what an unexpected pleasure,' he murmured.

'I doubt you'll see it in that light when you learn my purpose, sir.'

'Do I perceive a threatening note in your voice, Miss Fairmead?'

'Yes.'

'I'm all agog.'

'Will you answer one thing first?'

'My dear, I'm at your disposal.' His glance moved slowly over her, resting on the low decolletage of her gown before meeting her eyes.

'Did you compromise Adam last year because Mrs Tully preferred him over you?'

A light passed through his eyes. 'My dear Miss Fairmead, I really don't know what you're talking about.'

'Now it's my turn to talk of playing games, sir,' she said, reminding him of their conversation on the verandah at Bourne End. 'You know exactly what I mean, just as you knew exactly who the lady was in the miniature you were looking at so adoringly. You hadn't bought it that day, you'd been carrying it around with you for a long time; indeed, I'd hazard a guess that it reposes in your pocket at this very moment.'

Before he could stop himself, his hand moved instinctively toward his pocket. He realized he'd given himself away, and gave a lightly ironic laugh. '*Touché, ma chère.* Very well, I admit to reacting out of male pique that the lady was foolish enough to spurn me.'

'And did you also choose a way that would harm Gregory because Margaret had chosen him rather than you?'

'My, my,' he murmured, 'you're an extremely perceptive creature, my dear. Yes, I see no reason to deny it. I wanted her, but she hardly knew I existed. I would have been more vindictive, but she didn't matter all that much to me, she was but a fleeting fancy. Mrs Tully, on the other hand, was much more than that. I lost her because of Drummond, and I wasn't about to let that pass without striking back.' His eyes glittered. 'Nor was I about to let your interference in my affairs pass unchallenged, my dear, but then you no doubt know I've carried out my threats concerning the *billet-doux*.'

'Oh, yes, I know,' she replied, holding his gaze, 'but the time has come to put a stop to your iniquity, sir, and unless you put right the many wrongs you've done, I intend to see to it that you're disinherited after all. And, believe me, I can do just that.'

'You're a kitten, my dear, not a tiger, so pray don't give yourself airs and graces to which you cannot aspire.'

'There's nothing of the kitten about me, sirrah, as you'd be wise to remember. I have only to go to your father right now and tell him what you've really been up to, what you're *continuing* to be up to, for him to wash his hands of you completely.' She smiled a little, heartened by the increasingly guarded look in his eyes. 'Oh, yes, you were right to think I'd told him more than you wanted; indeed, he and I had a very interesting discussion. I know full well how he'd react now to hearing everything I know about you.'

'You're wrong, my dear, for he'd never disinherit me.'

'No? Don't call my bluff, sirrah, for it will be the worse for you.'

'You haven't the willpower to break the old man's heart.'

'Oh, but I have. Lives are now at stake, sir, and I put that consideration before your father's heart.'

'Lives?'

'Your lies and schemes have led to a duel. Gregory has called Adam out, and they face each other with pistols at five in Herne's Glade. You are the only one who can stop them, and I intend to see that you do; otherwise, I'll go to your father straightaway. I'm not going to let you get away with anything more, you've damaged too many lives already, so unless you wish to see your own life damaged still further than it has been already, I advise you to take my threat very seriously indeed.'

For a long moment he looked at her, then he turned away slightly, giving a low laugh. 'So, Gregory and Adam are to duel at dawn with pistols, eh? May I ask why?'

'Ostensibly because Gregory has learned of my meetings with Adam, but I think their real reason is all that happened last year.'

She looked coldly at him. 'Which is where you come in.'

'You surely don't expect me to toddle off to Herne's Glade to tell them I'm terribly sorry they've arrived at such a fix, because it's all been my fault? Come now, I'd be filled with shot myself!' He gave a mocking laugh.

'I don't ask you to go there, I merely ask you to write a full confession.'

'I think you're forgetting something, Miss Fairmead.'

'Lady Bowes-Fenton? No, sir, I'm not forgetting. It's as I've already said, lives are now at stake. Tell tales on her if you wish, it will make no difference to me, I will still acquaint your father with the full extent of your sins.'

He smiled a little. 'Fire with fire?'

'Yes. Blackmail is your weapon, sir, but is equally effective in the hands of others, and if you think me incapable of using that weapon, you'll be making a grave mistake. I have nothing to lose and everything to gain by turning that weapon on you, just as you have everything to gain by writing the letter I want, and a great deal to lose by refusing. By putting pen to paper, you can be sure of my silence. . . .'

'And I can be equally sure of being pursued on the road to Falmouth by those I've harmed,' he said dryly.

'Not if I give you my word they won't follow.'

'Such word is easy enough to give, but impossible to carry out.'

'I think I can persuade both Adam and Gregory not to come after you.'

'To *think* something isn't good enough, my dear.'

'It's all I can do. Write the letter, it's your only sensible course. Surely it's better to be sure of remaining your father's heir, and to take a slight risk that you'll he pursued along the highway, than it is to be certain of penury, and certain, too, that I won't miss a single opportunity to point an accusing finger at you.' Her eyes and her voice were steady, for he had to be convinced that she meant every single word.

His glance flickered away. 'What a formidable wife you would have been, Miss Fairmead,' he murmured.

'Do we have a deal, Mr St John? Are you going to write the letter, or must I go and tell tales to your father?'

'I think, Miss Fairmead, that it's time to see the error of my ways. Very well, I'll write your letter, provided, of course, that I have your word that you won't speak to my father.'

'You have that word,' she replied, barely able to conceal her elation.

'And you, being a true lady, will, of course, keep that word,' he said softly.

'For which you, being an undeserving toad, have just reason to be exceeding grateful,' she countered.

'No doubt,' he murmured, going to the writing desk and flicking back the tails of his coat as he sat down. 'What exactly am I to say?'

'That you were responsible for what happened to Prince Agamemnon, that you did it because you were jealous over Mrs Tully, that you chose to hurt Gregory as well because you were annoyed that Margaret chose him over you, that you forced me to agree to a temporary betrothal in order to part your father from some of his money, and that you lied in the letter to Adam when you said I'd surrendered everything to you.'

He glanced at her. 'Quite a catalog, is it not?'

'Are you proud of it?'

He smiled a little, and didn't reply. Taking up a quill, he dipped it into the ink and began to write. He didn't see Helen close her eyes, weak with relief that her plan was working. Once he'd finished, all she had to do was get to King Henry Crescent and stop Adam from leaving for Herne's Glade. She glanced at her watch again. It was nearly four. Or so she thought.

For a long time the only sound in the room was the scratching of the quill. Another stagecoach arrived in the yard, approaching from the other direction and not passing the window, although the glow of its lamps shone in for a brief moment. She could hear sounds from within the inn, the clatter of pots and pans from the kitchens, the shout of an angry man who wished to complain to the innkeeper, and the humming of a maid as she hurried past the door.

At last Ralph finished, putting down the quill and sanding the letter with irritating thoroughness. He blew the surplus away, studied the letter for a moment, and then handed it to her. 'I trust this will suffice.'

She took it, and read.

I trust that this missive, written under duress, but truthful for all that, will go some way toward righting the many wrongs of which I've been guilty. Last year I gave full vent to my wrath over losing Maria Tully's affections to Drummond, so much so that I concocted the whole wearisome business of Prince Agamemnon. It was none of Drummond's doing, I compromised him out of spite, paying Sam Edney well for his cooperation. There was also an element of spite in choosing that particular method of hurting Drummond, for by calling Bourne End's good name into question, I punished Gregory Bourne for having the audacity to win Margaret Fairmead, a lady for whose hand I for a while entertained hopes. Among my more recent sins has been the coercion of Miss Helen Fairmead into agreeing to a temporary betrothal. I needed the match in order to persuade my father to stump up, and I made her do my bidding by threatening to broadcast her asso-ciation with Drummond, and also by threatening to expose a past indiscretion of another lady, who shall remain nameless. This second threat had proved very effective in the past, for-cing Drummond to keep silent over my guilt concerning Prince Agamemnon, even though he knew full well I'd done it. Lastly, I confess to having written a letter containing noth-ing but lies about my so-called relationship with Miss Helen Fairmead. I have never had my way with her, and she has never played a double game; indeed, it is my belief that she loves Drummond with all her heart.
Ralph St John

'Will it do?' He was studying her.
'Yes.'
'Then we are quits?'
She nodded, folding the letter.
He took out his watch, studying it for a moment and then snap-ping it closed and putting it away. 'I suggest you make haste, Miss Fairmead, for you haven't much time left.'
'I have only to get to King Henry Crescent,' she said, hurrying

toward the door.

'Do that, and you'll find your bird has flown. He's bound to be on his way to Herne's Glade at this very moment.'

She halted, staring at him. 'Why do you say that?'

'Because it's half past four, and if the duel is to take place at five. . . .'

Her breath caught, and she looked quickly at her own watch. It said ten past four. An icy wash of dismay swept over her. She'd forgotten to wind it again! All this time it had been twenty minutes later than she'd realized! Her eyes fled to the window. Outside the light was the faintest of grays, where only a short while before it had been inky black. Was it already too late?

With a cry of concern, she gathered her skirts and opened the door, hurrying out into the passage and almost cannoning into the landlord. She didn't wait to apologize, but dashed on. Behind her, she heard the man address Ralph.

'Mr St John? It's time to leave, your father sent me to tell you.'

'Very well.'

She glanced back briefly and saw Ralph standing watching her, then she pushed open the coffee room door and entered the noise and crush of travelers.

As she emerged into the courtyard at last, the light was perceptibly gray, although dawn had yet to break. Mary was standing by the berlin with Peter, and she turned anxiously as her mistress appeared. 'Miss Fairmead?'

Helen ran up to them, clutching at Peter's arm. 'Drive straight to Herne's Glade, we haven't a moment to lose! Don't spare the whip, I beg of you!'

He was galvanized into action, turning to vault up onto the box. Helen and Mary clambered inside, slamming the door behind them as he snatched up the reins and whistled the startled team into action. The berlin lurched forward, turning sharply in the confined space, and then springing forward as he urged the horses beneath the entrance, and out onto the highway. The wheels rang on the cobbles, and the hooves clattered, striking sparks. Peter's whip cracked, and the carriage flew along the quiet streets.

Helen sat rigidly on her seat, blinking back tears as she stared out. Mary sat opposite her, and after a moment leaned timidly forward to touch her hand. 'What is it, miss? Wouldn't Mr St John do as you wished?'

'I have the letter, Mary, but I fear it may be too late. My watch. . . .' Her voice caught, And she couldn't say anything more.

Awful realization crossed the maid's face, and she sat back without another word.

Helen stared out at the eastern sky. It seemed that it lightened with every breath she took.

CHAPTER 24

Windsor Great Park was silver-gray as the berlin drove at headlong pace back along the Ascot road. A light mist was threading between the trees, and birds rose startled from the branches as the pounding of the horses' hooves thundered across the silence.

Helen was striving to remain collected, but all the time the same guilty accusing thought swung around and around in her head: Why, oh, why, hadn't she remembered to wind her watch? But for that vital small omission, she'd have reached King Henry Crescent in time. Now it might already be too late, the duel could already have taken place. She glanced at the watch again. The hands pointed to twenty to five, which meant that it was now five o'clock, the very moment set for the duel. Her heart felt like ice in her breast. Please, don't let it be too late; don't let the duel happen before she got there. . . .

It seemed an age before the great copper beech towered over the track, and Peter swung the berlin sharply off the road to Hagman's, urging the lathered team along the bumpy, rutted way to the glade. He was just flinging the horses forward as fast as they'd go when something ahead made him rein in again sharply.

'Miss Fairmead! It's the Bourne End landau, it's drawn up just in front and Mrs Bourne's standing by it. She's very distressed.'

As the berlin lurched to a standstill, Helen's heart seemed to stop. Fearfully she lowered the glass, leaning out to look ahead at the other vehicle. Margaret was standing beside it, being comforted by her maid, and the sound of her sobs carried quite clearly. Helen's heart began to pound again. It was too late, the duel was over!

With a choked cry, she flung open the berlin door and alighted, running desperately along the few yards of rutted track separating the two vehicles. 'Margaret? Margaret, am I too late?'

Margaret's distraught sobs caught, and she turned quickly, the plumes on her little blue velvet hat trembling. She wore a blue spencer over a cream sprigged muslin gown, and would have looked very Mayfair and stylish had it not been that she was so overcome with emotion. Her eyes were red and puffy, and her lips quivered as she stared blankly at her sister, almost as if she didn't recognize her.

'H-Helen?' she cried after a moment.

Helen seized her hands. 'Am I too late? Is it over?'

Margaret stared at her. 'How are you here. . . ?'

'Answer me, Margaret! Is the duel over, am I too late?'

'N-no. I c-couldn't stay and watch, I h-had to come away.'

Hope surged through Helen. 'I must stop them!' She pulled away, running back toward the berlin.

Margaret called helplessly after her, 'There's n-nothing you can do. They w-won't listen to you, or t-to anyone!'

'I have Ralph's confession!' cried Helen, waving the letter aloft and not looking back. 'They *must* listen now!'

Peter whipped the weary horses into action almost before she'd managed to close the berlin door, and the vehicle jolted forward yet again. In a blur Helen saw Margaret's stunned face, and saw the realization of hope. As the berlin sped away along the narrow track, Margaret was climbing back into the landau, ordering it to the glade as well.

Herne's Glade appeared ahead at last, visible through the silky swathes of fine evaporating mist. Adam's bright red curricle was drawn up beneath an immense overhanging oak, and near it stood a surgeon, his top hat pulled low over his forehead. Several saddle horses were tethered nearby, and a groom was with them, watching what was happening in the center of the misty glade. With their appointed seconds standing to one side, Adam and Gregory were facing each other, having turned after taking the required twelve paces. Their shirts were ghastly white, and their pistols were already leveled, the barrels glinting in the cold dawn light.

Helen leaned fearfully out of the berlin window, crying out

desperately. 'Stop! You *must* stop! Gregory, I can prove Adam's innocence!'

For a beat of the heart they remained motionless, but then slowly they lowered the pistols, turning as the little carriage hurtled into the glade, followed by the landau.

Peter reined in once more, halting the foam-flecked team, and Helen fumbled with the door in her haste to open it. As she alighted, she was vaguely aware that William Lamb was Adam's second, and that she recognized Gregory's second, having met him at the dinner party, although she couldn't put a name to him. As Margaret alighted from the landau, hurrying across the glade toward the duellists, Helen went up to Gregory, hesitating a moment before giving him the letter.

'Before you read it, I must have your word that you won't go after Ralph.'

'I won't give any promise, Helen.'

'I gave him my word, Gregory. Please allow me to keep it.'

He looked into her pleading eyes, and then gave a brief nod. 'Very well.'

She turned to Adam. 'Will you promise as well?'

'I don't owe St John any consideration.'

'I know, but I still ask you. Please, Adam.'

'As you wish.'

Her hand shook as she gave the letter to Gregory. 'Read it,' she said, 'for every word exonerates Adam.

He handed his pistol to his second, and then began to read. Margaret pressed close to his side, reading as well.

Helen glanced again at Adam, wanting so much to see warmth in his eyes, but she found only an impenetrable veil that allowed her to see nothing of his thoughts. She swallowed back the pain, for her past lies still counted against her, and nothing would change that. But at least she'd stopped the duel, and cleared his name, so that he could no longer say he owed her nothing.

Margaret finished reading, and raised contrite eyes to her face. 'Oh, Helen, we've been so wrong, so very wrong. . . .'

Gregory nodded, folding the letter. 'It seems we have. Dear God, how completely Ralph gulled us.'

Margaret touched Helen's arm. 'But how did you obtain this

confession, how on earth did you persuade him to tell?'

'I blackmailed him. At the Farrish House ball I found out that his father wasn't taken in by his lies; indeed, I found out that Mr St John Senior is a very agreeable and shrewd person. He'd guessed that Ralph had been telling less than the truth, and he persuaded me to tell him a little of what I knew, which was enough to persuade him that Ralph had to be stopped, hence the threat of disinheritance unless Ralph agreed to return immediately to Jamaica. Mr St John also said that if he found out anything else, he'd disinherit Ralph anyway. I knew so much more about Ralph, including the fact that he'd been continuing to interfere most vilely in my life even after the confrontation with his father, that I suddenly saw how I could use the self-same threat of disinheritance. I had only to threaten to go to his father, and that is what I did. With the help of Mary and Peter, I got away from Bourne End and went to the Golden Key to face Ralph with my ultimatum. It worked.' Helen looked anxiously at her sister and brother-in-law. 'You mustn't blame Mary and Peter for assisting me; they did it because they too wished to stop the duel – especially because they cared about you, Gregory.' She looked at him.

He nodded. 'No blame will attach to them; indeed, I'm grateful, but Helen, you do realize, don't you, that this letter makes no difference to the duel? Maybe I was wrong about Adam's part in the past, but I'm not wrong about his dishonorable intentions toward you.'

'You *are* wrong about that as well,' she replied, taking the letter from his hand and thrusting it toward Adam. 'Just as *you* are wrong about something as well, my lord. Pray, read the letter.'

'Nothing St John has to say is news to me, Miss Fairmead, for I know the exact extent of his crimes.'

'No, you don't. Please read the letter,' she insisted.

'As you wish.' He handed his pistol to William Lamb, and then began to read.

She watched, and knew the precise moment he reached Ralph's vindication of her virtue. A light moved through his eyes, and he looked quickly at her.

She met his gaze squarely. 'I didn't play you false with him, I was merely his helpless pawn, but you wouldn't believe me. And *you*,'

her glance encompassed the others as well, 'wouldn't believe me
when I told you Adam hadn't attempted to seduce me. There's no
earthly reason why this duel should proceed, Gregory, because not
only was Adam innocent of tampering with Prince Agamemnon,
he's also innocent of improper intentions toward me. If anyone is
guilty of impropriety where virtue is concerned, that person is me.'

Gregory raised an eyebrow. 'Helen, if you expect me to
believe. . . .'

'Oh, I do, sir, I expect you to believe, because what I'm going to
tell you is the truth, I'd swear it on my parents' memory if required
to. I've behaved very badly indeed since leaving Miss Figgis's
emporium of decorum; in fact, I doubt that that good lady would
recognize me if given a description of my antics.' She swallowed,
for a blush of shame colored her cheeks. 'Gregory, when I arrived
at Bourne End, you were curious as to what hour I'd set off in
order to reach Ascot so early in the afternoon. I glossed over a
reply, for the truth was that I'd spent the previous night at the Cat
and Fiddle Inn, Upper Ballington, forced to do so by the weather
and by Lord Swag. Afraid for my reputation, I decided to adopt a
false name, and so I pretended to be the widowed Mrs Brown.'

Margaret gasped in dismay. 'Oh, Helen!'

'I know it was foolish, but it seemed safe enough at the time. I
would continue with the journey in the morning, and no one
would be any wiser. But it wasn't as simple as that, for in the courtyard I was saved from certain death by Adam's quick thinking, and
when he asked me to dine with him, I didn't hesitate to accept. I'd
do it again, so help me, for in spite of my monumental gaffes, I
enjoyed that evening more than was wise. I basked in the flatter-
ing and charming attention of a man whose very smile devastated
me, and when later that night I saw him again rescue someone, this
time a maid from the brutish attentions of a drunken coachman,
my fate was sealed.' She looked at Adam then. 'I fell hopelessly in
love with you that night, and if a liberty was taken when we finally
parted, it was a liberty I didn't attempt to spurn.'

'Helen, you don't have to say any more. . . .' he began.

'But I do, I have to tell them everything.' She began to recount
her every thought and action over the past weeks, and when she'd
finished, she looked at them all. 'My conduct doesn't bear close

inspection, does it? And my reputation will never amount to much, not after all this. If you persist in this duel now, Gregory, you'll be persisting for a nonexistent cause – my good name.' There were tears in her eyes as she looked pleadingly at him. 'Please believe me, Gregory, and stand down from this duel. You and Adam have no ax to grind any more, all obstacles have been removed from your friendship. He doesn't owe you an apology for anything, but you owe him one, for you've been totally in the wrong throughout.'

He glanced at Margaret, who slipped a hand into his. 'She's right, Gregory, we do owe Adam an apology.'

Gregory turned to Adam. 'I don't know how to begin. . . .'

Adam hesitated, but then held out his hand. 'I understand how you were misled. I'm glad to extend my hand in friendship again.'

Gregory's face broke into a relieved and glad grin, and he swiftly accepted the proferred hand.

As Margaret hastened to make good the rift as well, Helen turned away unnoticed. Tears were blinding her. She'd told all now, and the full extent of her foolishness would soon be common knowledge. And she would have to face the raised eyebrows of society on her own, a woman who by her own admission had behaved with unbecoming boldness.

She slipped away to the berlin, pausing only to speak to Peter. 'Please drive away, Peter.'

'Yes, miss. But where?'

'Anywhere, just take me away from here.' She climbed inside, closing the door softly behind her. Mary was still seated inside, and now reached out to comfort her mistress, who gave in to the tears of wretchedness.

Peter urged the tired horses away, and the berlin's wheels left an arc on the wet grass as it turned around in the glade and then drove off.

Margaret broke off in mid-sentence, turning in dismay. 'Helen? Helen, come back!' She made to hurry after the carriage, but Gregory caught her hand.

'Let her go, it will do no good to follow.' He glanced at Adam, who was standing gazing after the berlin, a pensive expression on his face.

Peter urged the team along the bumpy track toward the copper beech, and then turned toward Hagman's, feeling that Helen would rather go there than return to Bourne End. In the berlin, Helen felt as if her heart was breaking. It was all over, once and for all, and she'd lost the only man she'd ever love. Hot tears stung her eyes, and a hollow ache echoed inside her, as if her soul had gone. Ralph had played a part in her misery, but when it came down to it, she had no one to blame but herself; she was the author of her own downfall.

She gazed blindly out of the window. The air was much more luminous now, with the sun almost above the eastern horizon. Mist still clung between the trees, becoming more dense as they neared Eleanor's Lake. The boathouse appeared ahead, silent and deserted after the celebrations of the night before. The pleasure boats were moored along the jetty, and the great golden barge was still adorned with its floral decorations.

Peter reined the exhausted horses in, climbing down from his box and coming apologetically to the door. 'I can't drive them any more, Miss Fairmead, they're quite used up.'

Still overcome with tears, she nodded. 'Yes, of course. I-I'll walk for a while.' She alighted from the carriage, followed by Mary, who was very anxious about her.

'I'll stay with you, miss.'

'No, I'd prefer to be alone. I'll be all right, please don't worry.'

Without waiting for the maid to say anything more, Helen walked away, her steps taking her automatically toward the lakeside path. There was no music in the air this time, no Mozart or Vivaldi, just an early morning chorus of birdsong. The lake lapped softly against the shore, the water smooth and almost without a ripple. Swans glided silently over the glassy surface, and she could hear the ducks somewhere among the reeds further along the shore. The rhododendrons were as if seen in a dream, their foliage indistinct, their blooms subdued but still of discernible color.

She didn't know why she was walking to the clearing where Adam had so finally spurned her, but her steps just took her there. The grass was wet with dew, and as she looked toward the water, she saw the pleasure boat where he'd waited for her the night before. Her skirts dragged through the grass as she walked down to the shore, and the boat swayed a little as she stepped inside. The cushions scattered on the boards were faintly damp, but she didn't notice as she sat down on them, reaching up to undo the ribbon in her hair. Shaking the long tresses loose, she closed her tired eyes, bowing her head so that her hair tumbled forward over her shoulders. She wept silently, her face hidden from the world.

She didn't hear the curricle drive up to the boathouse, or the brief exchange of voices, she knew nothing until the boat swayed suddenly, and she looked up to see Adam stepping aboard.

In Herne's Glade he'd discarded his coat and waistcoat for the duel, and he'd left them behind now. His shirt was unbuttoned at the throat, and his cravat hung loose. He wore no gloves or top hat, and his black hair was windswept from the speed with which he'd driven. His gleaming top boots were as impeccable as ever, marked only with the moisture from the grass.

She stared up at him for a moment, and then turned wretchedly away. 'Please leave me alone, we have nothing more to say to each other.'

'On the contrary, there's much to be said.' His gaze moved over her, taking in the cascade of honey-colored hair and the way her shoulders trembled as she strove to hide her misery.

'I think you said it all last night, Adam,' she said quietly. 'You made yourself very clear indeed then.'

'I was wrong.'

'You were still prepared to believe it of me.'

'Had you given me reason to trust your word?'

She bit her lip, blinking back fresh tears. 'No.' Her voice was barely audible.

'We have to talk, Helen.'

Taking a deep breath, she managed to nod, closing her eyes again as he got down on the cushions beside her, lounging back with that effortless grace that was so much his mark. His very closeness made her tremble still more, for in spite of everything her senses betrayed her. She still wanted him so much, still needed him so much; still loved him so much. . . .

He looked at her. 'Helen, you aren't the only one with confessions to make, I have some of my own. I'm ashamed of myself for treating you as I did right here last night, and in mitigation I can

222 *Sandra Heath*

only say that I was driven by anger at learning your real identity and I was bitterly jealous that you'd apparently given to Ralph St John that which I so dearly craved myself.'

She swallowed, gazing at the prow of the boat without really seeing it. 'If that was how you felt about me, why didn't you just show Ralph's letter to Gregory when he confronted you? Why did you let him believe you had tried to seduce me?'

'A gentleman doesn't tell tales on a lady, least of all on the lady he loves, even if she has apparently betrayed that love.'

Slowly she looked at him. 'Loves? You said *loves*,' she whispered.

'Oh, yes, Helen, I love you; I think I've loved you from the moment I plucked you from beneath that stagecoach at the Cat and Fiddle.' He smiled, reaching up to brush his fingers against her cheek. 'I held you close in those brief moments and it was a sensation I more than enjoyed. A sensation I enjoyed still more, was kissing you on the lips just before I left. You were so adorably original, so refreshingly different, that I knew I had to see you again. You proved tantalizingly enigmatic, my mysterious Mrs Brown, and each time we met, you made more certain of my complete subjection.'

She stared at him. 'You – you still love me?' she breathed.

'With all my base male heart.' He reached up to brush his fingertips against her cheek. 'Can you forgive me for saying those things to you last night?'

Her senses were reeling. 'If – if you forgive me for deceiving you.'

He drew her down to the cushions. 'Oh, my darling, you're forgiven a thousand times over.'

Her whole body was alive to him. 'I tried to tell you,' she whispered, tears of utter joy filling her eyes.

'My poor darling,' he said softly, 'for it was a quite impossible confession.' He leaned over her, running his fingers softly through her hair.

She closed her eyes as he bent to put his lips to her throat, and desire stirred richly through her. 'A totally impossible confession,' she breathed, submitting to the enticing warmth that was enveloping her.

'Look at me, Helen.'

Slowly she opened her eyes, gazing up at him.

'I have one last thing to ask of you.'

'What is it?'

'Will you marry me?'

Her heart soared. 'Do you really want me?' she whispered.

'Oh, what a foolish question,' he murmured, bending his head to kiss her.

Her lips parted beneath his, and an unbelievable happiness sang in her heart. She didn't need to give him an answer, he knew by the warmth and ardor of her response that she was his.

Also by Sandra Heath
and soon to be published:
A MATTER OF DUTY

ALTAR-BOUND

Handsome and wealthy Lord Christopher Highclare made it painfully clear why he was asking a virtual nobody like Miss Louisa Cherington to be his wife. He had made a promise to her dying brother to do so, and was honor-bound to keep that vow.

Proud and beautiful Louisa made it just as clear why she was accepting this man who not only made no pretense of loving her, but made no secret of the ravishing woman who was his mistress. Louisa, too, was bowing to the wishes of her late brother, who wanted to rescue her from poverty and the peril of Captain Geoffrey Lawrence, the notorious rake who was in hot pursuit of her.

Thus these two were bound to marry – and bound to wonder what would happen then. . . .

A MATTER OF
DUTY